~*The Duke's Daughter* ~

Part 2: Highs And Lows

Shana Granderson, A Lady

CONTENTS

INTRODUCTION

At the end of Part 1, William Darcy saved Lady Elizabeth Bennet's life, but at what cost? After a short look into the future, part 2 picks up from the point that Part 1 ended. We find out very soon what William's fate is. We also follow the villains as they plot their revenge and try to find new ways to get money that they do not deserve.

Elizabeth finally admitted that she loved William the morning that he was shot, is it too late or will love find a way? As there always are in life, there are highs and lows and this second part of three gives us a window into the ups and downs that affect our couple and their extended family.

DEDICATION:

This book is dedicated to the love of life, the holder of my heart. You are my one and only and you complete me.

ACKNOWLEDGEMENT & THANK YOU

First and foremost, thank your E.C.S. for standing by me while I dedicate many hours to my craft. You are my shining light and my one and only.

I want to thank my Alpha, Will Jamison and my Betas Caroline Piediscalzi Lippert, and Kimbelle Pease. Your assistance is most appreciated. A special thank you to Kimbelle who had been a great help and has dedicated much time and effort to making this book better.

Thank you to my professional editor Tameka Harmon. Cover art created by Veronica Martinez Medellin.

My undying love and appreciation to Jane Austen for her incredible literary masterpieces is more than can be expressed adequately here. Without her I would never have been inspired to write.

I also thank all of the JAFF readers who make writing these stories a pleasure.

CHAPTER 1

August 1812...

K aren Younge, her brother Clay, and Johanna Álvarez were seated in the Happy Leprechaun Inn near the small harbour in Bundoran, County Donegal in Ireland. It had been three long months since they had been forced to flee Fowey in Cornwall for this Godforsaken little town. They finally had what they believed was a fail-proof plan to get their revenge on the Bennets and Darcys, one which would gain them at least two hundred and fifty thousand pounds.

Karen did not care about the money; all she wanted was to make the uppity Lady Elizabeth Bennet suffer. Mrs. Younge was delusional, and like her dead lover, George Wickham, she had no intention of returning the woman unharmed to her husband, a duke! She almost had an apoplexy when the three-week-old London paper had reached Bundoran. The whore was a Duchess! As Karen sank deeper into her delusion and reality faded into the background, she was ever more determined to punish the object of her obsession.

Mrs. Álvarez was most vexed. Her son Tony had disappeared over two *months* ago! She had urged Younge to mount an exhaustive search, which he begrudgingly did after she had agreed to part with a further ten percent of her stake of the ransom. His crew had searched everywhere in the little town and questioned many of the denizens. None remembered seeing the young man since the day she declared he was missing, and there was no information other than what they had already known, which was only that he was missing. Irrationally, Johanna blamed the same people who had her husband hung, and swore to exact further revenge. She knew the truth, but had to keep up the pretence that her son was dead.

Around the same time that Johanna's son was lost, three of the *Stealthy Runner's* crew had disappeared. As this had happened before, it raised no alarms, and Clay Younge was more than satisfied with the three men he had found to replace them. A Dennington Line ship, the largest type of ship that could safely fit in the small harbour, had arrived a few days after his men had absconded. Three sailors caught pilfering from the ship's supplies to sell on the side had been summarily discharged and thrown off the vessel, which made the Dublin to Bundoran run once a month, with brief stops in ports at other small coastal towns along the way. Clay considered them to be his type of men and had approached them with an offer to join his crew.

There were two things that he should have noted, but had not. One, the man who had taken care of the spy following his sister in Fowey the day they had departed, was one of the three that taken off. Two, if he had watched the men, he would have seen that they carried themselves as men who had been in the military. They were, in fact, demobbed marines that were part of the many the Dennington Line employed for security.

~~~~~~~/~~~~~~~

Do not worry, dear reader, I will tell you all that transpired in the previous four months...

Four months earlier...

Lady Anne Darcy refused to leave her son's side as his fever raged. To no one's surprise, Lady Elizabeth Bennet was right next to her. She had been assigned a guest chamber in Darcy House after no one had tried to gainsay her when she informed her parents, and anyone else who would listen, that she would help nurse Mr. Darcy back to health. She felt that it was the least she could do for the man who saved her life. Both her companion and lady's maid were in residence with her.

Earlier that day Lady Elizabeth had confessed her love to

William's mother. If she was expecting the lady to be surprised at her admission, she was sorely disappointed. Her Aunt Anne informed her that anyone who saw them together, could see that there was love between them, even if they had not yet acknowledged it to each other. As Lizzy thought back, she remembered a number of comments, which now made sense as she considered them in this new light. Lady Anne had hugged the daughter of her heart tightly. They had a battle to fight first. There had to be a way to bring her son's fever down if he was to survive.

Fitzwilliam Darcy was in a place that he did not recognise. On one side was a short, straight path, easy to walk toward...yes, his honoured Papa! On the other side was a steep path, one that would be hard to climb, and there was a lady there, but he could not make her out though her voice was familiar. No, there were two voices. One sounded like...Mama! The other he thought he recognised; however, in the fog and distortion in his mind, he could not place it other than that he was sure her voice meant a great deal to him. He was exhausted and he knew that if he went toward his father he would get to rest, to be at peace, and he would never have to leave his Papa again. But what of his Mama? What of the woman with the other voice? If he went to his Papa, would he ever hear them or see them again? Would he ever see his beloved sister again?

Lady Anne was beside herself; the fever was climbing, her son's breath was getting shallower, and he was fighting for each breath. The physician had said that it was in God's hands and that they should all pray, but given the severity of his fever, he did not hold out much hope. While they again cooled his skin with a wet cloth, Lady Elizabeth remembered something that she had read in a text in Longbourn's library.

"Aunt Anne, have Carstens fill a bath with cold water, and if there is any ice in the house, have him put it in the bath," Lizzy announced.

"Cold water and ice?" Lady Anne could not imagine what the younger woman was about.

"Yes, I read about it being done in extremes cases when the

fever was high like William's is." She took his mother's hand and looked her in the eye. "If I am correct, it will help him, if I am not, then we have already lost and it will have made no difference. We have nothing to lose and much to gain." The orders were given, and over the protests of the doctor, the bath was filled with ice and cold water.

It was just too hard, so Darcy decided that he needed to go to his father. He could not fight up the hill; he had no more strength. He started walking toward his beloved Papa who looked just as he had when his son had last seen him, hale and healthy. A few more steps and he would be in the safety and warmth of his father's outstretched arms as he had been as a young boy. Just as he was about to grasp his father's hands, he felt as though he had fallen through the ice while skating on the small pond at Pemberley. He felt cold like he had never before experienced. It was as if he was pulled by some unseen force that he had no power to resist. The shock of it had spurred him forward, toward the voice he knew he had to reach; he started to force himself up the steep path. Fighting, he was fighting! The cold had shocked him into action, so as hard as the steep path was to negotiate, he would follow it; he would not take the easy way out! He could see his mother and Georgie waiting for him with open arms in place of his father, and then he saw the face that belonged to the voice he recognised. He loved that voice and the face that went with it, it was his Elizabeth! She was talking, but he could not make out what she was saying, then he heard her clearly say... "I love you."

~~~~~~~/~~~~~~~

Juan Antonio Álvarez, AKA the *Spaniard,* had not believe that Wickham would succeed. He felt nothing about double-crossing him, having one of his men give him and his whore a permanent smile, then dumping the bodies in the Thames. Why should he settle for twenty thousand when he could have the whole one hundred thousand, minus a little for Withers? He looked over the note again. They had the lady at a house of ill repute which he owned. He took two of his men, who acted as his primary bodyguards, with him, and they rode the short distance to the house of Madam Cheri.

Álvarez was already counting his money in his head, so when his conveyance was swarmed by redcoats and runners as soon as it halted, he could not comprehend what was happening. The doors were wrenched open and his foolish men, who had tried to point their pistols threateningly at their captors, paid for it with their miserable lives, the cabin filling with the acrid smoke of discharged pistols. Álvarez, already stunned, was now temporally deaf, his ears ringing from being near the weapons when they had discharged in the cramped space.

The *Spaniard* was roughly pulled onto the ground by two soldiers and clapped in irons. It dawned on him too late that his greed and Withers had led him into a trap. He would never see any money, in fact, he likely would not see more than a fortnight's worth of sunrises before he had a date with the hangman. Being the coward that he was, he gave up all of the information about his 'empire', which would be well on its way to being dismantled, and many of his 'associates' would be in custody by the time he had his date with the hangman.

~~~~~~~/~~~~~~~

"Why is she here?' Darcy asked himself. *'Why do I see her apparition with Mama and Georgie, and why do I feel like I am surrounded by snow? Why did she say that she loves me?'* He felt a sense of warmth suffuse his body as the scene before him changed. The next thing he saw was the park at Pemberley. He no longer felt the bone jarring cold, he felt warmer and more comfortable. As he stood and looked out over the park, his father rode up on his steed, Goliath. Darcy did not know how, but he was sitting on Zeus and riding with his father as he had so many times in his lifetime.

"By Jove! You had the right of it, Lady Elizabeth," Mr. Bartholomew exclaimed as he felt his patient's forehead. "There is still a fever, but it is much lower, just above normal. I will have to make note of what was done here to use in similar cases in the future," he gave the lady a half bow to indicate his appreciation for her actions.

"Elizabeth, I think that you just saved my William's life!" Lady Anne said with thanks evident in her voice, tears of joy flowing freely as she hugged the younger woman.

"If I did, it was naught but his due as it was his selfless and brave action that saved mine," the lady said.

"Elizabeth," Georgie said in a timid voice, "did you mean what you said when you begged William to come back to us?"

"What do you mean, Georgie," Elizabeth blushed, realizing she must have made her declaration aloud.

"You said that you loved William. Is that true?" the younger girl asked.

"We will talk about this and much else once William is on his way to recovery, my sweetling," her mother said gently. "What now, Mr. Bartholomew?"

"Your son is not out of danger yet, your ladyship" the physician reported. "His fever is much lower, but until it breaks it could go up again," he saw that the ladies were about to interject so he continued, "however, we will use the method that Lady Elizabeth introduced if his fever again rises so precariously."

As the sun was starting to rise, Ladies Elaine and Catherine entered Darcy's chambers. When they were told what Lady Elizabeth had done, and the change that it wrought on their stricken nephew, Elizabeth Bennet was repeatedly hugged and kissed by the women in his family. William was much loved by his relatives, and their relief at his apparent improvement was immense.

For the first time in two days, Lady Anne, coaxed by her sister Catherine, agreed to go take a bath and climb into her bed to get some much-needed sleep. Lady Elizabeth was ordered to do the same by the Countess of Matlock, who with a look let her know that there was no room for debate. Once a promise was elicited that they would be woken if there was any change for the worse, both ladies left their charge in the capable hands of his two aunts and his sister.

As they rode, seemingly flying across the field of Pemberley at a speed that surpassed anything that Darcy had ever attained on Zeus prior to now, he heard his father's voice in his head:

"As much as I would have liked you to wait with me until your

mother joined us, it gives me much pleasure that you have decided to take the harder path, the one that will lead you back to those who love you. You could not have chosen a better daughter for me, William. Lady Elizabeth will be the making of you."

"But Papa, she used to hate me! It is only recently that we became friends." Darcy explained.

"You think her indifferent to you, son? Then answer me this, why is she with you and willing you to return to the mortal world? Why did she tell you that she loves you?" George asked, his brow arched in challenge.

"She did say that, did she not father? But I too would not have minded staying as I miss you so very much. Did you know that your accident was in fact a murder committed by George Wickham?" Darcy looked directly at his father to assess how he took the news.

"I did my son, but that is in the past now, I want you to look to the future. Protect my beloved Anne and Georgie." George soothed.

"Will I ever see you again, father?" Darcy asked quietly.

Before he could answer, his father and the horses were gone and Darcy was standing on the summit of the hill he had thought would be too hard to climb, then everything went black.

~~~~~~~~/~~~~~~~~

If it were not for his best friend's fight for his life, Charles Bingley would have been the happiest of men. He had been granted a courtship with the woman that he loved beyond all others a month earlier than he had planned to make his proposals to her. He had felt that he should wait as he had not wanted to be seen as insensitive to Darcy's fight for life. Bingley had visited Darcy House earlier in the day and the news had been very promising; it seemed that Darcy had taken a definite turn for the better. With such good news, Bingley felt that it was time to propose to his beloved Franny. He was on his way to visit his sister Caroline and his newly gained brother Graham in their home, Phillips House on Portman Square in London. The added attraction was that his Franny was being hosted by her brother and new sister.

He was shown into the drawing room where Caroline Phillips

was conversing with her sisters, Louisa and Franny. On seeing her brother, the mistress of the house stood and hugged him in welcome.

"Is my brother at his place of work, Caroline?" he asked his youngest sister.

"He is, yes. He is assisting Sir Randolph with a case as we speak," she smiled, pride in her husband obvious, then her demeanour rapidly changed to one of concern. "How is Mr. Darcy?"

"We can thank God. The fever has broken, with much thanks to Lizzy. He is resting much more comfortably now. He has not woken yet, but the doctors are somewhat hopeful that he will soon." Bingley offered what he knew to ease their worry.

"What did Lizzy do?" Caroline asked the question all three ladies wanted answered. Bingley shared the tail of how Elizabeth Bennet had taken charge and what she had insisted be done when Darcy's fever was so high that the doctors were advising his mother and family to prepare for the inevitable. At the end of his telling, there was not as much surprise for Lizzy's efforts as he would have thought there would be.

"That is my cousin," Franny said with a big smile, "she is more circumspect when it comes to judging others now, but when she is sure that she is correct about something, she will allow no one to gainsay her."

"It seems that all of Lizzy's reading has paid handsome dividends for Mr. Darcy," Louisa opined.

"Franny," Bingley turned to the woman of his dreams, "may I speak to you, in private?" Miss Francine Phillips had a good idea why the man that she loved and respected required privacy and nodded, blushing as pleasure radiated from her very being.

"You may use Graham's study, Charles," Caroline informed him, "but the door will remain cracked open and if you do not return in ten minutes, you will find yourselves interrupted!" Caroline warned her brother, only partially teasing.

Once they were in the study, Bingley stood before the woman that possessed his heart and took her hands. "Franny, I used to have an 'ideal' woman in my mind. It was not until meeting you that I recognised that all of the attributes that I was looking for in that fictional ideal woman were physical. I thank God that I have matured and come to realise that the physical is the least important element when one is selecting one's life mate." Franny raised her eyebrows in question, was he intimating that she was homely? Bingley saw the questioning look and realised that she may have misinterpreted what he said. He was momentarily mortified, but soon regained his composure.

"Franny, I was in no way implying that you are anything but beautiful; let me try to speak coherently though, I find myself rendered almost mute by your internal *and* external beauty." She smiled, letting him know that she was mollified. "What I mean to say is that I now know that love, respect, felicity, intelligence, character, and compatibility are much more important than any the physical characteristics I *only* used to look for. To me, you are the most beautiful woman in the world! You have my love, and you meet and exceed every important item that counts. Your beauty is but an added bonus to all of the multitude of positive attributes I see in you, Franny." He could not miss the look of love and pure adoration that she was giving him, so he sunk to one knee.

"Miss Francine Hattie Phillips, my love for you is deeper than the deepest ocean. When I am with you, I know that I am home. You complete me and make me want to be the best version of myself that I can be. Franny, I know we have only been courting for a month, but you must know that had I been given leave to do so, I would have requested a courtship in Hertfordshire. You are the only one for me, and I will spend the rest of my days making you happy. Franny, will you do me the honour and fulfil my every desire by agreeing to become my wife? Will you marry me?"

"Yes, yes Charles, yes I will marry you. I too have long known my path through life would not be complete unless I was by your side." Bingley stood as he heard the words that he had long dreamed of hearing. "I have loved you for months now, and I knew that Papa had restricted you to waiting until I had experienced some of the Season before declaring yourself, but you are the only one for me, Charles." It will never be known if his betrothed wanted to say anything more as she was silenced when Bingley's lips captured hers. He had intended to pull back, but the taste of her captured his every sense, and when she responded, the kiss fell headlong into passion. "Though maybe a short betrothal would be best." She offered shyly, her breathless request making him groan as he tried to collect himself, her heaving breast not helping him find it.

"I will do all in my power to satisfy our needs," he promised quietly, her tell-tale flush making him take a step back from the temptation she probably was not yet aware she issuing. "We should get back before I take that invitation, Franny. I want you far more than I have ever wanted anyone and having to walk away from you will hurt me for many hours tonight." He watched her eyes to see if she understood his meaning, relieved she obviously did.

"Do not be so sure, Charles. You, at least, have known some form of relief. I need you more," she promised softly as she waited, her eyes met his to see if he caught her meaning, and was rewarded with a strangled groan as he pulled her in and kissed her again, this time without worrying if he would scare her as he now knew she was aware of passion and want; he was the luckiest man alive that she wanted him as she did. When he pulled back her eyes were glazed with want and it took some seconds to blink it away.

"A short betrothal, or we could just elope. Right now, the latter is not looking like so bad an option." He teased to help her calm, grateful it worked when she laughed.

"If they make us wait too long, I will demand you take me to Scotland and damn the scandal," she agreed playfully, smiling when his laugh filled the study.

"I think we will have a marriage that many hope is ahead of them when they say their vows." He lifted her hand to kiss it, not trusting himself to bring her much closer or he would kiss her again and they had to be out of time. Not wanting to take any chances, the ecstatic couple returned to the drawing room. Words were not required, and they were accosted by two joyous sisters who wished them happiness, the arched brow he received from Louisa adeptly ignored. Bingley reluctantly took his leave of his betrothed and headed to Bennet House where the Phillips' were being hosted by the Duke and Duchess.

~~~~~~~/~~~~~~~

As the afternoon sun shone though the partially open curtains in the master's chambers at Darcy House, those sitting with the patient went silent. They could see his eyes fluttering in an effort to open. It had been almost a full day since his fever broke, so his trying to wake up was not unexpected, had, in fact, been prayed for.

Darcy thought that he was dreaming again when he opened his eyes to find that she was sitting opposite him close to his bed. She was staring at him with her fine, hazel eyes with the green and gold flecks within. He tried to talk but he could make no sound beyond a croak because his throat was parched. He watched as the lady that held his heart poured some water into a glass from the pitcher beside his bed, Richard very slowly helped him sit up a little. He took small sips to avoid getting sick, as Elizabeth held the glass to his lips.

"Oh, my sweet William, welcome back to us," his mother smiled at him with tears of joy in her eyes. "We were so worried for you, my son, but now that you have woken all will be well."

"Richard, will you please go inform my sisters and Georgie? She would never forgive us if we do not notify her right away that her brother is awake," his Aunt Anne requested.

Darcy sipped water from the glass Lady Elizabeth held for him. His mind was foggy, and he was trying to remember what he had dreamt, or heard, or both. "What d-day is it?" he croaked once the water had eased some of the dryness of his tongue and throat.

"It is the sixteenth day of April, William," his mother informed him. "You have been in and out of consciousness since the ninth of the month my son." She answered his questioning look. The doctor asked the ladies to exit the chamber so he could examine his patient. A short while later he pronounced Mr. Darcy well on the way to recovery and said to summon him if any further assistance was required. As the ladies re-entered, he thanked Lady Elizabeth for her help before leaving the room. Darcy did not have a clue as to what the doctor referred, and before he could ask his sister flew into the room in a blur of blonde hair and skirts. She was followed at a more sedate pace by his two aunts.

"William," she exclaimed, "I am so glad that you have awoken." Georgiana assessed her brother. "If you want to rest so you do not have to attend your duties, William, there are better ways to achieve your ends rather than getting shot!" she teased him, which was unusual enough to surprise him into a smile, her own reflecting the relief of seeing her brother conscious and coherent again.

As soon as his sister said the word 'shot', the events of that day flooded back. "Elizabeth, you were not harmed?" he asked, his voice gaining some strength due to his concern for his beloved. He did not notice that she blushed when he used her name, though the three elder sisters gave each other knowing looks.

"No, William. Thanks to you, I was unharmed," she said. She did not realise that his hand had found one of hers, but when she did, she made no attempt to withdraw it. "You saved my life. If it were not for you, I would have been the one that the bullet would have struck."

"I could not allow that miscreant to harm the lady...my cousin." He blushed and cleared his throat. "Where is that blackguard?" he demanded.

"In hell where he deserves to be, I hope," Lady Catherine spat out with asperity. "Do you remember that the dastard boasted about murdering my brother before Lizzy's footman ended him?"

"I do remember that; though until now, I was not sure if it

was a dream," he paused to take a few more sips of water as his throat was again getting dry. He requested, and was told what had happened the day he was shot. Richard informed him about Wickham's accomplices and the *Spaniard's*, who in fact was Juan Antonio Álvarez, upcoming trial. There was little doubt that he would be found guilty and hung. Besides his participation in Wickham's ill-advised scheme, he had been tied to over ten murders and an untold number of lesser crimes. The one known as *Scarface*, Victor Withers, was spared for his cooperation, and he and his family had been transported. The one member of the conspiracy who would have been killed by Wickham's request and Álvarez's order, Mrs. Karen Younge, had disappeared. The runners agreed that as she had not broken any laws, it was not worth expending resources to track her.

Darcy opined that she had likely fled to Fowey in Cornwall, where her not-so-secret brother, Clay Younge, operated his smuggling enterprise. Richard suggested, and Darcy agreed, that they would send some men to locate her and keep watch. As long as she stayed there and minded her own business, they would leave her alone.

Darcy's family filled him in on all that had occurred during the sennight that he had been unconscious, and how Elizabeth was one of many who refused to leave him until she knew that he would be well. His left shoulder was still hurting very much, but Darcy was determined not to take any of the laudanum that the doctor had left for him. He hated the way that it made him feel.

"What did the doctor mean when he thanked Elizabeth for her help?" He asked when he remembered what Bartholomew had said before he exited the room, not missing her renewed blush.

"She saved your life too, William," Miss Darcy blurted out with the excitement and relief of having her brother awake. When he looked at Elizabeth with a questioning look, his mother, Georgiana, and his aunts filled him in on the treatment that she had demanded for him when his fever had risen too high. Her being at Darcy House the whole time had to mean that she felt more for him than as a cousin, or was it only gratitude? When he began to analyse the way that she related to him, the way that she looked at him before he saved her, it hit him. She had tender feelings for him prior to his being shot.

"Thank you, Elizabeth," he said as he squeezed her small hand, which was still ensconced in his hand.

"If I saved your life, William, then we are but even as you saved mine," she informed him. As the doctor warned them, Darcy soon became very wary and drifted off to sleep. He was kissed by his aunts, sister, and mother. Richard teased him by making as if he was about to kiss his cousin too but instead shook his hand.

Before Elizabeth left, he squeezed her hand again. "We will talk when you wake, William. Sleep well," she said as she left his chambers to be replaced by his valet and a nurse. After she left William's room, she sought out Lady Anne in her private sitting room where she was embordering a handkerchief for her son.

"Aunt Anne, may I please talk to you before I return to Bennet House?" Elizabeth asked tentatively.

"Yes, my dear, you know I always have time for you," Lady Anne welcomed the lady she suspected would be her daughter-in-law before too long. "Close the door and come sit with me on the settee. Should I ring for tea?"

"No thank you Aunt Anne, I partook with William not too long ago," Elizabeth said.

"Lizzy, you are usually more direct, why do you seem so tentative?" Lady Anne asked curiously.

"I want to do something for William," Elizabeth began. "He is the most honourable man that I know, even before he saved my life from that debauchering dastard."

"Anything that you do would be welcomed by William Lizzy, surely you do not doubt his feelings for you?" Lady Anne asked not understanding why the young lady was having so much trouble articulating her wishes.

"My confidence in his feelings is extremely high Aunt Anne," she responded and blushed a little as she remembered her utterance that Georgie heard. "As I unwittingly announced, I love him too."

"Then why do you need to ask me if you would like to do something for my son?" Lady Anne asked the direct question hoping that Elizabeth would clarify what she was trying to say.

"It involves what you told me about your husband and my oath of secrecy, I would like to…" Elizabeth explained what she desired to suggest to her cousin and why the oath between his father and her late husband would not be violated if granted. She made sure that Lady Anne understood that her feelings for William were not in any way tied to the decision made, so if Lady Anne refused, the matter would be forever dropped, and nothing would change between her and William.

"In talking to the Regent and the Queen, you would not technically be breaking your word to me as they know the full story," Lady Anne said thoughtfully. "I assume that you would like to canvass your parent's opinion as well?" Lizzy nodded. "The truth is that I never fully agreed with George's decision, I supported him, but I always felt that he would have made a great Duke of Derbyshire. As long as anything done does not breech the agreement made between the King and my late husband, you have my blessing to talk to your parents and your cousins."

"Thank you, Aunt Anne," Elizabeth said pleased that Lady Anne had given her permission to proceed. "William deserves this more than anyone else that I can think of." Elizabeth stood and kissed the aunt of her heart on her cheek and bade her goodbye.

For the first time since Darcy had been wounded, Lady Elizabeth felt like she could return home and that nothing bad would happen while she was across the square. She asked Miss Jones to collect her belongings and return home with her while her maid placed her clothing in a trunk. Biggs summoned two footmen then escorted the ladies back to Bennet House.

Biggs had not said anything to his lady, but he had noticed

that there was a marked decrease in the number of ragamuffins begging around the environs of Grosvenor Square since the failed kidnapping attempt. It was now obvious to him that the criminal he shot had used young waifs to spy on his Miss Lizzy. He grudgingly gave the man some credit for being cunning enough to pull his spies back after one had almost been apprehended outside of the Gardiner and Associates warehouse.

Elizabeth was welcomed back to her home with open arms. When she asked where Tom was, she was informed that he was at Ashby house visiting his betrothed. She discovered that he was not there, he was at the Bennet House with Lady Amy. There had been negotiation between the couple and their two sets of parents, it had been agreed that they would marry the first Friday in June, the fifth, which would give them a two-and-a-half-month betrothal. Elizabeth knew it was longer than the couple had desired, but she was sure that it was less than the Earl of Ashbury had demanded; his wife must have helped him recognise that a compromise was in order. As she expected, they would marry from the Ashby's home, Ashbury, in Surrey.

Her family was much relieved to hear that William had awoken, that the physician had declared that he was out of danger, and that he only needed to rest and recuperate. The younger Bennet twins were excited that with her brother on the mend, they would see Georgiana soon. They had visited her to make sure that she was well, but nothing beyond short visits. They could now plan a shopping expedition for an agreed upon date. They decided to visit Darcy House on the morrow to ask Georgiana to join them and then they would ask Retta, quickly excited that they would all be together again soon.

Elizabeth requested an audience with her parents and was invited to join them in the Duke's study. They were concerned that aught was wrong until she opened the conversation explaining that she had fallen in love with William Darcy. She hastened to note that it was not out of gratitude for his saving her life but for the man that he was, the man she had learned to appreciate. She huffed at the knowing looks that she received from her parents. It seemed that everyone had already been well aware of what she had only recently admitted to herself.

In order to get her parents approval of her plan to honour William, she explained what she wanted to do, and that it was with Lady Anne's blessing on condition that for now, what she imparted would not leave the study.

CHAPTER 2

Lady Elizabeth Bennet was on a mission; now that she was finally able to admit to herself and others that she loved William Darcy, and he was well along the road to recovery, she decided that the time had come to help her cousin, the Prince Regent, right a wrong that had been denied his father. The King had not been able to honour George Darcy without violating the oath he made to the man who saved his life. When Elisabeth laid out her plan to her parents, both had given their unreserved support.

Elizabeth sent a note to Buckingham House requesting an audience with the Regent and his mother, the Queen. Her courier returned with a note from the Queen's lady-in-waiting, the Duchess of Kent, inviting her to meet with her cousins at eleven that morning. An hour later, Elizabeth was in an anteroom waiting for the Lord Chamberlain to summon her. At two minutes before the hour, the expected summons was delivered. Lady Elizabeth Bennet was escorted into the ostentatiously decorated drawing room which had more gilt gold than she had seen in a single room. She made a deep curtsy to her cousins and waited as one did not address the Queen or Regent before one of them spoke and addressed one first.

"You requested this audience, Cousin Elizabeth," the Regent drawled. "How may we be of assistance? We have to admit that your note intrigued us."

"I thank you for your beneficence in sparing me time, Your Royal Highness and Your Royal Majesty." Elizabeth looked first to the Regent and then to the Queen. "Cousins, over the last months, I have become very close to Lady Anne Darcy. She shared the story of how Mr. George Darcy saved His Royal Majesty's life in '76, and the oath that the late Mr. Darcy extracted from His Majesty the King at that time."

"Very few, outside of this drawing room know of George Darcy's heroism that day, and none save our mother know that he saved us that day as well, Cousin Elizabeth," the Regent said, a very pensive, faraway look in his eyes. "We were not yet fourteen and were with our father on that particular journey. The King had us hide in the carriage, telling us not to move for any reason other than his command. If Mr. Darcy had not stopped that madman, he would have killed our father, and then he would have searched the coach and found us. Father only issued the command for us to exit the conveyance after Mr. Darcy had departed."

"Mr. Darcy saved the King and you Cousin, his heir?" Lady Elizabeth believed that her purpose there that day was all the more righteous.

"That he did, Cousin, that he did. And now we understand that the son has saved our cousin's life," the Queen stated. "It never sat well with us that we were not allowed to acknowledge his heroism and service to the Crown, never mind his decline of any reward."

"I think I have a solution for you, my royal cousins," Elizabeth offered with a sly smile.

"We are interested to hear your suggestion, Cousin Elizabeth," the Regent sat forward in his throne-like chair.

"The promise that was made was specifically between the King and the late Mr. Darcy, was it not?" Both the Queen and her son nodded to indicate that it was so. "If that is true, Your Royal Highness, I do not believe that *you* are bound by said promise, are you? Your Royal Father made the pledge for himself alone, and only to Mr. Darcy, did he not?" Elizabeth waited, smiling when she saw both royals understood what she was suggesting.

"How does the Duke of Derbyshire fare, Cousin?" the Regent asked with a mischievous glint in his eye, his question implying how he decided to go forward.

"He is much improved, Cousin. He will be walking in the next few days, and completely released from the doctor's care any day now," Elizabeth offered the news to her cousins with supreme pleasure.

"As soon as you see that he is able to make a visit, we ask that you notify us and we will invite the Duke, the dowager Duchess, and Lady Georgiana to meet with us here," the Regent said with satisfaction as he winked at Lady Elizabeth. "We expect all of our Bennet cousins to be present as well, Cousin Elizabeth."

"By your leave, Your Royal Highness, may I inform the Darcys?" Elizabeth requested and received a nod of approval from the Regent.

With the plan in place, Elizabeth curtsied then backed out of the drawing room and departed for Bennet House. From the Regent's final remarks, she knew that he would elevate the late George Darcy posthumously; hence both Lady Anne and Georgie would be elevated as well, which would make her William, at least she hoped that he would be her William, His Grace, the Duke of Derbyshire.

~~~~~~~/~~~~~~~

Lady Elizabeth and her parents were shown into the drawing room at Darcy House. Lady Anne was present with her daughter, sister, brother, and sister-in-law. "To what do we owe the honour of your visit?" Lady Anne asked after she requested some refreshments.

"Do we need a reason to want to be with our family?" Elizabeth asked, then with a mischievous grin added, "Your Grace." "Lizzy, what have you done?" Lady Anne asked. Her brother, sisters, and daughter were lost and looking from one to the other in question. The Duke and Duchess were grinning, and both Anne and Elizabeth seemed to be privy to information that none of the rest of Lady Anne's family was.

"I went to visit Cousin George today..." Elizabeth started.

"You did not, did you, Lizzy?" Lady Anne gasped.

"I most certainly did, Aunt Anne, and my cousins were very keen to right a perceived wrong." Seeing that Lady Anne was about to interrupt her, Elizabeth proceeded before she could, while those who had no knowledge about what they were talking about sat in confused silence. "You told me that the promise was between His Majesty, King George III, and your late husband, did you not? *Only* between them?" Lady Anne nodded as she puzzled out how the lady her son loved had achieved what she suspected had been done without anyone violating the King's oath to her beloved late husband.

"Anne, please tell us what is going on," her brother Reggie fairly demanded.

"If I understand what Lizzy has so slyly intimated, and seeing the smiles on both Sarah and Lord Thomas, then William is now his Grace, the Duke of Derbyshire. If I am correct..."

"What did you just say, Anne? How can William be a duke and what Cousin George..." Lady Catherine's her mouth snapped shut as she realised precisely which cousins Elizabeth was speaking of.

"As I was about to say, *if* I am correct then I am now her grace, the Dowager Duchess of Derbyshire, and Georgie is Lady Georgiana Darcy, the daughter of a duke." Other than the three Bennet's smiling and nodding, the rest of the new dowager duchess's relatives sat as still as granite.

"Anne, as you seem to understand what Lizzy is about, please tell us how this happened," Lady Elaine requested, the first to voice the request many wanted to make.

"I will tell you, but I want William helped down first. He is dressed and was planning to descend later today." Lady Anne rang for Killion and relayed her instructions. A quarter hour later, the new Duke of Derbyshire walked slowly into the drawing room with Carstens close by, in case he needed assistance. He lit up as soon as he spied Elizabeth in the room, and she had the same reaction when she saw him enter, none surprised when he sat in an armchair next to Lady Elizabeth.

"Go ahead, Lizzy. You did this, you tell him," Lady Anne smiled at the sight of the two of them together.

"There is much to tell you, William." Lizzy looked directly at him, and his look of concern proved that he was worried that she might say something that would separate them. "As of a few hours ago, you are now his Grace, the Duke of Derbyshire." It was not what he feared, but what she said shocked him to his core. She spoke fast to get it all out before she lost her nerve, "Your mother is the dowager Duchess, your father the late Duke, and Georgie is Lady Georgiana." He was silent for a minute. Lady Elizabeth knew that when he was thinking about a weighty issue, he would be silent until he was ready to speak, so she waited quietly.

He simply asked, "How? Why?"

"William," Elizabeth said as she realised that in her desire to do something good for the man who she loved, she had omitted to ask his opinion beforehand; this she now saw as a gross oversight on her part, as it could be something that he did not desire. "If you do not want to accept the honour, I will speak to our cousins. Nothing has been publicised so other that the Regent, the Queen, and those of us in this room, your family's elevation is unknown." As she thought about her actions, that she knew were driven by her desire to do good she recognised that they were presumptive in the extreme, it was not her decision to make.

Before William answered, his mother relayed the whole of the story to her children and siblings. When she was finished, Lizzy added the information of which not even Lady Anne had known about, the Regent being saved that fateful day along with the King. If the members of the Darcy, Fitzwilliam, and de Bourgh families were stunned before, they were flabbergasted after the telling of both parts of the story.

William who had been considering what Elizabeth had said in contrition for not speaking to any of the Darcys beforehand, wanted an important question answered before he made a final decision. "The Regent did this, and in no way contravened the oath that his Majesty the King made to my late father?" Darcy verified. "Elizabeth nodded vigorously. "If that is the case," William said after a delay to think, "Then I will happily accept the elevation for my family. In future Elizabeth, I would appreciate being consulted on any life changing information *before* you act." He said in mild rebuke.

Once her brother had made the decision, Lady Georgiana was the first one to regain her speech. "My Papa saved the King, and without knowing it, the Regent as well?"

"Yes, Georgie," Elizabeth confirmed.

"Yes, your Grace," Elizabeth replied impertinently. "The oath was in the name of the King, and only between himself and your father. It did not preclude the Regent from his actions," Elizabeth explained. "I do not know why your father refused the King's offer, but as I understand it *this* is not an offer. It is done, and as soon as you feel that you are able to take a carriage ride, I am to inform my cousins so that you may be invited for your investiture."

"I will have another ally in the Lords," the new duke's Uncle Reggie stated with glee.

"Who said I will join the Whigs, Uncle?" Darcy teased.

"Anne, you are a duchess, a dowager one, but a duchess none the less. If I was prone to that sort of thing, I would be calling for my salts right now," Lady Catherine joked. She did not miss the irony that she, who used to be so concerned with the distinction of rank, was now the lowest ranked person in the room.

"I am Lady Georgiana Darcy?" the newly elevated young lady exclaimed. "William is a duke, just like your father, Lizzy."

"Yes, Georgie," her mother could see that her daughter was still processing all the changes to their family. "William will be the second Darcy to be the Duke of Derbyshire. Your Papa, my dear George, will be named the first in his line."

"William, did you know the Derbyshire duchy has four estates and much wealth associated with it? The main estate, the duke's seat, is Falconwood which is located near the north-eastern border between Derbyshire and Cheshire. In fact, I believe the last duke added an estate in Cheshire so that Falconwood straddles the two shires today. All was held in abeyance until the Crown bestowed the title on someone, and it seems that someone is you," the Duke of Hertfordshire informed Darcy.

"If I remember correctly, the secondary title is Marquess of Dovedale and the estate of Dovedale will belong to the marquess, when you decide to gift the world with a son."

"William, is Dovedale not five miles the other side of Lambton?" Lady Anne asked.

"I believe that you have the right of it, Mother." Darcy turned to Bennet, "I also know of Falconwood. With the estate that was annexed to enlarge it, I believe it is larger than Pemberley."

"As far as I know, all of the income from the estates has been held in trust for more than thirty years since the former Duke passed on to his eternal reward. If my sources are to be believed, the amount generated from the four ducal estates plus the Marquess's is an enormous fortune. It is in addition to the wealth that was originally part of the dukedom. Now that I think about all of the wealth that you have just inherited, you will be as wealthy as the combined Bedford and Hertfordshire dukedoms, or close to it."

"I never sought any of this, although I have accepted it," Darcy was stunned and stared at Lord Thomas as he absorbed the information. "We are wealthy enough without the Derbyshire estates and fortune."

"In my opinion, the dukedom could not be in better hands, your Grace," Lady Elizabeth replied, her approval evident when her eyes met his. "Most would see nothing but the wealth, but from what I know of you, William, your first concern will be the welfare of the people who are dependent on you."

The new Duke inclined his head toward his love in appreciation of her words and made an un-Darcy-like spontaneous decision. "Bennet, would you grant me a private interview with Lady Elizabeth, if she has no objection?" Thomas Bennet looked at his daughter while the occupants of the drawing room held their collective breath. She gave her father a slight nod to indicate that she had no objection to hearing what Darcy wanted to say to her. Her father granted the request, and everyone present exhaled in relief. The rest of the party left the drawing room so that Darcy would not have to strain himself to stand and walk to his study. Once the door was closed except for the inch or two required for propriety, he tried to stand but the lady skewered him with a look of warning, daring him to exert himself in that fashion. He wisely remained seated.

"Elizabeth, do I presume too much believing that you are no longer indifferent to me; that you may, in fact, have tender feelings for me?" he asked hopefully, knowing that his future felicity was dependant on her answer.

"No, William, you are not mistaken. In fact, my feelings are in fact far more than just tender." She replied softly.

Lord Fitzwilliam Darcy felt relief and a warm feeling suffused his entire body. "You are too good to trifle with me. You must allow me to tell you how ardently I love and admire you, Lizzy. It has been many months now that I have known that you are the only one for me. I pray that your love of me is not just gratitude for saving your life, but for me, the man. Not the Duke, just me, plain William Darcy." He looked at his beloved hopefully.

"Firstly," Elizabeth said, looking directly into his eyes so he could see the truth of her words, "My asking for your elevation was in no way because I wanted to marry a duke. My only requirement for a husband was deepest and truest love, not a title! I truly believed that I was doing it for you! It was never about me, although I fully acknowledge that I went about it the wrong way, and should have consulted you *prior* to talking to my cousins. I too love you and would not care if you were still Mr. Fitzwilliam Darcy, wealthy or not. As I stated earlier, I am still willing to go back to my cousins and have them rescind your elevation."

"I know that your motivation was not selfish Elizabeth," he said as he returned her look, showing her that he meant his words completely. "I made my decision and I did not make it because I felt that you wanted it or not, I considered the impact on my family and future generations of Darcys, and made my decision on that basis alone," he reassured her. She could see that he wanted to say more, so Elizabeth placed her finger on his lips softly.

"I have to say this William," she said as her expressive eyes begged him to allow her to finish what she felt that she needed to say. "My parents taught me, and all of their children, the best principles, the way to relate to everyone based on the worth of their character, not their position or wealth. For the most part, I did that, but I took the story of what *that woman* almost cost mama and papa as a lesson to mistrust and be quick to judge, as I did with you." Elizabeth saw that he was about to interject so she continued before he could say anything. "I was guilty of some of the same things that I accused you of William. I may not have looked down on those that I thought below me, but I let my pride and my belief that I was not wrong in my judgements pass quick and harsh judgements, and was in my own way, selfish and petulant.

"You once told me that my setdown of you caused you to hold a mirror up to yourself and see who you were becoming, and that drove your desire to change." William nodded to indicate that it had been so. "I went through similar introspection and I learned that my judgement is far from infallible, and because of that, I have learned to take a step back, look at all sides of an issue, and then come to conclusion. Seeing how contrite you were the next day after the assembly started me questioning myself, but I had too much pride and prejudice to allow myself to own up to my errors yet. After talking to a number of people, culminating in my conversations with Aunt Anne, I did see that I had been very wrong, not just in my judgements but in making them in the first place. As we are told, 'remove the tree from your own eye before you try and remove the splinter from that of another,' and that is what I have tried to live up to.

"Acknowledging my own failings made me revaluate everything and led me to see you, the real man, not the one that I had deemed you to be. All of that led me to the point that fateful day when I finally allowed my heart to win the battle with my head that it should have weeks before, that I love you, William, and always will."

"My love, we both made mistakes, I appreciate what you have told me, but my eye is now to the future, a future that has you in it by my side," he said closing the issue, then he looked at her with a grin. "Now," he said, lightning the serious mood, "when did you fall in love with me, my dearest loveliest Elizabeth?"

"It has been coming on so gradually that I was in the middle before I realised what I was about," she said, and he could see the love shining in her countenance. "While I fell in love with you before that day, William; before any of what had happened, and will soon happen, I confess I had admitted it to myself on my walk that momentous day. How could I not fall in love with you, William? Everything changed for me after our visit to Haven House.

"I know what you did to fund New Haven House," she stayed his protest with a finger on his lips before he could make it. "It is not *because* of your generosity, but that and much more forced me to look at the real you and I liked, no loved, what I saw. When we talk and debate, you are never condescending and respect my point of view, even when it is diametrically opposed to what you hold true. The short answer is no, William. Although I am very grateful for your actions to save me from harm, it is not the reason that I love you. It only enhances the love that I allowed myself to admit to before that event."

Darcy smiled a smile that Elizabeth had never seen before, one that revealed his dimples. "Lady Elizabeth Rose Bennet, if I did not know that you would censure me for harming myself, I would be on my knee. When I look to the future, I know that there is only one who I picture walking through life with, as a true partner, and it is you, my beloved Lizzy. It has been some time now that I have known that you are the only one that I could ever marry. I love you with all that I am. Will you grant my heart's fondest desire and agree to be my helpmeet, my partner in all things, my wife?"

"Once I allowed myself to admit my true feelings for you, I realised that you are the only man in the known world that I could ever be prevailed upon to marry. Yes, William, a million times yes, I will marry you." Lizzy replied softly

As she accepted him, she slid to the end of the settee and leaned toward him as he leaned toward her and their lips brushed, their first kiss chaste. They drew back a little, and their eyes met. He gently captured her face in his hands while her hands rested on his chest. They slid around his neck as he drew her to him, and with her in his lap, he kissed her hungrily, like he could never get enough. Passion flared, and her arms tightened around him to keep his kiss, to negate his pulling away before he even tried. When he moaned, she opened her mouth to taste it, and he took the invitation, his tongue sliding up hers so that he could penetrate her in some way, the satisfaction immense. Her tongue teased his, and when she suckled, he was almost unmanned. As much as they wanted to stay in this moment, they were cognisant of the fact that they would soon be checked on. Once they created a small distance between them, Darcy asked the next most important question.

"Please tell me that you do not want a long betrothal, my love," he asked huskily.

"If it were up to me, it would be next week, William. You are not the only one keen to say our vows. Tom and Amy will marry on the fifth day of June. What say you we request to have a double wedding with them? It is less than two months, but no one will be able to say that our marriage was a rushed or patched up affair," Elizabeth suggested. "If they want their own day, we will choose another. I am only suggesting the double wedding as I do not want to wait too long to be your wife William. The truth is that I would prefer a day that is just ours, I am impatient."

"As much as I would love to marry you sooner, Lizzy, I agree with you. Will you talk to Tom and Amy?"

"No, William, I will not. As the commencement of our partnership, we will talk to them, once Papa has approved our engagement and our plan. I will ask that a footman request that they join us if it is convenient to them as they are at Bennet house with Jane, Marie, and their husbands." Elizabeth put herself to rights and looked in a mirror to verify she was fit to be seen.

"I notice that you said *once* your father approves, not *if* he approves!" he teased with his dimple-revealing smile. She hoped that this was the second of many such smiles in which she would be the recipient.

"It seems, William, that we were the last in the family to acknowledge the fact that we love each other. I also may have let it slip that I loved you the night that the cold-water bath brought your fever down." She blushed.

Darcy put his head back and let out a full-throated laugh that led to a knock on the door, the Duke poking his head into the drawing room. "Is all well in here?" the bemused man asked. He saw how close they were sitting one to another and could not miss that the Duke of Derbyshire was holding his middle daughter's hand.

"Papa, I think that William may have something to ask you," she said with a huge smile as she stood and exited the drawing room.

~~~~~~~/~~~~~~~

Karen Younge had finally arrived at her destination of Fowey on Cornwall's coast. It had been a long, arduous journey which had taken a large bite out of her dwindling funds. She was determined to cause as much damage to her enemies as she could. Mrs. Georgiana Wick did not miss the sign at the Blind Bill Inn looking for a new housekeeper. Like she had when she applied for the position of Miss Darcy's companion, Karen Younge had forged some characters and presented them to the innkeeper. Truth be told, after running her boarding house she would be able to fill the position adequately.

She was interviewed by Mr. and Mrs. Grant Firth, the owners of the Bill. Both Tess and Grant were impressed by the well-spoken woman who seemed to have impeccable character, and after a short deliberation, hired Mrs. Wick to be their new housekeeper. At least if she had to go into service it would be in a position of authority. The next part of her plan was to find and make contact with her brother Clay so that she could start to plan her revenge for the death of her George.

Mrs. Wick did not consider disguising her appearance in Fowey as she was unknown and was sure that the circuitous route that she had taken would hide her tracks well enough. When four ex-soldiers took rooms at the Blind Bill, she did not give them a second thought, but they knew *exactly* who she was.

~~~~~~~/~~~~~~~

As soon as Lady Elizabeth entered the parlour where the rest were sitting, all the mothers present noted the look of bliss and love radiating from her countenance.

"Lizzy, is there any news that you would like to share?" Lady Sarah questioned her daughter in anticipation.

"William asked you to be his wife, did he not?" Lady Anne asked with obvious pleasure. Not able to speak at that moment, all Lizzy did was nod vigorously.

"It seems that you have accepted my nephew," Lady Catherine observed, to which the nodding only increased in vigour.

"Yes, yes, he proposed, and I accepted," she was finally able to share her joy.

"We are to be sisters! Oh, I knew how it would be when you said you loved William on that night when we thought we would lose him," Lady Georgiana gushed. "I am gaining not just one sister, but many sisters and brothers..." She deflated, "James will be my brother," she whispered to herself, thinking that it would preclude a relationship between them in the future.

"He will not be your brother through blood, Georgie," her Aunt Elaine interrupted her thoughts, wrapping an arm around her niece to soothe her. "The family connection between you will be through marriage only. You can always think of him as he is now, a cousin." Georgiana brightened as she saw the truth in her aunt's words and immediately blushed at the presumptive thoughts she had verbalised.

"You have no idea how happy this makes me," Lady Anne said as she hugged her soon to be daughter. "There was no doubt in my mind that you two are a perfect match. It gladdens me that the two of you see what the rest of us have seen for months now."

"You owe me ten pounds, Reggie," Lady Catherine informed her brother, amused at the questioning looks around the room. "I wagered that William would propose in the next fortnight when Reggie said he had not noticed them circling one another for months now." She shot her brother a smug look.

"Welcome to the family, Elizabeth," the Earl of Matlock hugged his daughter's sister. "Well, I suppose that we are already family but now you will be my niece. Please call me Uncle Reggie from now on."

"Thank you, Uncle Reggie. I am very pleased to re-gain you as an uncle." Lizzy teased him.

"William will be so pleased that he and Richard will be brothers," Georgie said excitedly.

Lady Elizabeth realised that in her joy she had forgotten that once she married, she would replace Lady Anne as the mistress of all of the Darcy's estates and town homes. "Aunt Anne, I am grateful that I will get to learn how to be the mistress of Pemberley from you. I do not want to supplant ..."

"Lizzy, do not be silly. You will not be supplanting me or usurping my role! It is with the greatest joy that I will watch you become mistress and that I will be able to aid you as you see fit. From now on, could I be Mother Anne?" Lady Anne hugged the young lady that had been a daughter of her heart for some time, and would soon be her daughter in reality.

The Duke of Hertfordshire sat on the settee his daughter had vacated; just not as close to his future son as Elizabeth had been. "Lizzy seems to think that you have a question to put to me?" he asked as he arched an eyebrow like his middle daughter was wont to do, a trait that she had obviously inherited from her father.

"Yes, your Grace. I asked for Lady Elizabeth's hand in marriage, and to my supreme pleasure she accepted me. I now request your consent and blessing of our union." Darcy was silently praying that the man he hoped would soon be his father-in-law had no objections to him.

"Even as you behaved as you did in Hertfordshire when we were first acquainted with you, I could see that you were more than what you allowed others to see. My then future sons confirmed my belief, and you came and humbled yourself and apologised. Our Lizzy did not let you off the hook and was harsh in her judgement. Rather than run with your tail between your legs, you made some hard changes, letting the man that your mother and family always knew was inside emerge. Even before you threw your body in front of a bullet meant for my Lizzy, I knew that you were a man worthy of her hand, mayhap the *only* man worthy of her. So yes, William, you have my consent and blessing. Welcome to the family as a son rather than a cousin." Bennet shook Darcy's hand.

"Thank you, my Lord..." Lord Thomas cut him off.

"Firstly, we are the same rank. Secondly, I am to be your father-in-law so please call me Bennet or Father Bennet. You do know that you will be gaining two fathers–in-laws, do you not?" Bennet smirked.

"Two? I am not sure that I take your meaning," Darcy's brow furrowed as he tried to determine what Bennet meant.

"I forgot that you were not at Richard and Andrew's wedding, Marie was walked down the aisle by my brother Sed. He and Rose do not have children and have adopted my children as their own, so you will, in fact, be receiving two sets of in-laws." Bennet chuckled.

"Should I ask his permission as well?" Darcy asked pedantically and Bennet's laugh told him it was the right thing to do, even to make him laugh again.

"I will do so when next we meet. If I may change the subject? Lizzy proposed a double wedding when Tom and Amy marry. Do you object if the other couple agrees?" he asked, hoping that his beloved's father would not require a longer betrothal.

"Conditional on Amy and Tom agreeing, I see no reason why not, Son." Bennet agreed, having long known this day was inevitable, and was grateful he had a couple more months with his Lizzy; rather than seeking the special license some might demand given her nursing of him, this which would mean she would not be gone before a week was past.

Not too many minutes later, the rest of the family re-joined the two dukes in the drawing room as they waited for the three couples from Bennet House to join them.

Ten minutes later, they were joined not just by the three couples expected from Bennet House, but the younger Bennet twins and Wes and Loretta De Melville. The news was shared, and after a new round of congratulations and wishing the betrothed couple well, Elizabeth asked Lord Tom and Lady Amy to join her on a settee away from the rest. She made the request on behalf of herself and her William. Elizabeth made sure that they understood that she and William would not be upset in any way if they wanted their own day. Neither Amy nor Tom had any objection. Amy reminded them that the wedding was being planned for Ashbury, but she had no objection if they decided to marry in Town. The couples settled on marrying at St. Georges, the church at which all of the family worshiped when they resided in Town.

Once the news of the Darcys' elevation was shared, Richard Fitzwilliam, who could not have been happier that his cousin William was soon to be his brother, teased his cousin as often as he could with 'your Grace' this and 'your Grace' that until Lady Jane gave a small shake of her head to make him cease. The new Duke understood his cousin's rapid compliance as he had recently been on the receiving end of a Bennet daughter's wrath. He was sure that Richard would rather avoid that for as long as possible.

A family dinner was planned for the Saturday, two days hence for all of the extended family to celebrate the betrothals of both couples.

CHAPTER 3

Mrs. Wick had Saturday off so she decided that she would walk to the last known address that she had for her bother Clay. She knocked on the door and presented herself as Mrs. Wick, just in case her brother no longer used the house, not noticing the two men who had trailed her unobtrusively.

"I dunno any Mrs. Wick," she heard her brother's voice call from within.

"Clay, you reprobate, it is me, your sister Karen," she called out. Her brother poked his head out of the room he was in and saw that it was his sister. He had not seen her for almost five years and could not imagine what she wanted with him now.

"Come on in, Karen." He stated evenly. Once in the dingy parlour which had an open window to allow the sea breeze in with fresh air, Karen Younge relayed the whole of the failed plan to her brother. She knew that he would know it if she lied, so she related naught but the truth. She told her brother how she wanted to avenge her lover and beseeched him to assist her in her quest. She dangled the ransom as an incentive to attract her brother to join her scheme. What she did not know, could not have known, is that one of the ex-soldiers had placed himself below the window and heard all.

Once her brother agreed to help the delusional woman for five and seventy percent of all money they were paid, the two men stealthily withdrew and returned to the Blind Bill. They conferred with their two compatriots and agreed on a schedule to watch both brother and sister Younge, then sent a detailed report to their former colonel, with a request for orders and what action, if any, they were to take.

~~~~~~~/~~~~~~~

While Lady Sarah Bennet was dictating the finishing touches on the family dinner at Bennet House later that evening, Lady Elizabeth was at Darcy House visiting. She was seated in the private family sitting room with the three residents. The Darcy women had presumed correctly that her attention would be fixed on the Duke of Derbyshire for her visit, as it was but a day after their engagement. Lady Anne inclined her head toward the door, and she and her daughter stood.

"Mrs. Annesley will remain as a chaperone. It is good to see you, Lizzy, but Georgie and I have to select our gowns for tonight's dinner," she offered the excuse flawlessly to allow the couple some time to converse.

"Thank you, Aunt Anne. I would like to see your gowns before I leave," Elizabeth said distractedly while her eyes never left the handsome face of her betrothed.

Mrs. Annesley repositioned herself, so she was as far from the couple as possible while still preserving the rules of propriety. She smiled to herself, not missing the glow of happiness on the master's countenance. How well he looked when he was happy rather than the dour man that he used to be.

"I missed you, Lizzy. I know that it is less than six weeks until we are to wed, but I am an impatient man and cannot wait until we never have to part again," he said as he looked at her, captivated by his betrothed's fine eyes.

"You are not the only one who is impatient, William. I too wish it was our wedding day already," Elizabeth agreed with a dreamy, loving look. "For too long ago I tried to deny what our families could plainly see. Now that I have allowed myself to acknowledge that you are my soulmate, my true one and only, I cannot wait to start our lives together."

"When did you fall in love with me, Lizzy?" the duke asked his future duchess.

"Before I answer that question, William, I want to be sure that you know that I never desired your missing my sister's marriage to your cousins." She stopped him before he could interject with a hand on his arm, "I was not ready to see you when your family first visited Longbourn, but I am not sure if you know that I was ready to forgive you long before we met again in London."

"That choice was mine and mine alone, my love. My mother, Richard, Andrew, and others all told me in no uncertain terms that I would be more than welcome to attend the wedding and the festivities prior to it," Darcy related with a sad smile. "*I* did not feel that I was ready to face you, your family, or the citizens of Meryton yet. It was not your desire that I stay away but *only* my own. My mother was candid with me that she asked you to wait to forgive me, and I find that I cannot disagree with her, my love. It was not time yet. Please do not have any recriminations about then, we have both matured and grown. Neither of us is the same person we were at that time." He held her hands in his. "Now my dearest, loveliest Elizabeth, I am waiting for the answer to my question."

"I cannot fix a time or place, William, I was in the middle before my head allowed me to acknowledge what my heart already knew. After your apologies and obvious efforts to better yourself, I knew that you were an estimable man, one who I wanted to count as a friend." Darcy took her hands in his and bestowed a kiss on the inside wrist of each. The sensations his actions ignited left the lady breathless. She was only sorry that they were not alone and that his kisses were not ones she could return as her lips ached for him. She had tasted him after his proposal and could not wait for more. She blushed crimson at her wanton thoughts and tried to answer his question with some semblance of calmness.

"I already thought of you as a friend when we all visited Haven House. I overheard your conversation with Miss Cookson, and discovered your generosity, which you do not want made public. I knew then that my heart belonged to you. While I came to it in my own time, I wish someone had told me to pay attention to myself when I was with you, any clue to help me discover such happiness sooner. Once I agreed to three sets at

Anne's and Ian's ball, I was already well on my way to admitting that I loved you. It was not long after that my heart started to overwhelm my head, which led me to finally admit that my love for you involved all of my being. It was the morning of my walk that my heart finally won and told the rest of me to accept it as fact.

"As I told you when you proposed, although I will forever be grateful for your unselfish and heroic acts that infamous day, it was not what made me fall in love with you. I was already very much in love with you, William. I allowed myself to admit the morning of that walk that you were the only man that I would be prevailed upon to marry." The love and adoration shining from her eyes gave truth to her words. "And you, William? When did you fall in love with me?"

"If I am honest, my tender feelings started the night of my epic set down at the assembly." He squeezed her dainty hands to stop the protest he could see was on the tip of her tongue. "When I saw how mesmerising your eyes were, and that you so obviously cared not a whit for my position in society or my wealth, I knew that I was standing before a lady that would see the man, not what he could give her.

"I will not prevaricate. At first, I tried to rationalise my behaviour and was indignant, but even before my cousins and Bingley took me to task after the assembly, I had begun to acknowledge the truth of your words. I berated myself for possibly putting both of my cousin's relationships with your sisters in jeopardy. Owning that I was not always right, humbled me, which drove me to present myself at Longbourn to apologise the next morning. If I thought that the dressing down that I received from Andrew and Richard was severe, it was nothing to what I received from their parents, my mother, sister, and aunt on my return to Town."

"You were not the only one at fault, William. I was too strident in my opinions, too quick to judge, and to fixate such implacable resentment. I..." He silenced her speech with a quick, chaste kiss that caused Mrs. Annesley to raise her eyebrows, but she remained silent.

"No, my love, I deserved every word. As I worked to change my behaviour, I had more time to think about you, and I realised that you were, in fact, the most handsome woman of my acquaintance. By the time we met in London after the double wedding, I was well on my way to loving you. When you apologised to me, accepted mine without any reservation, and proposed that we start again, I was irrevocably lost and knew that you were the only woman that I would or could ever love. If I could not win your heart, then I would not have married, and Georgie's first son would have inherited Pemberley and all of our properties. Now our first-born son, who will be the Marquess of Dovedale, will inherit all of the ducal properties after I leave the mortal world, and if we are blessed with a second son, he will have Pemberley and the other Darcy estates, none of which are entailed. When you accepted me it was a dream come true. I never thought that I would be able to win your heart, but I am so very glad that I was proven incorrect in this too, my love. You are my everything, my heart, and with you by my side as my full partner, I am complete."

"It was a dream for me as well, the wish that you could fall in love with me after the way I abused you, William. Let us make a promise to each other, from now and for the future, let us only remember the past as that remembrance gives us pleasure," Elizabeth suggested a way forward with no more looking to their past missteps by either.

"I agree," he promised, already knowing that he would never be able to deny her anything she asked of him.

"Before I forget, William, Cousin George, the Regent, sent a note from his private secretary asking if you are well enough to come to Buckingham House for your investiture." Elizabeth smiled sweetly.

"I am well now, my love, so you may send a response that I am able to make the visit at the Regent's pleasure and convenience." He chuckled.

It was not long after that the Dowager Duchess and Lady

Georgiana returned. "Lizzy, I am so very happy that I will be gaining you and four new sisters when you wed William," the young lady offered joyously. "God did not grant Mama any more children after I was born, so I have never felt sisterly love until I met all of the Bennet sisters in November last year. Gaining four more brothers is a wonderful thing as well."

"Especially one particular brother," Elizabeth teased, and a blush started to spread across Georgie's face and got progressively redder.

"Do not tease your younger sister, Lizzy," Lady Anne corrected her elder daughter with mock severity. "Did I not already request that you call me Mother Anne?"

"That will be a pleasure Mother Anne. If you will excuse me, I need to write a note to my cousins." Lizzy was directed to the mistress's study to pen her missive. Seeing the questioning looks from his mother and sister, Darcy informed them of which cousins she referred to and about the subject of the note.

Before the Darcys walked across the square to Bennet House, a royal courier had delivered the summons from Buckingham House for the first Monday in May at eleven o'clock in the morning. All three Darcys were to be present. At the same time, a similar summons was delivered to both the Matlock and Hilldale Houses.

That evening it was a very large and merry family party that enjoyed dinner and convivial company, and many toasts were raised to the two betrothed couples. During the separation of the sexes, the matriarchs of the family were seated together discussing their favourite subjects; the Darcy's elevation, the betrothals, and upcoming double wedding.

"This is all Lizzy's fault, you know," Lady Catherine drawled.

"What is that, sister?" Lady Anne asked.

"That you are above me in rank now, a dowager duchess! I hope you do not expect me to use the 'your grace' appellation, Anne," Lady Catherine teased.

"How am I to feel then," asked Madeline Gardiner, "as I am the only untitled one here, and my husband is in trade?"

"You know, Maddie," Lady Rose Bennet, stated, "Sed had told me that the prevailing opinion among many in the peerage is that times are changing rapidly. It will not be too many years in the future when tradespeople will be the sought-after connections, and those of the peerage who only rely on income from the estates and no other sources will be the ones seeking you out."

"Only time will tell," Mrs. Gardiner responded then tactfully changed the subject. "Lady Catherine, I understand that the Duke of Derbyshire's proposal earned you ten pounds."

"Firstly, as we are family, Madeline, my name is Catherine, and yes, my nephew's timing earned me said sum," she said with a smile of amusement.

"Anne, you were the first to opine that Lizzy and William would become a couple once they both moved past their stubborn natures and admitted what you and then the rest of us could see as plainly as the noses on our faces," Lady Sarah Bennet stated as she looked at the group of younger ladies sitting together and talking.

"I was only the first to see where they were headed because I was able to observe them together more than the rest of you, Sarah. It was not long until we all saw the tender feelings developing between them." Anne explained.

"I pray that both Loretta and Wes make love matches like Tom and Lizzy have," Lady Pricilla, Countess of Jersey said wistfully.

"I am sure that they will, sister," Lady Rose Bennet assured her sister-in-law as she squeezed her hand. "How could they not with so many examples in the family?"

"Both of my boys made love matches and brought me daughters that I still have trouble telling one from the other when they are not with my boys," Lady Elaine looked toward her daughters who had made her sons so very happy.

"Add my Graham to that list," Hattie Phillips added, "and soon Franny will be saying her vows for her own love match."

"When do you depart for Meryton, Hattie?" Lady Sarah

asked.

"We leave on Monday morning. Most of the plans are in place and Franny has ordered her trousseau, so there really is no reason to delay our departure." She looked at Sarah, long loved as a sister, and was gratified the feeling was mutual as she had not had such a connection with her own. "Sarah, I do want to thank you for hosting the dinner before the wedding."

"No thanks necessary. You know how much we love Franny." Sarah smiled warmly as she again scanned those assembled and soaked in the evident happiness of so many.

"Is the date set for a betrothal ball for the two couples, Sarah?" Lady Rose enquired.

Sarah Bennet looked to Lady Anne for confirmation and seeing her nod, she answered her sister-in-law's question. "Now that William is well, we are about to start sending invitations out for Friday the fifth of June, ten days before the wedding."

As the ladies were busy with their discussions, the men were having a much more serious one. "I have heard from the men that I sent to Fowey in Cornwall to keep an eye on Mrs. Younge. She uses the name 'Mrs. Georgiana Wick' now."

"What hubris to assume to take Georgie's name combined with his," the new duke spat out. "How dare she?"

"Her name is not our problem, cousin," Richard Fitzwilliam reported. "It seems that the woman has not learnt from her 'dear' Wickham's demise, she is planning to avenge him with the help of her smuggler of a brother, Clay Younge." the former colonel then relayed the contents of the letter he had received. It stated that for much of the first week she had kept her head down and did her work, but then it detailed what the men had heard when Mrs. Younge made contact with her criminal brother.

"We will not wait around for this woman and her brother to try and hurt my daughter. I want them arrested as soon as may be!" Lord Thomas Bennet announced with no little anger and worry in his voice.

"What are you doing to protect our sister, Richard?" his

brother, Lord Andrew Fitzwilliam, asked.

"By the morrow, ten more of my ex-soldiers, accompanied by a contingent of runners, depart for Fowey. When I answered the missive, I instructed the men to keep a good vigil and to report back to me anything else they discover," he explained matter-of-factly.

"If anyone tries to harm my Lizzy again..." Lord William cursed at the very idea someone might.

"No one will harm her, William!" his Uncle Reggie interjected. "We are aware of her plans, and it seems that she is not cognisant of being observed," He noted. Unfortunately, his words would prove to be the opposite of the truth.

~~~~~~~/~~~~~~~

Clay Younge was a criminal, but not a stupid one. Once his sister had shared the extent of her former lover's attempt to kidnap the daughter of a duke, he was sure that a rich and powerful family like the Bennets would leave no stone unturned to find all involved in the botched conspiracy. Not wanting to take a chance, he assigned three of his best men to watch out for his sister. He was thinking about what he should do when he was approached by a woman in black mourning garb who was accompanied by a young man of perhaps of eighteen or nineteen years.

The woman asked if he was Clay Younge. "U' wants ta know?" he asked with disdain.

"I am Johanna Álvarez, and this is my son Anthony." She replied firmly.

"So what? I dunno know you, so why should I care u' you are?" he scoffed.

The lady proceeded to tell him that she was the widow of Juan Antonio Álvarez, the *Spaniard*, and she was seeking to pay back the people that had her husband and the father of her son hung while taking away the empire that they had built. As she was telling the man her tale, she recalled how she became Mrs. Álvarez.

Johanna Cross had been employed as a maid at one of the Span-

iard's brothels in St. Giles. She had not been there long when she observed that the Madam was skimming money to keep for herself. As a way to better her lot, she reported the facts to Scarface. *Later that day she was presented to Juan Antonio Álvarez.*

After the Madam received a permanent smile and a 'swim' in the Thames, Álvarez made the smart and intelligent woman his temporary Madam. She excelled at the work and soon she was in charge of running all four of his 'houses', and as a consequence spent more and more time with the man.

They had started lying together and she had become with child. He married her, and four months later, her Tony was born. He had been happy to have a son who he could train to take over the running of his empire one day.

In her own way Johanna had loved her husband and would not let the people that took him and their livelihood away go unpunished.

"Ow did you find me?" Younge asked.

"Your sister's former lover was very forthcoming with any and all information that my husband wanted, and he told us about you. My late husband, may he rest in peace, made note of your name, trade, and location," the widow informed him. "I made the assumption that your sister would come to you to help hide her, and so I took a chance that I was correct and brought my son with me."

Younge thought for a while then welcomed the woman whose aims aligned with his own, and who had a reasonable sum of money to her name that she had been able to spirit away before the runners had dismantled their empire. As they were talking, one of Caleb's men that had been told to keep an eye on Karen reported that there were four men watching the Blind Bill's housekeeper, and that one or two of them followed her where ever she went. They also seemed to be interested in their boss's movements. Caleb Younge had no doubt that these men were connected to the powerful people Wickham's scheme had targeted.

He ordered his man to ready his sloop, which was one of the

fastest smuggling vessels in the kingdom; at least in his opinion, and for another to retrieve his sister. If there was a man or men following Karen, the problem was to be dealt with. He, his men and his new confederate slipped out of a hidden door into a back alley and headed for the sloop as they lost the men posted to watch him.

Mrs. Wick was in the market buying fresh produce for the inn when her brother's man whispered that she was being followed and that she had to leave with him immediately. As the man who was assigned to keep track of her that day made to follow her, he was pulled into an alleyway from which he would never emerge by three of Younge's men.

Within two hours, Younge's sloop 'The Stealthy Runner' had slipped her lines and sailed toward France with Karen Younge, Johanna and Anthony Álvarez, and her normal crew of miscreants and headed toward France. As soon as she was over the horizon out of view of anyone on land, she changed tack and set the course for Ireland. The criminals decided that they needed to disappear for some time so the trail would go cold. They would use the time to plan, then, when they were ready, they would return to receive their perceived due.

CHAPTER 4

The Darcys, Bennets, and Fitzwilliams were in an ante-chamber at Buckingham house awaiting the summons from the Lord Chamberlain to enter the drawing room where the Queen and the Regent were sitting. A few minutes after the hour, he summoned them, then announced them all to the royals.

Once all were announced and deep curtsies from the women and genuflecting from the men had been offered, they were invited to sit. "We welcome you all and thank you for graciously accepting our invitation," the Regent drawled. "We are especially gratified to see that his Grace, the Duke of Derbyshire, seems to be hale and healthy again. We would like to thank you for saving our Cousin Elizabeth from that madman." He inclined his head toward Darcy who accepted the royal thanks with a single nod.

"Lord Darcy, did our cousin explain that not only did your father save my husband but also our son on that fateful day?" Queen Charlotte asked.

"Lady Elizabeth did tell me that, your Royal Majesty. I have always been proud of my late father, and am even more so now that I have heard of his heroism. He told no one save my mother, his beloved wife Lady Anne." Darcy radiated pride for his late father, the first Duke of Derbyshire in the Darcy line.

"Did we hear correctly that the dastard admitted murdering your father before he was dispatched?" the Regent asked.

"Yes, Your Royal Highness, that is correct," the Duke of Derbyshire replied, his anger building as he thought about what Wickham had taken from them, what he tried to take from him now. "If he had not been shot, I would have done the deed with my bare hands." The Dowager Duchess sitting next to him put her hand on his arm to calm him. Even though Georgiana knew what the murderer had done, she gasped at hearing his criminal deeds being discussed in such a forum.

"Cousin Elizabeth and Cousin Tom, did we hear that congratulations are due to both of you as you are both betrothed?" the Queen asked, knowing the answer to the question before she asked it.

"Yes, Your Royal Majesty," the brother and sister chorused.

"On behalf of my betrothed, Lady Amelia Ashbury, I thank you for your kind words, Your Royal Majesty," the Marquess of Birchington said as he bowed his head toward the Queen.

"You are betrothed to Derbyshire, cousin Elizabeth?" the Queen asked. "We heard that at one time your feelings were not so tender, if our sources are correct?"

"In cases such as this, Your Royal Majesty, a good memory is unpardonable," Elizabeth answered cousin with her trademark impertinence. The Regent let out a loud guffaw while his mother laughed silently into her hand.

Once the Regent had settled, he got to the business of the hour. "Derbyshire, you understand that by awarding the dukedom to your father posthumously we did not violate the agreement that he made with my father, His Majesty the King?"

"I do, Your Royal Highness," he agreed.

"Good. Before we commence with the investiture, we would like to explain why we invited the former Colonel Richard Fitzwilliam and his family here today." Richard tensed as he truly could not fathom that he was the reason that his family had been invited to attend the ceremony. "Wellesley has fully informed us of your heroism at the battles of Roliça, Elviña, and Buçaco." As the Regent saw the former colonel about to protest, he raised his hand to silence him. "As you well know, Wellesley does not give praise lightly, and we have verified everything with other officers who served alongside you as well as some of those whose lives you saved. For the services that you provided to the crown and your heroism in the field, we *are* elevating you. From this date forward you will be the Earl of Brookfield. We are awarding you the estate of **Broadmoor** in Nottinghamshire. Your first son will be Viscount Broadmoor. We do this with our thanks and that of the kingdom, even if most do not know of your actions by necessity."

The Duke of Derbyshire was then instructed to kneel and the Regent tapped his right shoulder with his ceremonial sword, the elevation then official and irrevocable. The new Earl kneeled in front of his Highness and received his tap on his shoulder. His family watched the investiture with pride and happiness radiating from their countenances. The Lord Chamberlain handed each new peer their patents and informed them that a royal decree would appear on the morrow in the papers.

,. "You had to better me and reclaim your place that I took when I outranked you after we married," Lady Marie Fitzwilliam could not help teasing her older sister as they walked out of St. James, very happy for both her sister and new brother. "Janie, I can scarce believe it, you are a countess!"

"*You* cannot believe it! Richard and I are waiting for someone to wake us or tell us it was all an intrigue by our cousins," Jane admitted as she walked between her mother and mother-in-law.

"This was never anything that I wanted," the Earl of Brookfield stated, still in a stupor.

"No one deserves it more than you, Rich," Andrew Fitzwilliam countered. "As much as you have tried to downplay your actions, the family has long known about them," his older brother added. Richard scanned his family, his eyes narrowed in accusation.

"No, son, not I nor anyone else in the family petitioned the royals for this or anything else. While you were being elevated, one of the royal advisors informed me that it was General Arthur Wellesley himself who informed the Regent and pushed for you to be recognised," the Earl of Matlock assured his son. He was as proud of his son as any father could be, in fact more so than he could express in words and of much lesser importance, it did not hurt that he had just gained another ally in the lords.

"Only one person here made a disclosure to her cousins that led to an elevation," the Dowager Duchess of Derbyshire teased her future daughter-in-law. "Although, I must admit that Lizzy sought my permission to speak to her parents and cousins, and I granted it to her." William should have known that his betrothed would not break an oath of secrecy to his mother and just shook his head in amusement.

"It did not take much convincing. Cousin George was delighted that I offered him a way to thank the Darcys for the service that your late husband provided them," Elizabeth reported proudly.

"I see," teased the Duke of Derbyshire, "you are determined to marry a duke!" he said with a huge grin. He was able to tease her as he knew that his new title had nothing to do with her wanting to marry him. "This duke is more than happy to make you his duchess, Lizzy."

~~~~~~~/~~~~~~~

The new Earl of Brookfield was beside himself with anger. When the men and runners that were dispatched to Fowey arrived, they found only three men, not four. A search discovered the body of Sergeant Hamms with his throat slit. If that was not bad enough, the Younges had vanished. After an exhaustive search and questioning many, it was discovered that the sloop that Younge used had sailed the same day that Hamms had disappeared. The report was that it seemed to be heading toward France, but as Richard related the information to his Cousin Darcy and Lord Thomas Bennet, they all agreed that the heading was more than likely a diversion.

Lord Thomas noted the name and description of the sloop. The information would be disseminated throughout the Dennington fleet with instructions to report any sightings of the *Stealthy Runner*. As they could have sailed anywhere, there would not be a formal search mounted. The Dennington Lines fleet was the largest in the realm and docked in ports large and small in every corner of the known world, therefore, it would be the most effective way to search for the sloop. The three men pledged money that ended up totalling ten thousand pounds to be invested for Hamms' widow and children, giving them an income of more than five hundred per annum, considerably more than what the ex-sergeant had earned. It would not make up for Mrs. Hamms loss of her husband or his children their father, but they would be cared for financially.

Richard Fitzwilliam pledged that those who murdered Hamms would be brought to justice, one way or another, and the steely look in his eyes left no doubt of his resolve. His family had seen that look before, the Younges and their cohorts had crossed a line that had lit the fire of fury in the normally affable man with a jovial disposition.

The two betrothed couples decided to take a walk in Hyde Park. Lady Elizabeth had not uttered one syllable in opposition to the eight footmen that would accompany them, including her and Amy's companions. Since that day, she had accepted whatever security measures that her father put in place to protect his family. Some of the guards, namely Biggs and Johns, would stay very close to the couples, and two sets of three would walk ahead and behind their charges. Even with Wickham dead and his co-conspirator out of England, the Duke of Hertfordshire would not take any chances. He gave his middle daughter a challenging look, daring her to try and gainsay him; it killed any possible protest before it was made.

As they walked over the infamous bridge, Darcy looked at his betrothed, both silently acknowledged that they would never walk over the bridge without remembering what almost happened. Seeing the pensive look on her fiancé, Lady Elizabeth gripped his arm tightly to get his attention.

"William, I think that even though you were shot here, this is a place that we should look upon with pleasant memories, not bad ones," Elizabeth stated, nodding at her betrothed's quizzical look. "There was much more good that happened here than bad. You saved my life, and it is in this park I finally admitted that I loved you."

"Then I agree, my love, there was much positive that day. Even after everything that he did, murdering my father, trying to kidnap my heart, what he tried with Georgie, I still mourn the person that Wickham could have been, the one that he was as a boy before his viscous propensities came to the fore," the Duke of Derbyshire said with sadness in his eyes.

"William, it is natural that you mourn the friend that was, but never forget that for far more of his life he was the person that died here while trying to harm me," she said as she looked into his eyes, her love there for him to fall into. "I think that we should hold true to our agreement and only think of the past as the remembrance gives us pleasure."

"It is a good philosophy, my beloved Lizzy," he said as he smiled. "I do have so much to be thankful for, for I will soon marry the love of my life." Elizabeth nodded vigorously in agreement with his sentiment. "My dearest mother was brought back to us by a miracle when the doctors had given up hope, Georgie was saved from the dastard and his paramour…"

"By *you*, my love, do not minimise the fact that had you not arrived when you did…" Lady Elizabeth interjected and then he cut her off.

"I know that, love, I just chose not to congratulate myself again," he blushed. "We are surrounded by a large, expanding, and loving family. Yes, we are wealthy, but all the wealth in the world would be meaningless without your love and the love of family. It scares me when I think how different life would have been if God had not released my mother back to us, rather than calling her to Him." Darcy shuddered as he said the last.

"But He did not take her, did He? How lucky am I? Soon I will have three mothers!" Lady Elizabeth added with glee. "My Mama, Aunt Rose, and Mother Anne, I am so very lucky, some have no mothers, and I am to have many!" Darcy nodded his head in agreement with her sentiment. He was fully cognisant of the fact that he would be gaining the Duke and Duchess of Bedford as an additional set of parents-in-law.

"Amy and Tom seem well suited," Darcy changed the subject, inclining his head to the couple walking ahead of them.

"They are, and I am happy to welcome Amy as another sister. I have no doubt that they will be happy." She agreed. "William, did you know that Tom's estate of Birchington is less than thirty miles from Pemberley?"

"I do. Tom and I have discussed our estates, his is across the border of Yorkshire, the same shire that the Bedford's primary estate is. With Jane's and Richard's estate not more than ten miles from Pemberley, and Snowhaven, and Hilldale not much farther, we will have a lot of family in close proximity after we are married," Darcy informed his beloved.

"I will miss Longbourn and the rest of my family, but I am sure that I will be very happy at Pemberley. Will I get to see it before we are married?" she asked hopefully.

"That depends on your father, my love. If he agrees, and we have time before the wedding and the ball, it would be my pleasure to show you our estate." He agreed and Elizabeth recognised the look that he got when he was deep in thought. "Mayhap we can suggest a trip that includes the Ashbys so that Tom can show Amy and her parents Birchington?"

"I think that is a wonderful idea, William." Before she could call out to Tom and Amy, Darcy suggested that before they head north, if it was agreeable to all, he would like to have his fiancée take a tour of Darcy House. She agreed and then called Tom and Amy who stopped and waited for them to catch up.

Lord Birchington and Lady Amelia heartily agreed with the suggestion. It was resolved that the four would talk to the various families and ask, cajole if needed, about taking a trip north after the Bingley-Phillips wedding.

~~~~~~~/~~~~~~~

The Tuesday before the Bingley-Phillips wedding Lady Sarah Bennet and her middle daughter arrived at Darcy House for the agreed upon tour; Lord Tom, Lady Amy, and her mother were touring Birchington House on Russel Square. All three Darcys met Lady Sarah and Lady Elizabeth, the Dowager Duchess introduced her housekeeper, Mrs Cheryl Killion, whose husband Henry was the butler.

"Now Lizzy, if there are any changes that you want to make, you will not offend me in any way. In a little more than a month you will be mistress of this and the rest of the Darcy properties, so it is only natural that you would want to make some changes as I did when I became mistress," Lady Anne squeezed Lizzy's hand, her heart filling with happiness at the idea of soon having her with them all the time as she loved the young lady dearly.

"I thank you, Mother Anne. *If* there is anything that *needs* to be changed, I will be honest about wanting to, but from what I have seen when I stayed here while William was ill, there will be little or nothing to change for my tastes." She smiled warmly, wanting the Darcys to know that she had no intention to make changes just because she could.

"I was informed that you never took a formal tour when you were nursing me, my love," Darcy noted, "and I understand that you saw little outside of my chambers and your own."

Lady Elizabeth acknowledged the truth of his statement, and with a nod from her mistress, the housekeeper commenced the tour. The house was very similar to Bennet House except for some cosmetic changes that the Darcys had made over the years. On the entrance level there was a wide hallway that led to the grand marble staircase ascending to the second floor. The ceiling in the hall was two floors above rather than one, on which was a very tasteful fresca. The hall itself was lined with tapestries, one of which showed the Darcy family trees and was hung next to the stairs.

There were three drawing rooms, a very large music room, a receiving room, and three smaller parlours on the first-floor ground level. In addition to those, there was a breakfast parlour, family dining parlour, and a formal dining parlour. A magnificent ballroom was down but a short hallway to the right of the double front doors. There were multiple crystal chandeliers and many wall sconces, it was nearly a twin of the ball room at the Bennet's house. On two of the four sides were a number of large floor to ceiling windows, and a set of large double doors that led out to a veranda with steps that ended at the entrance to a garden on one side of the ball room. The walls between the three dining parlours could be folded and rolled back to expand the ball room, if ever needs required.

The next stop was the guest wing that spanned the third and fourth floors. There were multiple suites that had two bedchambers with a shared sitting room, and a good number of single bedchamber suites with smaller sitting rooms. In addition, each floor had a nice sized guest sitting room. Between the two floors they could accommodate fifty guests with ease. On the fifth floor were the school rooms and the chambers for nursemaids, governesses, tutors, and companions. Thus far, Elizabeth had found nothing she would classify as a major change, although she had suggested some minor updates to a few of the guest chambers. The servant's quarters were spread between the attic and an area on the kitchen level.

The last floor they toured was the second floor, which held the family wing, and Lizzy learned that Lady Anne no longer inhabited the mistress' suite. She now had a full, two bedchamber suite one door down from Georgie's. There was a large family sitting room that could comfortably accommodate around five and twenty, and a family music room. The music room contained Lady Anne's harpsicord, a small square pianoforte, and a harp. The penultimate stop was the mistress's side of the master suite.

Lady Elizabeth's soon to be chambers included a very large bed chamber, a huge walk-in closet, and dressing and bathing rooms. Opposite the bed was a fireplace with a mantle that held miniatures of the family. To the left was a floor to ceiling window, and to the right were double glass doors that opened onto a balcony which overlooked the gardens. Try as she may, she could not hide her blush on spying the very large bathing tub in the bathing room. She had no doubt that it would fit two with ease. She felt wanton as she considered sharing it with William, and the ability to wash him with a cloth, then her cheeks flushed hotter as she pictured washing him without even that between her fingers on his wet, soapy skin as she slid them up and...down. A light brush of his hand on her back startled her out of her thoughts and she attempted to refocus, finding it difficult when he murmured that he wanted a full accounting of her thoughts when next they were in the room.

Between the mistress and master chambers was a spacious, private sitting room. Her future chamber and the sitting room were the only two spaces in which that Lady Elizabeth had asked for substantial changes. The wall coverings were a little faded and Lizzy preferred other styles of furniture. She told Lady Anne that she and Georgie were welcome to anything that wished and she would add its replacement to her list if not already on it.

The final stop on the tour were the master's chambers. As she had expected they would, her beloved William's chambers exuded masculinity with the walls a mix of hunter green and browns. She blushed scarlet when she saw the most enormous bed she had ever seen. Her betrothed changed colour as well when he noticed her reaction to seeing his, soon to be their, bed. His bathing room had a twin of the bathing tub she had seen in mistress's bathing room which caused her to blush all over again.

They returned to the green drawing room for refreshments, and Georgiana took Lizzy's hand in her own. "I know I have told you this before, but I am so happy that you will soon be my sister, Lizzy," she smiled brightly. "When you told Will that you loved him while he was fighting for his life, I just knew how it would be!"

"I am likewise as glad that I will be gaining you as a sister, Georgie," Elizabeth said as she hugged the younger lady.

"Has a decision been reached about all of us travelling north yet?" Lady Anne settled next to Lady Sarah.

"Thomas has agreed, but we are waiting to hear from the Ashbys. I believe we will have their answer when Tom, Amy, and Gillian return from Birchington House," Lady Sarah replied contentedly.

While all were enjoying their tea, Killion announced Lord Thomas Bennet, the Marquess of Birchington, Lady Gillian Ashby, the Countess of Ashbury, and Lady Amelia Ashby. After greetings were conveyed, Lady Gillian informed everyone that the Ashbys had agreed to join the expedition north set to leave after the wedding on the fifteenth day of May. The three Ashbys would meet the Bennets and Darcys at a coaching inn where the road from Meryton met the Great North Road.

~~~~~~~/~~~~~~~

As the *Stealthy Runner* neared the coast of Ireland, the feelings of resentment toward those that forced them to flee England grew exponentially with every conversation the co-conspirators shared.

Karen Younge had been expounding on her 'dear Wickham' *ad nauseum*. Her ravings annoyed Johanna Álvarez so much that she was tempted to tell the babbling woman about her 'love's' plot to have her murdered in order to claim a larger share of the ransom. As much pleasure as she would have derived from watching the reaction, Johanna decided to forgo. As long as the woman was angry, it served her purposes.

Clay Younge had chosen Bundoran in County Donegal for their base of operations. It was on the west coast of Ireland and far from Dublin, which would offer minimal risk of observation and why it was chosen. It was a smaller town with a harbour that would accommodate his sloop, but nothing too much larger than it. Clay opined, and Johanna had agreed, that no one would look for them there. They would bide their time and then they would strike, earning more in this one strategic plot than he had ever dared dreamed of before. They felt that if they took time to plan, unlike Wickham they would succeed in making the toffs pay the demanded sum.

The day they docked, they set up lodgings, and Johanna had the task to get her hands on any papers for news, as one would normally want when coming to port. To that end, the post office kept a two-week supply of Dublin and London papers as those who docked could as easily hale from one or the other. As they looked for any news of themselves or of note about the incident in the park, Karen Younge read something that made her furious. She learned that the prig who always denied her George his due was a duke! Not only that, he was engaged to that Bennet trollop who had humiliated her love, and, she was sure, had been instrumental in his death. As she was ranting at the unfairness, Anthony Álvarez, Tony as he was known, swore that he would do anything that he could to exact punishment on those that had had his papa hung and destroyed their empire.

When Johanna Álvarez and Clay Younge heard about Darcy's elevation, they only saw the possibility of exacting more money than they had so far suggested to request. Both suffered from the same affliction that had been the *Spaniard's* downfall: insatiable greed.

~~~~~~~/~~~~~~~

The pre-wedding festivities and the celebration of Charles Bingley marrying Francine Phillips was most enjoyable. The new Mr. and Mrs. Bingley had just been sent off on their wedding trip which they would spend at the Darcy's Seaview Cottage near Brighton. After the final guests departed, the Bennet and Darcy carriages were loaded to begin the journey to Pemberley after meeting the Ashbys at the appointed coaching inn. Lady Georgiana Darcy was pleased to learn that the Marquess of Netherfield was home after completing his studies and graduating with honours from Cambridge. His presence always made her feel warm inside, observations of those around her proved that she was starting to understand how it felt to be in love.

With many outriders and footmen guards, the convoy departed Longbourn for the meeting point with the Ashbys. They would arrive at Lord Paisley Hastings, the Duke of Leicestershire's estate Saturday afternoon, and sojourn there on the sabbath. The estate was just across the border of Northamptonshire, less than a day from Pemberley and Birchington. Lord Paisley was good friend of both Thomas and Sed Bennet, and had welcomed the chance to host them when they broke up their day of travel to two.

Lady Elizabeth Bennet, the daughter of a duke, was full of happiness and anticipation for what her future held with the man that she loved above all others.

CHAPTER 5

After a very restful sabbath, Monday morning, just after sunrise, the carriages started on the final day of travel, which would set their arrival at Pemberley just after two o'clock that afternoon. It was just past that hour when the carriages turned off the road toward the Darcy's estate.

Lady Elizabeth was granted permission to join the lead carriage with Darcy, his mother, and sister at the last rest stop of the day. The carriages passed the gate house under the metal arch that proclaimed 'Pemberley' in bold, brass letters between the two pieces of iron that made the arch connected to a stone pillar on either side of the gates. The gatehouse keeper had opened the gates wide as soon as he spied his Grace's coach and that of his guests. He kept a weather eye out for the new Duke, having been advised the previous afternoon by the housekeeper that very important guests were expected to accompany his Grace to Pemberley, one being his betrothed; therefore, soon to be mistress of the estate. Burris doffed his cap and bowed as each carriage passed him by. As soon as the convoy of carriages and the numerous outriders had passed, he closed the gates and fired two pistol shots in the air, sending a lad waiting halfway on a horse galloping toward the manor house. He notified the housekeeper, Mrs. Reynolds, and Mr. Douglas, the butler, of the master's and his guests' imminent arrival.

Elizabeth was naturally excited to see her future home, but the excitement she felt building in her companions made her own build to an almost fever pitch. She was about to see the home that her betrothed loved dearly; that had helped form him into the man that she loved. On either side of the drive leading to the manor house was the most magnificent forest, she could imagine endless rambles and rides on Mercury through the majestic trees. After thirty to forty minutes of traveling through the forest and a turn toward the right, the carriage started to negotiate an incline. They could hear the horses breathing harder as they strained to pull the conveyance up the hill. The carriage was just short of the crest of the gradient when Lord Fitzwilliam Darcy rapped on the roof with his cane and the carriage rolled to a stop.

As they alighted the carriage, the occupants in the other carriages followed, Elizabeth's betrothed asked her to close her eyes and she shot him a questioning look. "Do you trust me, my love?"

"As you have already saved it, with my life, William!" she replied emphatically. After she closed her eyes, she felt him take her hand in his, then he led her to the crest of the incline, and requested that she open them. She blinked a little as her eyes adjusted to the sunshine, when her vision cleared, she saw the most magnificent of sights. Elizabeth had her betrothed on one side of her, and Mother Anne on the other, Georgie was bouncing up and down on the balls of her feet in excitement on the other side of her brother. "Oh, my. Of all of this I am to be mistress?" she teased, having had a very good idea of Pemberley's magnificence from the discussions she had shared with the Darcys during the last two hours of the journey, and the many instances it had been referenced during their acquaintance.

"I thought you said that your courage always rises when faced by anything intimidating," Darcy retorted, pleased she so obviously approved of their home. His easy and playful reply earned him a smile that lit up her eyes.

Elizabeth again surveyed the vista before her, impressed by the large, handsome stone manor, though really more of a mansion, situated well on rising ground. The stonework, the same used on most houses in the area, seemed to glow with a golden hue as the late spring sun light shone on the facade. Behind the structure was a gently rising hill with more verdant forest on the slope. To the left, Elizabeth could see a vast vegetable and herb garden and a conservatory. Beyond that were the extensive and well-maintained stables. She was certain that Mercury would be very comfortable in his new home.

Both in the centre and to the right of the manor house was an area with benches sporadically placed among various flower beds full of colour with a fountain in the middle as a scenic centrepiece. Everything that she saw called to her, letting her know that she was finally home, that feeling proving without a doubt that she would love her new home just as much as the current Darcys did. She could already count so many places that she could sit and read while soaking in the beauty of Pemberley.

In front of the manor house, Lady Elizabeth saw verdant gardens that, although well-maintained, did not look overly manicured and ordered as some were wont to do. There was a stream that wound its way lazily through the vista until it connected to a lake of clear blue water that reflected the rays of the afternoon sun onto the face of the house just beyond the formal gardens. In the centre of the formal gardens Lizzy could see a divine rose garden that sported more benches placed at random intervals for one to sit and enjoy the sights and aroma. From the discussions they had, Lady Elizabeth knew that the gardens were Lady Anne's pride and joy, especially the roses.

There was a gazebo in the garden where she could imagine many relaxing hours spent outdoors reading or enjoying the company of her soon to be husband, mother-in-law, and new sister. On the other side of the stream, nature was allowed its head with no attempt to improve what nature and God had designed.

"Do you approve of our home, my love?" asked her betrothed.

"William, the estate is stunning. I understand now why you, Mother Anne, and Georgie light up whenever you talk about Pemberley. I have never seen a place that nature has done more, and where the natural beauty has been so little counteracted by the awkward tastes of man," she gushed.

"I just knew you would love our home," Georgie enthused

with a glow of happiness and pride in her home.

The Dowager Duchess took Elizabeth's hand in her own. "With you here as William's wife, we will be a whole family again, Lizzy." A tear rolled down her cheek as she thought how much her George would have loved Elizabeth.

"Not a bad little home you have here, William," the Marquess of Birchington teased.

"It is rather small, Tom," the Marquess of Netherfield added. "Not quite up to the standards that our Lizzy would expect it to be."

"Boys!" Lady Sarah admonished, that one word enough to silence her sons and the Duke of Hertfordshire and the Ashbys laughed at the interplay.

As William looked at the glow on his betrothed's face, he smiled at her, "I am very pleased that you approve, Elizabeth, especially as your approval is the most important one to me."

"I would have to be a dullard not to approve of Pemberley. Mother Anne, your gardens look enchanting. I hope that you will allow me to assist you with them from time to time," Lady Elizabeth stated as she squeezed Lady Anne's hand.

"You will always be welcome to assist me, Lizzy. And each mistress of Pemberley gets her own garden that she can design as she desires," the Dowager Duchess informed the daughter of her heart. "It will be no different for you."

As Lady Sarah Bennet watched the obvious love that her daughter had for her soon to be mother-in-law, her beloved husband pulled her aside to ask if all was well as they watch their daughter fall in love with a home that was not theirs. She promised that she was well and that she felt only joy that their Lizzy would be so happy, both in her marriage and her new home. Sarah Bennet had always understood that the heart had an unlimited capacity for love, and that loving another did not displace those already present within. It was the very reason that she was the most perfect of mothers to all of their children, and never once hesitated to share their children with their brothers and sisters, and take the Phillips' to her heart. The

Duchess, however, did not miss the wistful look on her beloved husband's countenance. He would miss the debates and chess matches with his middle daughter, but they would see each other in Town each season, and there would be visits to each other's estates, and in small compensation he had heard talk of the magnificent library that Pemberley sported, so there could be more visiting than was expected.

They returned to their conveyances for the short trip down the hill to the house. The coaches came to halt in the internal courtyard where the housekeeper and butler were waiting to welcome them at the base of the stairs that led to the massive entrance doors. As if by magic, footmen, all wearing the distinctive green and gold of Darcy livery, materialised, opened the doors, and placed the steps for the occupants to descend.

Pemberley's butler and housekeeper had both heard glowing reports from the Killions in Town, and looked forward to seeing the wondrous lady to whom his Grace was betrothed. Mrs. Reynolds had no doubt that it was all true as she had read the letters from the mistress, as the Dowager Duchess had described how the young lady had overruled the doctor and saved Master William's life.

Douglas had been promoted from head under-butler to butler, and had held the post for fifteen years. Mrs. Reynolds had been hired on as an assistant housekeeper when Darcy was but four; and after training under her predecessor for two years, she was promoted when the previous housekeeper, who had held the post for over five and thirty years, had retired. All retainers who did not have family to live with after retirement were awarded one of a good number of pensioner cottages that the Darcys had built for their loyal staff over the years.

The lady who would be their new mistress seemed to be without artifice from the information Lady Anne had provided, and her short observation of the future duchess supported it, but she would reserve final judgement until she had more time with the lady. There was no missing how truly Lady Anne cared for Lady Elizabeth, and the changes in the former Miss Darcy,

Lady Georgiana, were astounding. Mrs. Reynolds smiled as she watched her 'dear boy;' the love he exuded for his betrothed obvious when he was not willing to let her hand go after he helped her down from the carriage, the long look they shared making them both blush as she had allowed him to keep her hand.

Lord Tom Bennet, his betrothed, and her parents would depart for the three-hour journey to Birchington in the morning, allowing them to break up the days of travel. As they entered the house and headed to a drawing room off the main foyer, Elizabeth could not fail to notice that like Darcy House, Pemberley exuded wealth and comfort; however, while filled with the best of everything, it was in no way ostentatious or gaudy. One example of this was the furniture, it was obviously acquired for comfort rather than to impress. Lady Anne's impeccable sense of style and decorating was on display here as it had been in London. The house had four stories above the ground level, with an extensive cellar and cold room below.

There was a sweeping grand marble stair case that rose up from the rear of the entrance foyer, with various doors leading off either side of the hall. The ceiling went all the way up to the third floor and it was very tastefully painted with a fresco, obviously by the same artist who had painted the one at Darcy House. As they congregated in the drawing room, Lady Elizabeth was looking forward to the extensive tour that they would take on the morrow; Lady Anne informed everyone that after they changed from the road and rested, that aperitifs would be served an hour before dinner in the same large orange drawing room that they were in.

The party was shown to their chambers and the Bennets, who would remain at Pemberley, were assigned chambers in the family wing. Lady Elizabeth was placed between her parent's suite and Lady Anne's. Mary and Kitty's suite was next to Lady Georgiana's. As the mutual attraction between the youngest Darcy and Lord James was not a secret to anyone, he was placed in a suite with his older brother and would be joining them for the trip to Birchington on the morrow.

As they walked toward the stairs, Lizzy turned to William. "When I come to live here, William, am I to be given a map so I do not get lost for days on end, and starve and wither away?" Elizabeth teased him, her brow arched with impertinence, which caused a round of good-natured laughter from the whole party.

"When my George first brought me here as his wife, I was intimidated and I grew up at Snowhaven, which is large and a castle, however it only lasted a very short while and I never did get lost," Lady Anne shared playfully.

"I will remind you once again, my dearest Elizabeth, that you have always told us on more than one occasion how your courage always rises at every attempt to intimidate you, so I have no doubt that you will soon know your way around." Darcy smirked, his sense of contentment at watching her smile because he had teased her increasing in proportion with it. "Besides, I would hear your heart calling out to mine and I would find you." He kissed each of her wrists earning him a very becoming blush from his lady.

The plan was to visit Lord Tom's estate for a week then return to Pemberley for a few days before they all returned to town. Prior to the departure, the two couples had agreed to an engagement ball, which would be given by the Duchess of Bedford in honour of the betrothals of her nephew and soon-to-be niece, on the first Friday in June, ten days before the marriage ceremony. Queen Charlotte had responded to an invitation expressing her regrets but noted that Princess Elizabeth and Prince Edward would attend on the family's behalf. The ball would also be the official introduction of the new Duke of Derbyshire and the Dowager Duchess to the Ton in their elevated rank. Ladies Elaine and Catherine were assisting Lady Rose with the planning of it and it would be held at Bedford House on Russell Square.

While neither couple enjoyed being gawked at, they understood that it was a necessary event from which they could not be excused. Lord Tom Bennet was a lot closer in disposition to his sister's betrothed than he may have liked to admit as he too preferred quiet events with not many people. Similar, to his sister Lizzy's ability to make Darcy smile, so too his Amy would add liveliness and mirth to her future husband.

Dinner at Pemberley was served in the smaller family dining parlour. The footman serving the diners could not help but smile for it was the liveliest dinner that they could remember since before the previous master had passed.

After in a letter, William informed the Steward, butler and housekeeper without any demand to keep the information secret, the true cause of the previous master's death. It was most shocking to find out that the late master had been murdered by the wastrel son of the late steward. It was generally agreed that it was a kindness to old Wickham that he had not lived to see the depths of the depravity to which his son had sunk.

During the separation of the sexes, the Duke of Hertfordshire approached his soon to be son-in-law. "William, when will I see your magnificent tribute to books that I have heard so much about?" he asked with a smile.

"Tomorrow, Bennet. It will be the last stop on the tour; and I will have you summoned when we are about to enter the library," Darcy promised. "I promised your daughter that we would all see it together; she is desirous of seeing your face when you first enter."

"I will have to survive until then, then," Lord Thomas replied ruefully. "If Lizzy has decreed it so, who am I to gainsay her?"

"William," Tom Bennet called out to Darcy, "I understand that you have a fencing room here..."

"Do you want to see if you can last more than two minutes before William vanquishes you, Tom?" Lord James teased his brother.

"Remind me, brother, how long did you last against our soon to be brother?" Lord Tom asked with as he smirked.

James mumbled an answer that was not heard by the others and when prodded by his brother said distinctly, "One *whole* minute!"

"All of the stories of your prowess with the sword are true then, Derbyshire?" the Earl of Ashbury inquired, receiving vigorous nods from the other three men. "My two sons and I are Oxford men. Even there we heard stories about Fitzwilliam Darcy and his skill with both foil and pistol. I am too old now, but mayhap one day my sons can test their skill against your vaunted abilities."

Darcy inclined his head toward the Earl, "I welcome any who are willing to spar with me, Ashbury."

As Mrs. Reynolds passed the family dining room during dinner she could not stop her smile spreading from ear to ear. It had been many years since the sounds of joy had infused the hallways of Pemberley. That her Master William was happy there could be no argument, but the effect on his small family was remarkable as well. She had not seen Lady Anne glow with happiness like this since her before her beloved husband had been murdered, and the little miss had been filled with sorrow and recrimination since she was almost duped by her father's murderer at Ramsgate. From conversations that they had, the housekeeper knew that the Dowager Duchess would never remarry as there could never be any other than her late husband, in the housekeeper's opinion, she had no need. She smiled again and each of her smiles reached her eyes and were genuine, not forced. Hannah Reynolds, even though never forgetting her place, almost felt like a member of the family, she thanked God above for the restoration of the spirits of all three Darcys.

~~~~~~~/~~~~~~~

The Younges and the Álvarezs' found the only decent inn in Bundoran, the Happy Leprechaun, near the small harbour that served the town. The sea and harbour were critical to the town as there was only one road that came to Bundoran, County Donegal, and it was down a steep hill which made it hard for carts and carriages to negotiate. It was the reason that Younge had chosen this out of the way hole-in-the-wall location in which to stay as they laid low and planned their next moves. On the other side, however, as is true in any small town, they had to be very careful to not talk out of turn and become the focus of the town's gossips.

The *Stealthy Runner's* captain, his sister, Johanna, and Tony Álvarez took rooms at the inn for the foreseeable future, making the landlord ecstatic as he normally only rented his rooms for a night or two, and only when the Dennington Lines ship, the *Coastal Trader*, docked in the port once a month. Clay Younge pumped the landlord, Rory O'Rourke, for information. The loquacious man informed him that the trading ship, a sloop almost twice the size of Younge's ship, arrived around the middle of each month with goods and supplies for the town, adding that she was due to arrive in the next week or so. He was also informed that they made a run from Dublin to Bundoran and a few other remote, coastal towns of Ireland.

As the *Coastal Trader* was a regular visitor, there would be no danger from those aboard, though they may make note of another sloop being in port when it is often them. He would have his men meet them here in the Inn for a port or two so that they could listen for any information and swap news as only sailors can. He himself would watch for visitors that were not regularly scheduled. He had no idea that the Dennington Lines were owned by the two Bennet dukes nor that every vessel they owned that sailed the waters around the kingdom, or anywhere in the known world, had received a detailed message telling them to look out for the *Stealthy Runner* and her crew of miscreants. They had provided descriptions of the Younge siblings and some of the crew. The instruction was clear, that if seen to report directly back to his Grace, the Duke of Hertfordshire, but to take no action unless otherwise instructed.

By a stroke of luck, there were two floors that had four rooms each, and once Johanna learned which floor the Younge's rooms were on, she made up an excuse to take rooms on the other floor. It had been harder and harder for her to keep her resolve to not tell Karen Younge about the plans that Wickham had intended for her. She was ever more determined that once they got paid the ransom, she would hire some men to dispose of the delusional woman.

Tony Álvarez was certain that the cause of avenging his father was a just one. In a similar fashion to the way that Mrs. Younge forgot all of Wickham's myriad faults after his death, Tony had relegated the cruelty and disdain of his father to the recesses of his subconscious. The truth was that the *Spaniard* had been neither a good father nor a decent husband. He spent as much time 'testing' out the new wares at his brothels as he did at home, and when he was at home he was quick to temper. He never struck his wife but did not spare the rod when it came to his son. The man had claimed that it was to toughen the boy up, but the sad truth was that Álvarez was a bully and derived pleasure in the infliction of pain. There was one very good thing he did for his son, while grooming him to one day take over his criminal empire, he taught the boy to be suspicious of everyone and divine their motives for himself. The father was driven by paranoia, but the son had learned the art of critical thinking. He had loved his wife in his own way, as much as he was able to love anyone, which was the reason that she was spared physical abuse.

Tony had dreamed of one day inheriting his father's criminal enterprise. His drive to seek revenge was more for the vast fortune lost when the authorities found the *Spaniard's* cache of hidden money, gold, and jewels than for the love of his father. He and his mother had a few times discussed what they would do after they received their share of the ransom. One option was to leave the realm for good and set themselves up in the New World, establishing an enterprise similar to the one that had been taken from them in England. The young man did not know any other way, and the plans being discussed around him only helped convince him that there was no other path for him to follow.

CHAPTER 6

Lords Birchington and Netherfield and the Ashby's arrived at Birchington after but a four-hour carriage ride from Pemberley. Birchington was a large estate, about two thirds the size of Pemberley, and the main Bedford estate, Longfield Meadows, was a little larger than Pemberley. The Marquess would inherit the Meadows, along with the rest of the Bedford properties and assets, when he ascended to the dukedom, and he prayed that it would be many years in the future until that happened.

Lord James Bennet wished that he could have remained at Pemberley, but he knew that there was at least two years before he could declare himself for Lady Georgiana, and only then if the feelings that he believed existed between them were still present. He knew that he was in love with the lady and could not imagine falling out of love with her, and he hoped that he was correct in his observations believing she had tender feelings for him because he did not want to think about his world without her in it as his future helpmeet.

Lord James remembered how happy they were to escape the spring rains that had seemed to inundate London of late. He and the rest of the Bennets loved riding and were frustrated by the rains keeping them from their favourite pastime in Hyde Park or other open spaces where they could give the mounts their heads. While his brother was giving his betrothed and her mother a tour of the manor house, James and the Earl of Ashbury were planning a long ride in which they would allow their horses to gallop at full speed for some portion, as much for the horses as for themselves. James smiled as he thought back to his Aunt Rose admonishing Uncle Sed not to ride in the rain and the obstinate man doing so anyway. There was no one that loved riding more than his Uncle Sed.

Birchington's topography was much like that of Surrey where Lady Amy had grown up. Unlike Derbyshire to the west, Yorkshire was much flatter. As they pulled up to the manor where the butler and housekeeper awaited them with footmen at the ready to unload the baggage, the Ashbys admired the house.

It was a three-story structure in the shape of half an 'H' with a circular drive and a protective *porte-cochère* under which carriages could halt to ensure the occupants stayed dry no matter the weather. In the centre of the drive was a grass area with several benches. The formal gardens were to the left and right of the drive. Lord Ashbury could see that his daughter would be very happy here, and he could not miss the love that she had for her betrothed that was returned in full measure.

"Tom, your estate is beautiful," Lady Amelia stated as she looked around from inside the carriage.

"Soon to be *our* estate, my love," her betrothed corrected her, earning him smiles from her parents. As soon as the conveyance came to a halt, a footman placed the steps and Tom Bennet exited then turned to assist first his betrothed and then her mother from the coach. Once all five had exited, he introduced the senior staff to their soon to be mistress.

"Lord and Lady Ashbury and Lady Amelia Ashby, may I introduce Mr. Jacob Franklin and Mrs. Loretta Browning, the butler and housekeeper at Birchington. Mr. Franklin and Mrs. Browning, the Earl and Countess of Ashbury and my betrothed, Lady Amelia Ashby." The servants made their bow and curtsy which was acknowledged by the Ashbys then the party entered the house while the footmen removed their trunks.

"The chambers in the family wing are prepared as you instructed, my lord," the housekeeper informed the master once they were in the entrance hall.

"I assume that you would all like to change and refresh yourselves?" Tom asked, and his guests nodded their agreement.

"Thank you, Mrs. Browning, I will show my guests to their chambers." He placed his fiancée's hand on his arm and covered it with his other hand. "Amy, father Maxwell, and mother Gillian, please follow me. James knows where his are so he can find his own way," Tom teased his younger brother. Lord Tom showed them to their chambers and pointed out the gallery that they would see as part of the tour just beyond the family wing. The Earl and the Marquess of Netherfield confirmed their plans to ride as soon as they had changed into riding attire.

~~~~~~~/~~~~~~~

Among other things, the Earldom came with a townhouse on Portnoy Circle in Mayfair. A week after the elevation, the new Earl and Countess of Brookfield had taken up residence in their town home they renamed 'Brookfield House'. With the assistance of Bennet House's housekeeper and butler, the new town home was fully staffed. Jane Fitzwilliam liked her matronly housekeeper, Mrs. Maureen Carrington, very well. She ran a very tight ship and had come with wonderful characters, and best of all she and Mrs. O'Grady, Bennet House's housekeeper, were best of friends. The new butler was one Mr. Jeffrey Thatcher, the younger brother of Humphry Thatcher, the Bennet's butler in Town who had been an under-butler for over five years. As happy as he had been in the Duke of Cornwall's household, he jumped at the chance to advance without having to wait for his mentor to retire. Brookfield House was a large house and the Fitzwilliams were very pleased with it.

Previously, both Fitzwilliam couples had resided at Hilldale House and the twin sisters had enjoyed still living in the same house for at least some of the time. While Jane and Marie would miss being in the same house in Town, they had long known they would eventually separate, and were grateful that they were marrying men who were close and understand and support their desire to stay close to one another.

For the third morning in a row Lady Jane Fitzwilliam, Countess of Brookfield had been sick in the morning. Her lady's maid suspected the cause, but as her mistress had not sought her council, she remained silent on the subject. Lord Richard Fitz-william was worried; his Jane had been ill and he wanted to assist her in some way.

"Jane, my love, do you object if I summon Mr. Bartholomew to examine you?" he asked with no little concern.

Lady Jane, who had missed her last two courses, suspected what her ailment was because her breasts were tender; she agreed that he could summon the doctor so they would both be sure. Lord Brookfield also suspected the cause, but he too wanted to hear from a physician to be sure.

As far as Jane knew, Marie was not yet with child, but if she was *enceinte,* after her husband, she wanted very much to tell her twin. Once things were confirmed, and her mother and father returned from Pemberley in a little more than a sennight, she would share her news with them as well as with Mother Elaine. As if thinking about her sister conjured her, Lady Marie and Lord Andrew Fitzwilliam arrived just after the footman was dispatched to request that Mr. Bartholomew attend the Countess.

"I was just thinking about you, Marie," Jane hugged her sister. "Welcome, Andrew, what brings you two here this morning?"

"Has Aunt Rose sent you a message yet?" the Viscount asked.

"We have not checked our post this morning," Lord Richard stated. "Why do you ask?" As he had asked his brother the question, Mr. Thatcher knocked on the sitting room door and entered with a silver salver with but one missive on it. Richard removed the note and nodded his dismissal of the butler.

"I believe that is the same note Aunt Rose sent us," Marie opined. Seeing the questioning looks from her brother and sister she explained. "Uncle Sed is ill. You know he is too obstinate to refrain from riding in the rain and it seems as if he took ill two days ago. He has had a high fever but insists it is nothing and has joked with Aunt telling her that no one dies from a trifling cold." Richard read the note from their Aunt and confirmed that it held the same news that Marie and Andrew had shared.

"You know how concerned Aunt Rose is when Uncle Sed is

ill," Jane Fitzwilliam stated. "After Mr. Bartholomew calls, we will hie to Bedford House. Will you two join us?"

"Are you with child, Jane?" Lady Marie asked as her twin intuition kicked in.

Knowing that she could not hide anything from her twin, Jane admitted her suspicions, "It could be so, Marie, which is why we are waiting for Mr. Bartholomew. We are seeking confirmation."

A half hour later the doctor arrived, and after a short examination the Earl of Brookfield was called into his wife's chambers where he was informed that the physician believed that his wife was about two months with child and that their first son or daughter would enter the world in November or December. After Bartholomew left, the four siblings rejoiced at the news. Marie had always been sure that she would become pregnant first, but her courses had come last week so she knew that she was not yet in that state. Marie felt a surge of envy that her sister had attained the state that she had not, but so too was she extremely happy for her brother and sister.

Once the discussion of the new life to come was concluded, the four donned their outerwear and had the carriage summoned to take them to Russell Square.

~~~~~~~~/~~~~~~~~

The younger Bennet twins, who would have their come out the coming season as they would turn eighteen in March of next year, and Lady Georgiana were riding around the park during the tour of Pemberley. They planned to return in a few hours and had taken a picnic meal with them for luncheon and were escorted by the Darcy footmen, a groom, and their companions.

The tour of the manor house commenced with the public rooms on the entrance level of the mansion. The tour was led by the Dowager Duchess with the assistance of Mrs. Reynolds; and Lady Elizabeth was accompanied by her mother. The Duke of Derbyshire would join them when they were to tour the library as he wanted to be sure that no one other than himself showed that particular room to his betrothed and her father, both bibliophiles like himself.

The entrance hall was over two stories high and had a shining marble floor in shades of whites and greys. The first stop was the Duke's oversized and comfortable study, and next to the master's study there was a large and comfortable study for the mistress. Everything was well organised, just as Elizabeth had expected it would be, and there were neat piles of separated correspondence on the enormous desk. Behind the desk were floor to ceiling bookshelves full of well-worn books. There were two comfortable chairs facing the desk, and a settee on one side underneath a pair of large windows that faced out onto the park.

There were two public drawing rooms, a music room with the new Broadwood Grand pianoforte that the master and mistress had recently gifted to Lady Georgiana on the occasion of her sixteenth birthday. There was also a nicely appointed receiving room, three parlours of varying sizes. Like Darcy house, Pemberley had a breakfast parlour and a small dining parlour that could seat thirty with ease, and a larger dining parlour that could seat up to one hundred people. When touring the mistress's study, Lady Elizabeth surreptitiously looked at Lady Anne, knowing that in about a month she would be taking over the role of mistress from her, but sure that she would receive all the support she needed to make a success of her new role.

The last stop on the entrance level was the huge ballroom where Lady Anne informed the Bennets that the last time Pemberley hosted a ball was before the death of her late husband, George. The ballroom was at least twice the size of the one at Darcy House and had six huge crystal chandeliers and many sconces on the walls. On both the left and right side of the ball room were floor to ceiling windows with double French doors in the middle. One side led to a broad set of stone stairs that allowed access to the gardens behind the house and the benches therein. The other side fronted onto the park and had a large veranda, the same one that ran along the entire side of the house and could be accessed from the main drawing room. There were three points on the veranda where one could walk down to Lady Anne's rose garden in the front of the house; from there, one could take the walking paths that ran through the various beds of plants. Like many grand houses, the walls in the three dining parlours that separated them from the ball room could be rolled back if needs be.

As they were about to exit the ball room, Mrs. Reynolds pointed out the entrance to the kitchen in a corner of the common wall between the ball room and the dining parlours where the rest of the service area was located. Lady Anne had informed her housekeeper that the Bennets treated their servants as well as the Darcys did, so Mrs. Reynolds was not surprised when Master William's betrothed and her mother asked to see the kitchen, the pantry, the storerooms, and the housekeeper's office.

The housekeeper was not blind, she could clearly see the looks of pure love and adoration that were surreptitiously directed at one another when the other was not looking when she had observed them together earlier. What she noted was more reinforcement of her feeling that Master William had finally met a woman worthy of him. '*Lady Anne was correct; this is the only woman for our master. Pemberley will be a lively home again!*' She could did not miss how happy and easy in company the master was around Lady Elizabeth. She assumed that it was due to the love he radiated towards the lady that he was betrothed to.

In the kitchen the future mistress, and Lady Sarah were introduced to the baker and assistant cook, Gertrude McInnis, who had been born in Scotland but had been raised in England and was said to make the best shortbread anywhere in the country. Also introduced was the French chef, Claude-Michel Henri. The guests created a very favourable impression, both with the servants and their master, by giving a cordial greeting to all present from the scullery maids up. A hallway was pointed out to the Bennets by Lady Anne that led to the female servants' accommodations. Married servants were assigned to small two bedchamber cottages not far from the house, and the single male servants had accommodations in the attic.

The ladies took the stairs upward. They took a second stair-case that bypassed the second floor where the family chambers were and proceeded to the third floor where guest chambers were located. Lady Anne informed them that the fourth floor was for guests as well, and that it was almost a mirror image of what they were about to see. Each guest floor had thirty suites with two bedchambers and a shared sitting room, and fifteen smaller suites with one bedchamber and no sitting room. There were two large and airy sitting rooms on each of the two floors for those who did not have one in their suite or wanted a place to sit with more people.

"Do you see that which you want to change, Lizzy?" Lady Anne asked.

"So far very little but a few minor updates where I noticed some paper was frayed, but other than that, nothing, Mother Anne," Elizabeth responded. "In fact, how am I to follow those who have impeccable taste as both you and my mother have? I demand that you live forever so that you will always be able to give me advice on decorating and so much more," Lady Eliza-beth teased, only half joking.

"No false modesty, Lizzy," Lady Sarah admonished her middle daughter gently, "anyone who knows you knows that you have a very well-developed sense of décor." Elizabeth in-clined her head as she accepted the compliment from her mother.

"If you choose to, Lizzy," Lady Anne said, "we can skip the fourth and fifth floors. The fifth floor are the school rooms, a music room, and the chambers for nursemaids, governesses, tu-tors, and companions."

"Thank you for enlightening me, Mother Anne, and I too think we can skip those floors. Where are we to go now?" she asked.

"To the family floor, Lizzy. Lead on please, Mrs. Reynolds," Lady Anne requested. The housekeeper guided them to an al-most imperceptible door in the panelling that she unlocked which revealed stairs that took them to the family wing below. Lady Elizabeth was excited that it seemed her new home came with secret passageways. Once they entered the family wing through a panel that once closed was almost invisible, they started in the nursery that Lady Anne pointed out was connected to the mistress's chambers.

The nursery was a suite of eight chambers and two rooms. One was a bedchamber for a wet nurse that could sleep two if they were needed. There were five bedchambers, four for children and a larger one for a nurse. Two chambers, the ones closest to the mother's chambers were, for babes. There also was a storage room and a small dining parlour for the nurses and their charges once they were able to eat solid food.

They used the inter-leading door to enter the mistress' suite, which would soon be Lady Elizabeth's. Like she had at Darcy House, Lady Anne had taken a suite in the family wing after she had completed her year of deep mourning. She had made the change as she started her half mourning which was another year complete. Lizzy was amazed at the size of the chambers. The suite consisted of an enormous bedchamber with its own sitting area that led out onto a balcony, overlooking the rear of the house; the trees on the rising hill became a part of the forest on the crest of the hill. There was a walk-in closet that, when added to the dressing room, exceeded the size of her bedchamber at Longbourn.

Lady Elizabeth imagined what it would look like with her gowns hanging within, and how they would be organized. Surely the day dresses would be closest to the front in case she ever needed to quickly change, as all new mothers are wont to do once she was blessed with her beloved's children. As she considered if everyone could see her blush, it burned hotter when she saw the enormous brass tub in the bathing room off her dressing room, just like the pair that she had seen at Darcy House. Elizabeth imagined the tub with her and her betrothed in it. Ladies Anne and Sarah gave each other knowing looks as Elizabeth's blush became a deep crimson while her focus did not shift. They gave her a moment because it was healthy to want your husband, then refocused her attention.

The mistress' chambers had been updated just over two years previously, so the only request Elizabeth had was to change the colour of the wallpaper. She favoured light greens rather than the whites and golds currently framing the room.

"Mother Anne, is there anything that you want of the furnishings in the chambers?" Elizabeth asked as she lightly touched the vase with roses on the table by the windows. "The reason that everything is new in here, Lizzy," she said as she touched her new daughter's arm in appreciation for her selfless thoughts, "is that anything that I wanted is in my suite already. William insisted that I take them when I moved out of the master suite as my George was not here to share it with me. As he could not get me to stay in the chambers, I compromised with taking some of the items. Do not tell him I would have preferred a few new things as well." She tried to smiled when Elizabeth laughed. "I also told William to move into the master's chambers when I left to support the beginning of his tenure as master."

"Then should something break when you are reading or turning around because you are startled, I will promise to go shopping with you in support of your 'loss'." Lizzy offered, helping Lady Anne laugh again to ease the surge of pain.

"I thank you for the offer, Lizzy. I believe I shall take you up on it." Lady Anne nodded,

"Anne, am I correct that roses are your favourite flowers?" Lady Sarah asked as a change of subject to support the redirection from maudlin thoughts.

"Yes, Sarah. I love my roses above all other flowers. We have them year-round at Pemberley as the gardeners keep a selection growing in the conservatory," Lady Anne offered as they transitioned to the shared sitting room.

"I cannot imagine you changing a thing in here, Lizzy. This is precisely the sitting room I would have designed with you in mind," Lady Sarah offered as they entered the sitting room. Elizabeth's smiled with unaffected joy as she thought about sitting on the couch reading with her William in front of a roaring fire during the long winter evenings.

"You are right, the room is otherwise perfect, Mother. Except," she turned to the housekeeper, "Mrs. Reynolds, two additional pillows for the settee, not one. You never know when I will need to throw one, and if his Grace gets as lost in Homer as I sometimes get, a second one may be required as I will not want to give up the one I am lounging on." Lizzy smiled brightly as her mother and mother-in-law laughed and Mrs. Reynolds made a note. Whether or not Lady Elizabeth meant it, they would be added to her settee. The room truly did not need any changes as her William used it all the time, therefore it was up to date and very comfortable. "I love the furniture and colours, and especially the fact that there are bookcases so that there will always be reading material for myself and William here," she said wistfully.

"I agree with your mother, Lizzy. This is the perfect proof that you and William are so well matched," Lady Anne gave a cryptic smile to Lady Sarah as they had privately agreed it had taken too long for Elizabeth and William to come to the point.

They proceeded into the master's chambers, which Lizzy believed perfectly epitomised her William. The décor was very masculine, almost the same as Darcy House, the walls hunter green with some light browns. Lizzy blushed all over again when she saw that the bed in his bedchamber matched the enormous one that she had seen in his chambers at Darcy House. Her escorts again gave her a moment to enjoy the sensation as the more want increases, the more the trepidation and fear will be easily overcome. The master's chambers had a bathing room as well, but his brass tub was of a size that would only hold one. Elizabeth's eyes again fell on the bed they would share at Pemberley and she could barely stop herself from climbing into his bed just to be surrounded by his essence.

From the master suite, they descended the main stairs where they met the two dukes waiting for them at the doors that led to the library. Lady Elizabeth saw that her father was waiting with bated breath, and she could well imagine how much he was anticipating seeing what lay beyond the wide double doors. Truth be told, she was no less excited than her Papa was!

"Close your eyes and give me your hand," William requested. As she placed her delicate hand in his much larger one, Elizabeth felt a shiver slide under her skin from her hand down to her toes when their ungloved hands touched. As Darcy opened the doors, even before she opened her eyes, she knew that she was to behold something exceptional as she heard her father gasp in wonder.

"Open your eyes, Elizabeth," Darcy murmured, and when she complied, she was dumbfounded. Never in her wildest imagination has she envisioned such a place. The library went all the way up three stories with spiral staircases on either side that allowed access to the second and third floors. There were ladders on wheels on each level to access the upper shelves. There were books and items like a globe filling almost every space available. If she lived five lifetimes, she doubted that she would be able to read half of the tomes she could see, let alone all those she could not.

"Put a bed in here when I visit you, Lizzy, as wild horses will not remove me from this magnificent library," her father teased, only half in jest and his wife swatted him on the arm playfully.

"There will be no hiding from your family in this room, Thomas," she said with authority.

"Yes, dear," was the only reply that the Duke of Hertfordshire made as he drank in what his eyes could scarce behold.

"Oh, the smell of the leather and the number of books. William, you told me your library was large, but that was an unjustified downplaying of the truth! This is beyond my imagination!" Lady Elizabeth looked at him with wonder then again at the library that was part of her very soon to be home.

"This collection is the work of many generations, starting with Pierre D'Arcy in the time of William the Conqueror. He was gifted the land that Pemberley stands on, and soon after our name was changed to Darcy. He brought a large collection of tomes with him from France, books that were hand printed and today are preserved as they are very fragile. They were mostly religious; and the collection was started when there was limited availability of hand-printed books. He started collecting available books in English just after he had the original house built. Even then the library was the largest room in his house. Every subsequent master of Pemberley, including myself, have added to the collection. You see the results surrounding us in this room." Darcy smiled as he could not have hoped for a better reaction.

"My George loved this room, and he passed that love onto both of my children," Lady Anne said wistfully as she again thought about her beloved late husband.

Lord Thomas Bennet remained in the library as his wife and Lady Anne retired to the latter's private sitting room. Darcy and his betrothed prepared to take a ramble in the park to introduce Lady Elizabeth to some of the myriad walking paths at Pemberley, escorted by Biggs and Johns.

CHAPTER 7

The butler at Bedford House ushered the four Fitzwilliams into her Grace's sitting room where they found Aunt Rose in a state of worry. Tears were rolling down her cheeks when they walked in and her adopted daughters sat on either side of her, each taking a hand in theirs. "My Sed has never had a fever like the one he has now. The doctor used the cold bath like Lizzy used on William, and thank God, it seems to have brought it down." Aunt Rose nodded at the hope she saw in their eyes.

"Then there has been some improvement in Uncle Sed?" Andrew Fitzwilliam asked carefully.

"Yes, Andrew, his fever seems to have broken now, but I am so worried," she admitted as more tears rolled down her cheeks. "In all the thirty years since we married, I have never been so worried for my Sed."

"Should we send an express to Derbyshire, Aunt Rose?" Jane asked.

"You know that your uncle does not want to worry Thomas and the rest of the family, but yes I think we should let them know. Do make sure that you tell them that Sed thinks it is not needed for them to return," Lady Rose said with relief. Having the whole family around her would be a boon.

"Papa knows what Uncle is like; how he downplays anything connected to his health. I am certain that they will return as soon as they receive the news," Marie opined. As she spoke, Jane walked over to the escritoire and wrote the express. As soon as the missive was sealed, the butler was summoned and instructed to have the letter sent with all haste.

After confirming that their uncle was awake to receive them, and with the Duke of Bedford's long serving and very loyal valet, Mr. Adam Winters, the four made their way to his chambers. When the twins saw their surrogate father, they almost burst into tears but were able to somewhat control their reaction.

"Do I look so poorly that..." the Duke's inhale after but a few words, it was harsh to their ears, "Thomas's daughters got such...a shock seeing me?" he asked. It was obvious that he was trying to put on a brave face, but both ladies were beside themselves with worry. Their Uncle Sed had always looked younger than his two and sixty years, but if they were to admit the truth, he now looked considerably older than his age. They chose not to berate him for not heeding Aunt Rose's admonitions not to ride in the rain, he had always loved his stallion Apollo, and hated going more than one day without riding him.

Marie gained her equanimity before her sister, "Sorry, Uncle Sed, we are not used to seeing you ill," she managed knowing that it did not ring true, even to herself. She was sure that he understood their reaction to how bad he looked.

"You...did not ask...my brother to...return?" the Duke of Bedford managed between breaths.

"I did send an express to inform Papa that you are sick, Uncle, but we did not request that he return to London post-haste," Jane informed her Uncle whose eyebrows raised in bemused expectation as they both knew that the letter would be enough to have the Bennets leaving Derbyshire within a day of receiving it.

Lady Rose walked into her beloved husband's bedchamber saying, "Reggie, Elaine, and Catherine are with me in my sitting room, Sed. Reggie wants to know if you feel up to seeing him." The duke nodded and his nieces kissed him on his cheek as they followed their aunt back to the sitting room. The sisters passed their father-in-law in the corridor, and by their looks of solemnity he could tell that his friend was not in a good way.

When Ladies Jane and Marie entered the sitting room, the duchess was being comforted by the Countess of Matlock on one side, and Lady Catherine on the other. "I have Tom's and

Lizzy's betrothal ball all planned," Lady Rose said distractedly. "There have been no refusals to an invitation."

"Rose, I am sure that Lizzy and Tom will agree that they will not want to celebrate until our dear Sed is well again," Lady Catherine opined.

"That may be the case, Catherine," the duchess responded, "but if I know my Sed, it would upset him more if they cancel the ball because of him. He would not want that, and I would not suggest it to him as it would truly upset him." Elaine passed her a new silk and squeezed her hand.

"You have the right of it, Rose. I too know Sed will demand that plans not be changed," Lady Elaine nodded as she agreed with her friend. "At least the ball is at Bennet House so if he is not well enough to attend yet, he will not be tempted to force himself out of his sickbed to show his face." Lady Rose smiled as her friend had accurately stated just what her husband would do, his fighting spirit to rally with his family long joked about in their drawing rooms.

"It will be interesting to see what happens when Lizzy returns," Marie smiled as she thought about her younger sister. "You know that she can be as stubborn as Uncle Sed, but she has always loved him and listened to his council so he is the one person who will be able to sway her easily." Jane and her aunt nodded in agreement.

The Earl of Matlock and his sons returned to the sitting room and each man went to his wife. "We will all pray for him. My friend Sed is as strong as that horse of his, so I am sure that he will recover, Rose," Reggie said, as much to convince himself as the others.

Jane decided to change the subject. "Have the Gardiners, Phillips, and Bingleys been notified yet that Uncle is sick?" she asked.

"Thank you for reminding me, dear," Aunt Rose said gratefully. "I have been remiss and I should..." She was cut off by her younger niece.

"I am sorry to interrupt, Aunt Rose, but you have enough to

think about. I will write the notes and make sure that they are sent out," Lady Marie said, then went to sit at the escritoire to write, seal, and address the four notes as offered. The butler was instructed to send the three with London addresses with a footman, but that the one for Meryton was to be sent by express. The Viscountess realised that the other cousins would not be happy if they were not notified as well, so she wrote one more note and had it dispatched to Buckingham House forthwith. The Regent had always been close to Uncle Sed, so omitting the royal cousins would have been unpardonable.

~~~~~~~/~~~~~~~

Two days later the betrothed couple and their younger sisters returned from a lengthy ride flushed with exercise and smiling at the reminder of an amusement shared while they were on it. Darcy led them up a bridle path to the summit of a hill that overlooked the estate, it had a very good view of the peaks in the distance. As they were dismounting in the stables, a footman from the house approached the Master and requested that he and the ladies join their parents in the family sitting room as soon as could be. The five quickly followed and entered the sitting room where they first saw a grim-faced duke, his expression so unlike his usual sardonic smile it warranted their immediate attention. They then looked to his wife and saw she had shed tears and was being comforted by the Dowager Duchess.

"Papa," Lady Elizabeth broke the silence, "what has happened, why has Mama been crying?" she looked from one to the other for a reason.

The Duke said naught but handed his middle daughter the express that had arrived an hour previously.

22 May 1812
Bedford House

My Dearest Mama, Papa, and Family;
Uncle Sed is unwell. He caught a cold after riding in the rain and you know him too well to think that he would cease the riding be-

cause of some inconvenient weather.

At first it seemed no more than, as Uncle put it, 'a trifling cold', but it took a turn for the worse and Uncle had a raging fever. It was so high that the cold bath method Lizzy employed for William was used. It had the desired effect, and the fever broke, but all is not well.

When we first saw him, even our husbands gasped at his pallor. No matter how he protests that he is getting better, when he breathes there is a rasping sound and he needs to take as deep a breath as he can every few words when he speaks. He tires easily and sleeps for much of the time.

Aunt Rose is so very concerned. Uncle commanded that I not ask you to return as soon as may be, so I told him that I would inform you of his illness and leave the decision up to you, though I confess, I hope that we will be seeing all of you far sooner than had been originally planned.

Aunt Rose, my parents-in-law, and Aunt Catherine send their regards.

With much love,

Jane.

The three Bennet daughters all had tears of worry in their eyes after reading the missive. "We will return to Town, will we not Papa?" Lady Mary asked hopefully as she especially loved her Uncle Sed.

"Yes, Mary, we will return as soon as Tom and James arrive from Birchington," Lord Thomas too looked tired and worried. "William, we dispatched one of your grooms with a note to inform my sons, asking them to hie to Pemberley as soon as they are able."

"I sent Jim on the fastest mount available, William," Lady Anne informed her son who nodded his agreement.

Without planning it, Lady Elizabeth's hands found their way into her betrothed's and no one made a comment as she needed the comfort only her beloved William's touch could give. "We must pack," Elizabeth stated as she started to think of the practical tasks that must be achieved prior to the departure.

"The instructions have been issued, Lizzy," Lady Anne responded. "We will be ready to depart as soon as the party from Birchington arrives."

"They should reach us by evening, so we will depart as early in the morning as we can," the Duke of Hertfordshire stated.

Darcy agreed with his assessment and left to give instructions to his butler so that they would be able to depart before dawn on the morrow. He went to his study and composed expresses to be sent to the inns they would stay at and asked Douglas to have the steward work with the stable master so horses were sent ahead for the changes that would be needed along the way.

~~~~~~~/~~~~~~~

Within a minute of receiving the note from his father, Lord Tom shared the contents with his younger brother, and they sought out the Ashbys. As soon as they were apprised of the urgency of the situation, orders were issued to pack. They wanted to be heading toward Pemberley within the hour, two at the most.

Once the orders had been issued, Amy noted that her Tom was worried and rested her hand on his arm. "You are very close to your uncle, are you not, Tom?" she asked.

"I am. I have spent much time with Uncle Sed as he trained me to take over the duchy one day in the future..." His voice caught. He did not want to contemplate his uncle's mortality, but the thoughts were being forced upon him. "My prayer is that he will recover, and we will not be duke and duchess for many more years."

"That too is my prayer, Tom," Lady Amy said as she increased the pressure on her fiancée's arm. "We will pray often as it is in God's hands now. None of us know His plan; all we can do is hope that it is not your uncle's time to be called home to our Creator."

Not more than an hour later the coach, pulled by the six strongest horses Lord Tom owned, was on its way to Pemberley as fast as was possible, without harming the team. There was one rest break of less than an hour to allow the horses water and rest then they resumed their journey.

As dusk was falling, the Birchington carriage pulled into Pemberley's courtyard where the family waited for the occupants, they had been notified as soon as the conveyance rolled through the estate's gates. After greeting their parents, the Bennet brothers found themselves in a group hug with their three sisters, while Lord Ashbury conveyed his family's hopes and prayers that the Duke of Bedford would make a full recovery to the Duke of Hertfordshire.

That night the party was very much subdued, all went to bed early due to the intended departure time. The kitchen staff had baskets of comestibles in each carriage along with flagons of drinks so there would be no need to delay for breakfast. By a quarter hour before five, the carriages and attendant outriders had departed Pemberley.

~~~~~~~~/~~~~~~~~

The younger Phillips, the Bingleys, and the Hursts were in the sitting room with the duchess and her nieces when the butler announced that His Royal Highness, the Prince Regent had just arrived. The Regent was proceeded by a royal page that announced his highness, he received deep bows and curtsies from those present.

The Regent took his cousins hands in his own, "How is Cousin Sed faring, Cousin Rose?" he asked gently.

"He is as he has been this last week, Your Highness," Lady Rose reported. "The illness has not worsened, thank God, but there has been no significant improvement either, Cousin."

"We had to come see him for ourselves. We have always thought that our Cousin Sedgewick was indestructible. Our mother sends her best wishes, Cousin Rose, but could not come." The Regent paused before he went to go see his cousin. "Cousin Rose, would you like us to send you our royal physicians?"

"That is a most generous offer, Your Royal Highness," Lady Rose responded with a half curtsy. "However, you know my Sed well. He only wants the doctor that he knows and has used for many years. I do promise, Cousin, that if things take a turn for the worse, I will inform you, and overrule my husband with you. Together we may win." She offered a nod and the Regent's low chuckle and ghost of a smile was won before he was shown to his cousin's bedchamber. Once he left the room, the three couples took their seats again once Lady Rose had done so.

"I did not realise that Uncle Sed was so close to his royal cousin," Caroline Phillips stated softly. "It is extraordinary that the Regent would come here himself and not send an emissary."

"It was not unexpected as Sed and Cousin George were always very close," the Duchess explained. "Thomas, being so much younger than Sed, had a much more distant relationship with the Regent. It is an honour, to be sure, but sometimes family overrules the dictates of protocol."

"Knowing that the family is related to the royals, it was always almost abstract for me," Charles Bingley stated in wonder. "Being in the same room with our *de facto* monarch highlighted the closeness of the connection in ways that no amount of explaining ever could."

"I told you that I have the best connections, did I not, husband," his beloved Franny teased.

"A note from Thomas arrived this morning," Lady Rose changed the subject. "All of the party that travelled to Derbyshire will be in London by the afternoon on the morrow."

"What will happen with the betrothal ball, Aunt Rose?" Louisa asked. She still had to pinch herself that she was allowed to address two duchesses with the appellation of "Aunt".

"Catherine commented on the same thing, but I have spoken to Sed and he will not hear of plans being changed on his account," Lady Rose reported. "I could see that the thought of the ball or the nuptials being postponed on his account was very upsetting to him, so I allowed him to have his way. He will not relent on this."

"Let us pray that Uncle Sed will recover and be able to have a set with Lizzy at the ball," Graham Phillips offered hopefully. On his visit with his Uncle, he had a similar reaction to his twin cousins the first day they saw him; he was just able to mask it better. As much as he hoped and prayed for the Duke's recovery, he was not too sure that it would come to pass.

After a short visit with his favourite cousin, the Regent said his farewells and departed for Buckingham House with his retinue in tow.

~~~~~~~/~~~~~~~

The seven Bennets did not stop at their town homes to change, they went directly to Bedford House. The Darcys and Ashbys were in their own carriages for the last leg and would visit the Duke of Bedford on the morrow. No sooner had the two conveyances halted at the Russell Square house, than the seven made their way with all haste to the family sitting room where the butler informed them that her grace was with her nieces and their husbands.

It was a very emotional reunion that followed as the family commiserated together. After kissing his sister-in-law on both cheeks and giving her an encouraging hug, the Duke of Hertfordshire went directly to his brother's chambers. When he entered, he was stopped dead in his tracks. Thomas Bennet saw a very sick man, one who, no matter the hopes, would more than likely not leave his sickbed alive.

"Thomas...why are you...returned?" Lord Sedgewick managed to say between deep, rasping breaths. "I asked...Jane..."

"She did not beseech us to return, Sed, she honoured your request," the younger Bennet brother interrupted. "You must have known that as soon as we were informed that we would return, did you not?"

"I suppose...that...I knew. It is good...to see you, Brother. I have seen...you looking better." Even in the state that he was, Lord Sed Bennet was still able to joke with his brother. "Thomas, I...know that I...am not much longer...for this world. The...infection is in my...lungs. There is a...very hard conversation...that must be had...with my Rose." Seeing that his younger brother was about to interject, Lord Sed held up his hand to stay the protest.

"Thomas...I wish to witness...my niece and...nephew's marriage…before God…takes me…home to Him," the older Bennet rasped out.

"How long does Mr. Penrod think that you have, Sed," Lord Thomas asked, tears rolling down his cheeks and dreading the answer that he knew he would hear.

"A week…a fortnight at the…most." Sed admitted.

"I know it is hard for you to talk; will you allow me to talk to the family on your behalf?" Thomas asked and Sed nodded in agreement, "Is Penrod here?"

His older brother nodded again, "Resting in…blue chamber," was all he could manage. Lord Thomas summoned the nurse waiting respectfully outside of the room and instructed a footman to wake the doctor and have him join the family in the sitting room.

It was a very sombre Duke of Hertfordshire that returned to the family sitting room. As soon as his sister-in-law saw his mien, she knew that she was going to lose her Sed; that their prayers would not be answered. She started sobbing, supported by Sarah Bennet on one side and Jane Fitzwilliam on the other. When Mr. Frederick Penrod was ushered into the sitting room by the butler, he could see that the family was aware that the news was not what they wanted to hear.

"Sed told me what his prognosis is, but I would like you to elucidate us please, Mr. Penrod," Lord Thomas instructed the doctor.

"As you know, his Grace contracted a cold after riding in the rain a few weeks ago." The statement received nods from his listeners. "Unfortunately, the Duke did not tell his wife that he was ill until almost a week later when the fever started. Unfortunately, the fever was so high that we had to resort to an ice bath to help reduce it."

"By the time that I was summoned, it was no longer a cold but pneumonia. Everything known to us has been tried, and there was a brief period that we thought that his Grace may recover, but then the rasping sounds started to accommodate his breathing, which indicates that the infection is in his lungs." He looked at the Duchess of Bedford. "You have my sincere apologies for not informing you, your Grace, but your husband swore me to secrecy as he did not want to worry you until it was unavoidable."

"That is my...Sed," Lady Rose agreed between sobs.

"Thank you, Penrod. We need to have a family discussion now," Lord Thomas dismissed the doctor, and the butler closed the door after him. When they were alone, he shared the conversation that he had with his dying brother and conveyed his dying wish.

Once the family digested the news and the request, they all knew that none of them would want to deny Sed Bennet his wish. "We will need to discuss this with our betrotheds," Elizabeth stated the obvious. "I do not believe that William will object to marrying earlier. He can apply for a special licence on the morrow, if he agrees."

"The same is true of Amy," the Marquess of Birchington said, realizing that his ascendency to the Dukedom would come far sooner than he wanted, and he needed her to help him make it okay for so many of those that are dependent on them, or would soon be in their care. "If we are all in agreement, then William and I will go to the Archbishop's offices at Doctors Commons on the morrow."

"Sed is sleeping now, but when he wakes, I would like to tell him that his wish is being granted," Thomas nodded, his shoulders lowering as the weights continued to pile on compounded by the sadness which was almost overwhelming.

"We have to inform the cousins," Lady Sarah stated.

Once Lady Rose had calmed down, she told them about the exalted guest that had come to visit her husband and agreed that the royals must be apprised of the situation without delay. Footmen were dispatched in three directions, one to the Darcys, one to the Ashbys, and the last to Buckingham House. The first two carried notes that requested that the two families join them at Bedford House with all haste.

Two hours later the two stunned families heard the news

from the Duke of Hertfordshire. As their betrotheds had predicted, both the Duke of Derbyshire and Lady Amy Ashby agreed to the wedding that week without any reservation. It was decided that only family members would be invited to the wedding. Ladies Sarah and Gillian, as the mothers of the brides, would be in charge of the planning, and that they would notify the other family members who would be invited for the small ceremony. The very soon to be brothers planned to meet at Doctors Commons as it opened at ten o'clock the following morning. With the applications coming from a Duke and a Marquess, not to mention the connection to the royals, there was no doubt that the licenses would be approved and issued the same day.

Lord Thomas, accompanied by Lords Tom and William, went to see his ailing brother and had the pleasure of seeing him smile when he was told that his wish to witness the wedding would be granted. As hard as it was for him to breathe, it was a happy Lord Sed who returned to his slumber.

CHAPTER 8

The plans were set. The wedding would be held in the Bedford House ballroom. A very comfortable armchair with a footrest would be placed at the front for Lord Sed so he would have an unimpeded view of the ceremony; he would be carried downstairs in a bath chair by some footmen before the guests arrived. He was excited at the prospect of wearing clothing other than his night attire. A royal courier had brought a note from Buckingham House informing the Bennets that the Queen, Regent, Prince Edward, and Princess Elizabeth would attend the wedding. The Queen sent a Ming Dynasty vase for each couple as she had when the older twins married. The note indicated that the Queen's vicar, the Archbishop of Canterbury, would be happy to perform the ceremony. Fortunately, Reverend Moseby-Finch, the head clergyman at St. Georges Church, had responded that even on such short notice he was available to perform the rites of marriage, and would be present by nine that morning as the wedding was planned to start at ten. Lady Rose had written a note expressing her joy at the four royal cousins joining them and politely refused the use of the Queen's vicar.

The Phillips family had arrived in London from Meryton the previous day and were staying with their son and daughter on Portman Square so that Hattie and Madeline Gardiner had been available for any help that Ladies Sarah and Gillian needed to plan the wedding. Along with Lady Anne Darcy, Mrs. Gardiner had taken the responsibility for acquiring the flowers, and Hattie was in charge of decorating the Bedford House ball room, which would be divided in two. The ceremony would be performed on one side while the wedding breakfast would be hosted on the other side. Once everyone had transitioned to the wedding breakfast, the Duke of Bedford would be returned to his bedchambers.

Besides the family that was already in London, Lord and Lady Amberleigh, and Ian and Anne Ashby, Lady Amy's older brothers and their wives, would arrive on the morrow from Surrey, two days before the nuptials. Both brides had been seen by Madam Chambourg to consult on their wedding gowns, and her store was closed until they were ready.

The Duchess of Bedford understood that her husband's insistence that she continue to plan the betrothal ball was part of his plan to distract her from the truth of the seriousness of the illness that would soon take his life. As a compromise, and only if he were still with them, there would be a shortened wedding ball at Bennet House the night of the wedding. Outside family only a few close friends were invited. The supper set would be the final set and after the meal the ball would end. Ladies Catherine and Elaine were working with Bennet House's housekeeper to plan the ball.

The Duke of Derbyshire and his future duchess had been counting each day that passed until the fifteenth day of June separately as they were in anticipation of the day that would join them forever so they would not have to part again. Though they hated the reason of the accelerated wedding, neither repined marrying earlier. They, along with everyone in the family, were praying that God would deliver a miracle and spare Lord Sed as He had when He returned Lady Anne to her family when all seemed lost.

Both couples had agreed that, if necessary, they would defer their wedding trips until after the sad event, and three months of mourning, one month would be deep mourning and two months of half. They had all wanted to mourn longer, especially the deep mourning period, but the Duke of Bedford had extracted promises from all in the family that they would not. His wife had promised to keep to a half year of deep mourning and the next six months in half mourning as he did not want her to mourn him for the rest of her days. Lady Rose was the last surviving member of her original family. His Grace Sedgewick Bennet, Duke of Bedford, knew that his beloved Rose would be surrounded by loving family after he was called to be with God. His brother and sister had told him and Rose, in no uncertain terms, that if the predicted outcome came to pass, that his duchess would be welcomed into their household and would live with them for the rest of her days.

Sed Bennet was able to rest easier than most as he was supremely confident in his heir's abilities. He had educated him for the ascendency as well as any had ever been taught. Like his father and his siblings, Lord Tom Bennet had a vast ability to assimilate and hold information that could be recalled as needed. The Duke of Bedford was sad that his journey on the mortal coil would soon be at an end, but he was at peace knowing that he would see all of his family that he loved so well in God's Kingdom when it was their turn to join him.

~~~~~~~/~~~~~~~

The day before the wedding Lady Sarah knocked on her middle daughter's bedchamber door and was admitted by her daughter's French maid, Miss Jacqueline Arseneault. Lizzy called her Jacqui and both mother and daughter were pleased that someone familiar would be accompanying her across the square on the morrow. Lady Sarah had petitioned her husband, and it had not taken much convincing for him, to agree that Biggs and Johns would stay with Elizabeth and become Darcy footmen to continue to stand guard over her as they had done for the last number of years. After the murder of the man in Fowey, no chances would be taken with the safety of any of the family members.

The abigail left the room, and Lady Sarah and her daughter moved to the private sitting room attached to the suite. Once they were comfortable on the settee, Lady Sarah proceeded to give her daughter 'the talk.' It was, in essentials, the same talk that she had had with Jane and Marie the night before their wedding. As her middle daughter would become a duchess on the morrow, she addressed the change in rank that her daughter would undergo after the wedding.

"When I met your father, he was the Marquess of Netherfield, and I knew that one day he would become the Duke of Hertfordshire. It never intimidated me as I had a long time to get used to the idea that I would one day be a duchess. With William's elevation of such short duration, are you nervous about becoming a wife on the morrow?" her mother asked as she held Elizabeth's hand.

"Mayhap I should be, but I am not, Mama," Lady Elizabeth offered thoughtfully. "My relationship with William had a difficult beginning and I was still immature myself. I had allowed the stories of *that woman* to colour my judgements, and the way that I looked at the world. When I saw the tangible effects of my petulance, I was ashamed. You and Papa had tried to correct me, but I was too stubborn to change at that point.

"My behaviour was most shrew-like. There was nothing that I can do to change the past, and it was not my burden to carry. It was after talking to Mother Anne that I began to see things clearly. It took the perspective of one that was not close to me, well not yet, to help me see things in my own behaviour that I was not proud of. You know, do you not, that I wanted to forgive William much sooner, but Mother Anne asked me to wait?"

Her mother nodded, "I do. You are not the only one who had long conversations with Anne, Lizzy," Sarah Bennet said with a smile. "Your papa and I are very happy that you were able to see the problems in your own behaviour. We would have stepped in if you had gone too far; in fact, we almost did in William's case. You were not the only one angry with him, we all were, but the punishment did not fit the crime in our opinion.

"We spoke to Andrew and Richard the next morning before William made his first apology. They were the first ones who asked us to hold off before mitigating any of the repercussions that William would face. When Anne came for that first visit, she repeated the request, for the same reasons that she enumerated for you.

"Both of you learnt invaluable lessons about the consequences of bad behaviour, and jumping to conclusions without all of the facts. I dare say that it is behaviour that neither of you will ever repeat, Lizzy." Lady Sarah pushed an errant curl to the side as she waited for her daughter's response.

"You are correct, Mama, both William and I learnt and grew. No, I am certain that we will never repeat the same behaviour. To return to your concern about my being nervous. I was nervous about the marriage bed before your talk, but about being William's duchess, no I am not. We have been through so much together, I know that we will have a true partnership and there is nothing that we will not be able to face together," Elizabeth said resolutely. "Not only will William be there to help me, but you, Papa, Mother Anne, and the rest of the family will be there as well."

"After William missed your sisters' weddings, I am glad that he will have Richard standing up with him. How did you choose Marie over Jane as your matron of honour?" Lady Sarah asked.

"I love all of my sisters and brothers, but she and I have similar temperaments, that is if you ignore my past quick judgement," Elizabeth said self-deprecatingly. "Mayhap for that reason I have always felt a little closer to Marie."

"Jane and Mary too have a similar temperament, but Kitty, I fear, is a mix and it has been a pleasure to watch her become the young women she now is," Lady Sarah stated. "Is there anything more that I need to answer for you, Lizzy?"

"No, Mama. I want you to know that you are the best mother in the world, and I will miss seeing you every day," Lady Elizabeth said with deep feeling. "Before I forget, thank you for inviting Mother Anne and my new sister to stay at Bennet House for some days."

"It is our pleasure, Lizzy. Anne agreed that it will be good for you two to start your married life without a mother and sister underfoot." Lady Sarah stood and kissed her daughter on both cheeks. As happy as she was for Lizzy, she knew that after tomorrow there would only be two of her daughters left at home.

~~~~~~~/~~~~~~~

The Fitzwilliam brothers and their wives had been guests for dinner at Darcy House that night. During the separation of the sexes, the three cousins who would become brothers on the morrow were sitting in the master's study puffing on cigars and drinking some of the fine French cognac their father-in-law had gifted to Darcy.

"So, William, do you need any tips for tomorrow night?" Richard teased his friend and cousin.

"No, thank you, Richard," William gave Richard a death stare. "I may not be as experienced as an old soldier who once gallivanted all over the continent, but I am not without experience." The Duke of Derbyshire thought back to his eighteenth birthday.

They were at Darcy House the day after the family had celebrated the milestone with William who was in his second year at Cambridge. Father had told him to keep that evening open and not make any plans. Through the years, George Darcy had drummed into his son's consciousness the need to respect ladies, to never act the rake. Aside of the inherent disrespect, he pointed out the dangers of contracting the French disease or one like it.

They had left the house at seven that evening and arrived at a very good looking and well-maintained house a half hour later. His father informed him that they had arrived at one of the high-class brothels that members of the upper circle of the Ton were wont to frequent.

"Father," Darcy asked, "you have always taught me to respect women and never to use them as some do." He had wanted to add "like George Wickham does," but he decided to hold his peace.

"Yes, my son. Nothing tonight will negate my teachings. This is what my father did for me, when you marry you will want to have the tools to be a good lover for your wife. You enjoy learning, do you not?" George nodded once when his son agreed that he did. "Think of this as a different kind of education. All who work at Madam Juliette are ladies of the highest standard, and all are without disease. After my visit, I was chaste until I married you mother. What you choose to do is up to you, but I would recommend the same path I took." George

Darcy concluded.

Three hours later a much wiser and educated Fitzwilliam Darcy joined his father in the Darcy carriage, as he departed Madam Juliette's for the one and only time, he resolved to follow his honoured father's path.

The Duke was snapped out of his reverie as Andrew slapped his back. "Wake up, William, it is time to re-join the ladies. Is it not remarkable that come the morrow we will be married to three sisters? It is a pity that there are not two more Fitzwilliam or Darcy men for Kitty and Mary," Lord Hilldale joked as they headed back to the drawing room.

~~~~~~~~/~~~~~~~~

At Ashbury House, Lady Amy had just had her 'talk' with her mother. Like her new sister Elizabeth, she would soon be a duchess as well. The difference for her was that she had thought that she would have years to learn what was needed to be a duchess, she had not received the training to ascend to such a lofty title as her betrothed had. True, she was the daughter of an earl, but there was a big leap between that and becoming a marchioness on the morrow.

As she sat on her bed after her Mama had kissed her good-night, Amy wondered how it was possible to have turned the anxiety into excitement, she was relieved, no longer scared, and determined she would make sure she gave the same gift to her own daughters someday were God to bestow such a blessing. She thought back to the conversation that she had been party to with her soon to be mother-in-law and Lady Rose.

"Aunt Rose," Amy looked at her aunt and tears pooled in her eyes, "how am I to fill the role of Duchess of Bedford that you have filled so ably for so many years?"

"Amy, dear," Lady Sarah said soothingly, "do you think that Rose and I were not nervous when we married our husbands?" she asked. "When I married Thomas, he had already ascended to his dukedom, so thanks to the entrapment I never had any time as a marchioness before I became a duchess."

"That is true, Mother Sarah, but you would have been married

to Father Bennet if it were not for the perfidy that was perpetrated against him, and you had known him while he was a marquess," Amy tried to reason.

"As you have known Tom while he was a marquess," Lady Rose pointed out. "Is the reason that you are nervous because you feel like you will be usurping my position?" Lady Rose asked astutely. Amy nodded as more tears gathered, and her mother-in-law handed her a spare silk.

"You will not be usurping my position, you dear girl. I could never be the Duchess of Bedford without my Sed as my duke! It is the way of the world, has been the way for many more years than any of us have been in it, and there is nothing that you have done that had caused us to be where we are," Lady Rose told the young woman.

"Rose is correct, Amy, and you have an advantage that neither Rose nor I had when we became Duchesses," The Duchess of Hertfordshire stated.

"What is that, Mother Sarah?" the confused young lady asked.

"Us, Amy. You have us," Lady Sarah elucidated. "When I married Thomas, it was not many months after the former duke went to join his beloved wife in heaven. When I married, I became a duchess overnight, like Lizzy will. Rose had been married to Sed for seven years, all that time as his marchioness. Our mother-in-law Bennet passed not a year after Sed and Rose wed, so like I did, Rose had to learn on her own. We relied on each other as my sister-in-law had been a duchess for barely longer than me when I married my dear husband.

"You, Amy, are not alone. In addition to Rose and me, you will have Ladies Anne, Elaine, and Catherine to assist you when you need, not to mention the fact that you will soon be gaining six sisters. Among them will be a duchess, a countess, and a viscountess. My dear daughter, you will have more support and help than you will know what to do with!" Lady Sarah stated with authority.

As the soon to be marchioness thought back over the conversation, she acknowledged that the duchesses were, as usual, correct and pinpointed precisely the issue as well as why it was not one. She would have a support system like none other who had become a duchess. Her sister Lizzy too would have as much support as she required, but she suspected that Lizzy would take things in stride.

~~~~~~~/~~~~~~~

The morning of the wedding Thomas Bennet arrived at Bedford House, ahead of the family. He desired to talk to his brother before he was brought below stairs as the house filled with family. When he arrived, he noted that a company of royal guard were already stationed outside his brother's house. As he considered this, it struck him that it would soon be his son's house if the miracle that they were all praying for was not forthcoming.

Lord Thomas was ushered into his brother's chambers where he found his brother looking better than he had since the return from Derbyshire. Seeing Sed looking somewhat better gave him a modicum of hope. Lord Sed was seated in the bath chair with a blanket covering his legs while his valet of almost thirty years fussed with his master's cravat. Once his man was satisfied, he was dismissed and told to make sure that the brothers were not disturbed.

"You look better than I have seen you since you became ill, Sed," Thomas Bennet stated.

"Mayhap it is the excitement, but...I feel better today than... I have since this infernal sickness...took hold," he said and coughed into his handkerchief. His younger brother did not miss the red stain on the cloth. It seemed that his brother could talk a little longer without taking a breath, but the rasping and crackling sounds were still audible.

"I wanted some time to talk to you before the wedding, Sed," the younger Bennet brother stated, "as with the ceremony followed by the ball at Bennet House, I was not sure that I would get to spend any time just with you today."

"You know I always...have time to see my baby...brother," Sed smiled at his jest. "If Penrod is correct and I leave the mortal coil soon..." He took three or four deep breaths, or as deep as he was able, with the pain he felt in his lungs with each. "I leave knowing that Rose will be with those...she loves and love her in return." He took a pause to regulate his breathing. "Being involved in your children's'...lives as we were...made us forget... that we were not blessed...with our own."

"They are not just mine and Sarah's, Sed. You and Rose have been a second set of parents for them, and they love you as a such," Lord Thomas choked up as he spoke. "Marie was delighted when you walked her down the aisle to Andrew. You and Rose have been a very big part of their lives, and if God brings you home, it will leave a huge hole in all of our hearts." Both brothers had tears rolling down their cheeks and neither was embarrassed by the openly displayed emotions.

"Thomas, I am afraid that you will have to give Lizzy away on your own today," Lord Sed said with a smile. "She and William will have a love for the ages, you know. People will talk about them and the way that they came together long after all of us have departed this earth," the older Bennet brother predicted, and his younger brother found that he could not disagree with him.

It was not too many minutes later when the master of Bedford House's valet knocked on the door to let them know that the footmen were there to take his Grace below stairs. The brothers shook hands and as he left his brother's room, the Duke of Hertfordshire turned to gaze on his older brother one more time as he had a frightening premonition that he would not have many more conversations with his brother Sed after the wedding.

~~~~~~~~/~~~~~~~~

Soon to be eighteen-year-old Tony Álvarez was sitting on the dock in Bundoran's harbour watching the small boats as they were maneuvered by the man holding the tiller with skill acquired over many years of practice. For the first time in his life, he was beginning to question the wisdom of the path that his parents had set for him.

The young man was becoming confused. He had heard Karen Younge rant about revenge, but he was questioning *what* she was avenging. The man that she claimed to love was described by his mother as a blackguard of the worst order, and had been killed while trying to harm others. He took a risk, and then when it did not go the way he hoped, the victims were being blamed, not the ones that caused the situation.

In the few weeks that they had been in Bundoran, he had noticed how happy the locals seemed, none of them had empires to run, and none of them seemed to care about what others had. They seemed to find their bliss from within, not without, and without worrying about possessions they did not have.

After using the skills to fully consider all he knew, he had determined logically that his father's case was similar to that of the late Wickham's. He had made choices that had led to his downfall. As much as the son was starting to understand this, he was not ready to let go of his animus against those who had arranged for his father to be captured and hung. Tony did not like the polarizing thoughts that were swirling around in his head, and trying to shake them, young Mr. Álvarez returned to his room at the Happy Leprechaun.

CHAPTER 9

Her abigail woke her up just past the hour of six, as per Lady Elizabeth's instructions, and a bath was waiting for her. As Jacqui was washing her hair, she imagined how it would be the next time she took a bath at Darcy House, and possibly with two in the huge bathing tub she had seen on her tour. The thought of bathing with her husband made her stomach flutter and her body grew heavier with aching for his touch. It was but a few hours more that she would be required to wait, and then finally she would have the chance to express her need of him, and fulfil his obvious needs of hers.

There was no more waiting; she would wed her duke today. She was marrying for love, as she always swore that she would, and oh how she loved him! One of the things that had opened her heart to him was that he was generous to a fault. The Haven House administrator, Miss Ethel Cookson, had lately informed Lady Elizabeth that New Haven House was ready for occupation, and that in addition to his generous pledge, her betrothed had told Miss Cookson to come to him directly if there were any shortfalls or any other needs that arose.

Once she got past her own pride and prejudice, she had allowed herself to admit that he was the only man for her. He had bewitched her body and soul, and she loved him most ardently. From the moment that she had admitted it, she never wanted to be parted from him again. Elizabeth wanted to bring back the joy that had been absent from his life since his father was murdered, and she was honoured when he confided that he had at last began to heal because of her. During one of their discussions, he had told her that he had been walking through life as a shell of a man; going through the motions; not experiencing life; just living life going through the days; hiding from the world until he had fallen in love with her.

Just like she would help him, he would do the same for her. He already had. He grounded her and directed her passions to positive pursuits. She felt like she was floating on air when he smiled at her, and when he allowed his dimples to show, she felt like she could fly on the wings of angels. Lady Elizabeth Bennet always knew that she would only marry for the deepest love, but even in her imaginings she had not understood the depths that love could reach in its truest form as she had found with her William.

She exhaled in relief when she pressed her hand against the need building but restrained from releasing the tension as she would gain the true relief of having him as she had been longing for since she had first seen him in her dreams. The tension would only serve them better when she was finally in his bed, so she slowly slid her hand away, the last touch sending a shiver up her spine, as she revelled in the sensation before closing her thighs to avoid temptation and was eventually pleased she had. Not a minute later, Jacqui returned and helped her mistress out of the bath.

At Birchington House, the Marquess was dressed and ready by seven that morning, he was pacing back and forth, trying to burn off the nervous energy. It was all real now. Amy's belongings had been delivered to the mistress's suite yesterday, and in a few hours, she would be *his* marchioness. The real question was how long they would be the Marquess and Marchioness of Birchington. He hated the fact that his Uncle Sed had to leave this world for him to become a duke.

He had known it would happen one day; it was just far too soon. He would miss his uncle almost as much as he would if, heaven forbid, it was his father who was sick. Uncle Sed had prepared him, taught him everything that he needed to know, but still, he did not feel ready. He prayed fervently for the miracle of which they all beseeched of Him, then concentrated on the woman that held his heart. She was the love if his life, and he could not regret that they would marry a little more than a fortnight early. He hated the reason, but loved the consequence, as it was the idea of not sharing the moment with his uncle was unthinkable.

At Darcy House, his Grace was being shaved by his man Carstens. His poor valet had to request that he stay still more than a few times, but it was hard. Fitzwilliam Darcy was not a patient man, and it was only a few short hours that she would be his forever, but he was begging Father Time to speed up his clocks. He smiled at asking a fictional character for help, and Carstens had to halt his shaving once again to avoid cutting him.

He took a slow breath and closed his eyes, bringing a vision of her to soothe him. He was about to marry his soulmate. She was the *only* woman that he would ever have agreed to marry. If she had not returned his feelings, he would have been devastated and remained a bachelor. She loved him in return, had finally admitted it openly, and there was no mistaking that her eyes turned green as they filled with passion when he prolonged a touch or slid his finger along her side to barely touch the side of her breast. He bit back a smile as he diverted his thoughts until he could act on them, but there was no doubt in his mind that marriage to his duchess would never be drab or boring.

After he was dressed, he joined his mother and sister in the family sitting room where there was a tray with some fresh baked pastries, tea, and coffee. He helped himself to one of his favourites, a lemon filled pastry; the sweet and tart awakening his pallet delightfully.

"In two hours, I will not be the only sister, my cousins will be my sisters," Lady Georgiana bounced on the balls of her feet. "And Richard and Andrew will be our brothers!" she exclaimed.

"What about Tom and James," her mother teased.

"Tom will be my brother, but..." A furiously blushing almost seventeen-year-old could not yet voice her thought.

"But you can only think of James as a cousin?" her mother completed the sentence for her, and all Georgie could manage was a nod of her head.

"We will address those concerns later, please, Georgie. Right now, I need you to do the very sisterly thing and make sure I am at the alter for your sister, or I hate to think how she will exact revenge," Darcy teased her into a laugh, smiling when his mother's lit the room, her happiness at the finding of his evident for all to see.

~~~~~~~/~~~~~~~

Lady Amelia Ashby looked around her former room at Ashbury House. She had very fond memories of growing up between the estate of Ashbury and the house in London, but she was about to embark on a new adventure at a new estate and home in Town. She was not sure how long they would be at either, but again prayed that Uncle Sed would be spared for the sake of all her new family.

Before her mother's talk the night before, she had felt a level of trepidation about the marriage bed, and now she was anticipating it. The times that she and her betrothed had managed to steal a kiss, she had revelled in the feel of his lips sliding against hers, and for the two or three times she had opened and his tongue had teased hers as they tasted each other, she was almost weak at the knees with the dizzy after effects. She knew that Tom had some experience as they had discussed the subject one day at Birchington, but he was not a rake. She was very much in love with the man who accepted her for who she was, respected her, and did not want her to be other than who she was. Tom Bennet was the one; her one and only, and in a few short hours she would be his wife, irrevocably joined with him until death do them part.

She took one last look around then went to join her parents and her brothers and sisters in the drawing room for some refreshment before they departed for Bedford House.

The three families arrived at the Bedford's house at almost the same time. In keeping with the tradition that the grooms not see the brides before the ceremony, they were rushed into the house so that their brides could exit the conveyances at their leisure.

Lord James, who was standing up with him, accompanied his brother to the parlour off the ball room which for the day was designated as the grooms' waiting room. They found the Duke and Earl with reverend Finch and his curate. The curate checked his special license and found all in order, then verified the one that the Marquess had been issued. A quick check confirmed there was no impediment to the weddings proceeding.

Lady Anne, Mrs. Gardiner, and Mrs. Phillips had done a masterful job of decorating. The two ladies who had selected the flowers had chosen red and white roses that were simple but fit the day perfectly. Hattie, with the assistance of her two daughters, and Louisa Hurst, had decorated with white and red ribbons and bows so that the flowers and the ribbons matched well. Like the wedding itself, all was understated but elegant.

There was a raised platform in front of the two columns of chairs where the ceremony would take place, and to the left of the platform was another with the Dukes special chair, one on his right for his wife, and to his left four more very comfortable seats for the Queen and her three children accompanying her. Lord Sed was brought into the ball room and placed in his chair, aided by two footmen. Once he was seated, his valet covered his legs with a blanket. His duchess entered and sat next to him, taking his hand in hers.

Once the Duke of Bedford was comfortably seated, the family took their seats and at five minutes before the ten o'clock hour as the vicar, the grooms, and their attendants took their places. Everyone except for the patient rose as the royals took their seats, and once they had received their bows and curtsies, they sat then the rest of the family sat as well.

The Regent sat next to his cousin. As much as he did not want to, he had accepted that Cousin Sed would not recover baring divine intervention. He had sent his royal physicians who had confirmed his cousin's diagnosis and been honest about the fact that it would not be long before he succumbed. To the Regent's left was the Queen, followed by Prince Edward and Princess Elizabeth. Lady Anne was seated with her sister Catherine and her brother's family. Georgiana chose to sit near the Gardiners, Phillips, Bingleys, and Hursts, with Mary, Kitty, Wes, and Loretta. Lady Pricilla De Melville was next to her sister Sarah, with her husband Lord Cyril next to her.

On the hour, the string quartet started to play softly and May Gardiner, after executing a very proper curtsy to the royals, walked down the aisle dropping white and red rose petals as she advanced. She was followed by Lady Amberleigh, Isabelle Ashby, who was standing up for her sister-in-law walked down the aisle. Once she reached the platform, she stood next to James Bennet. Lady Marie Fitzwilliam came next and stood next to her brother-in-law Richard.

The string quartet ceased playing, paused, then struck up a lively tune. The Earl of Ashbury proudly escorted his daughter toward her intended. She had a cream satin gown with an empire waist, and a gossamer overlay. Her veil was adorned with pearls, and her hair was in an updo, held in place by pearl tipped pins. No one missed that she was glowing with happiness as her father lifted her veil, kissed her, and after replacing the veil, handed her to her groom who came to meet them. After the Earl sat next to his wife in the front row across from Lady Sarah, it was Lady Elizabeth's turn to make the walk to her destiny.

Darcy felt like he could not breathe when he saw her. She wore a similarly simple dress to Lady Amy, except it was white satin. Her sleeves were set slightly off her shoulders, and the cut in front displayed some of her ample breasts, but not too much as to be called indecent. Both the overlay and her veil had tiny diamonds sewn on which reflected the light like a crystal chandelier. She wore the emerald ear bobs and necklace that her groom had gifted her to go along with the emerald betrothal ring he had presented to her at Pemberley. Her hair was in a twist with some of her raven curls cascading down the sides. How he loved those curls and could not wait until he could run his fingers through her hair, as he had dreamt about doing for months now. Her pins were emerald tipped and matched her jewellery perfectly. The new Duke could see her eyes shining with love and anticipation through the sheer veil, the very eyes that had been the first thing about her which had captivated him.

Lord Thomas Bennet was the epitome of a proud father. His oldest son and middle daughter were, as far as he could see, marrying their perfect matches. As happy a day as it was, his heart was heavy when he noticed his brother's pallor as he neared him. It did not take a doctor to see that the prayed-for miracle would not be forthcoming. After he kissed his Lizzy and placed her hand on William's arm, he returned to sit next to his beloved Sarah.

The parson looked to the Regent for permission to commence and received a slight nod of His Highness's head so he opened the book of Common Prayer and began the wedding service.

"Dearly beloved, we are gathered together here in the sight of God, and in the face of this congregation, to join together this Man and this Woman in holy Matrimony; which is an honourable estate, instituted of God in the time of man's innocency, signifying unto us the mystical union that is betwixt Christ and his Church; which holy estate Christ adorned and beautified with his presence, and first miracle that he wrought, in Cana of Galilee; and is commended of Saint Paul to be honourable among all men: and therefore is not by any to be enterprised, nor taken in hand, unadvisedly, lightly, or wantonly, to satisfy men's carnal lusts and appetites, like brute beasts that have no understanding; but reverently, discreetly, advisedly, soberly, and in the fear of God; duly considering the causes for which Matrimony was ordained.

"First, it was ordained for..."

Not surprisingly, when the reverend asked if there were any objections there was silence except for Lady Catherine de Bourgh clearing her throat which produced many smiles from those that knew of her former aspirations for her nephew, and the irony of her warning all that if they interfered with his wedding another, they would incur her wrath.

Next the vicar asked, "Who giveth this Woman to be married to this Man?" He looked at Lady Elizabeth and her groom in turn. The Duke of Hertfordshire said, "I do." The question was repeated for Lady Amy, and the Marquess and the Earl of Ashbury stood and said "I do."

The two couples recited their vows, and the best men each handed his groom the wedding ring, first the Duke of Derbyshire and then the Marquess of Birchington recited: "With this Ring I thee wed, with my Body I thee worship, and with all my worldly Goods I thee endow: In the Name of the Father, and of the Son, and of the Holy Ghost. Amen."

The clergyman recited a prayer and then he concluded with: "Those whom God hath joined together let no man put asunder.

"Forasmuch as *Fitzwilliam* and *Elizabeth* and *Thomas* and *Amelia* have consented together in holy Wedlock, and have witnessed the same before God and this company, and thereto have given and pledged their troth either to other, and have declared the same by giving and receiving of a Ring, and by joining of hands; I pronounce that each couple be Man and Wife together, In the Name of the Father, and of the Son, and of the Holy Ghost. Amen.

"God the Father, God the Son, God the Holy Ghost, bless, preserve, and keep you; the Lord mercifully with his favour look upon you; and so, fill you with all spiritual benediction and grace, that ye may so live together in this life, that in the world to come ye may have life everlasting. *Amen.*"

It was done, Lady Elizabeth Bennet was Elizabeth Darcy, Her Grace, the Duchess of Derbyshire, and Lady Amelia Ashby was Amelia Bennet, Marchioness of Birchington. The curate led the newlyweds to the corner where the registry book had been placed on a table, and with the best men and matrons of honour as witnesses, the four newlyweds signed, and the last ritual was complete.

As had been agreed, the two couples first went to see Uncle Sed and receive his well wishes. None of the four missed that his gasping and wheezing had become more pronounced, but no one mentioned it. The brides kissed his cheek and the grooms shook his hand. The four then received their royal cousins' congratulations. As before, all other than Lord Sed stood, and the royals stood and headed toward the wedding breakfast.

Six footmen lifted the armchair with his grace in it to place him at the wedding breakfast as he was determined to see the celebration through. The two couples were surrounded by their immediate family, and Lizzy's three younger sisters took pleasure in addressing her as 'your grace' at every opportunity. Lady Sarah and Lord Tom split up, Lady Sarah hugging her middle daughter while her husband shook his son's hand and kissed his new daughter on the cheek. After her mother, the new duchess was embraced by her mother-in-law who had tears of joy in her eyes.

"How my George would have loved you, Lizzy," she said close to her newest daughter's ear. "On this happiest of days, I miss him, but I am comforted in the abject joy that I see in my son's eyes. You are the only one that suits him, daughter, and he is the only one that fits with you. God really does move in mysterious ways."

As Lady Anne moved on to hug and kiss her son, she was followed by Lady Catherine, who gave her newest niece a big wet kiss on her cheek. The great lady had grown to love Lady Elizabeth Bennet, and like so many others, could plainly see that she was the only one for her nephew. It was another half hour before all of the well wishes, hugs, and kisses were given.

Once all of the family was seated, the butler made the formal announcement. "Your Royal Majesty, Your Royal Highness, and your Highness, your Graces, my lords and ladies. Lord Fitzwilliam and Lady Elizabeth Darcy, their graces the Duke and Duchess of Derbyshire, and Lord Thomas and Lady Amelia Bennet, the Marquess and Marchioness of Birchington."

After the formal introduction, Reverend Moseby-Finch gave a benediction and said grace. The Queen and the regent took a small bite of food and the celebratory meal commenced. The newlywed couples went from table to table to talk to the various family members, and when the newlywed Darcys arrived at their uncle's chair, they were both taken aback by the way that he looked as he had worsened significantly. They, like the Duke of Hertfordshire, had taken a small measure of hope that morning when they saw their Uncle looking better than he had in recent memory, but they could not deny what they saw before them now. Uncle Sed was not in a good way.

The Duke of Bedford was clearly having a very hard time drawing breath, and no matter how he tried to hide, it was obvious that he was in a lot of pain. "Uncle Sed, I am as stubborn as you are, so do not try and protest. You need to allow the footmen to return you to your bed so the doctor can examine you," Elizabeth pleaded with her uncle. He was too weak to protest so he simply nodded.

"My Sed will be better once he has rested, he simply over-exerted himself today," Lady Rose informed her family. A footman pushed the bath chair so it was parallel to the arms chair while two others lifted their master and gently placed him in the bath chair. He was wheeled out, the concerned looks of his family following his progress including the Regent. Before Lady Rose followed her husband, the Regent beckoned her over and asked her to send a messenger to Buckingham House, regardless of the time, if Cousin Sed worsened any further, and she, of course, promised that she would.

Lady Rose turned and addressed the family before she followed her husband to his chambers. "You all know that my Sed would be very upset if his being tired causes the celebration of our niece's and nephew's wedding to be cut short. Please, carry on, and I will return with news as soon as I speak with Mr. Penrod." The Duchess of Bedford left the ball room and the celebration resumed, albeit much subdued.

A quarter hour later, Lady Rose Bennet returned and informed the family that the doctor concurred with her that the Duke needed to rest, and he was in bed and sleeping as she spoke. No one had their heart in the celebration any longer and the newlyweds and their parents discussed cancelling the abbreviated wedding ball scheduled for that night. When Lady Rose heard what they were considering she told them, in no uncertain terms, that neither her husband nor herself wanted the ball cancelled. If fact, she informed them, that before he fell asleep, her Sed had instructed her to attend to represent both of them.

Not long after the conversation the newlyweds made their rounds to thank their families for attending, then headed to the open carriage waiting in front of the house. The Duke and Duchess of Derbyshire entered their landau pulled by a matched white set of four while the Marquess and Marchioness only had to walk to the house next-door.

Fitzwilliam Darcy revelled in the closeness as his duchess snuggled up against him. As soon as the carriage turned out of Russell Square, he placed a not too chaste kiss on his beloved's lips. The driver was well trained and kept his eyes forward on the way ahead, while Biggs and Johns found very interesting things to look at not in the equipage as they stood in their positions at the rear. After the relatively short trip, the Duke and his Duchess arrived at their townhouse.

CHAPTER 10

Mrs. Betty Dodsley and Mr. Sam Hodges, the housekeeper and butler of Birchington House, had the servants arrayed for the new marchioness to greet when the newlyweds entered their home as husband and wife for the first time. The senior staff passed on congratulations on behalf of the servants.

"My husband and I appreciate your greeting us with this welcome and wishing us happy on this most special of days. Over the next few days, I will have time to meet each of you and hopefully it will not take me long to learn your names," the Marchioness addressed the assembled servants, earning her much approbation. "Mrs. Dodsley, my husband and I are going to get some rest before the ball. Please have a tray sent up at five this afternoon."

The housekeeper gave her new mistress a curtsy as the butler dismissed the assembled servants. Husband and wife quickly ascended the stairs and entered their suite. As soon as the door was closed, they dismissed their personal servants until they were summoned to prepare baths later that afternoon. Once they were completely alone, Lord Tom Bennet took his wife in his arms and kissed her, neither intending rest that afternoon.

The newlywed Darcys were greeted by the Killions. His Grace had conveyed his then betrothed's request that the servants not be pulled from their duties to greet the couple as she intended to meet with each and every one as soon as she was able to. The housekeeper and her husband welcomed the Duke and Duchess home and asked to let them know if they needed anything. To his wife's delight, he picked her up as if she weighed nothing and walked up the stairs, putting her down once they reached their shared sitting room. The tinkling sound of the new duchess's delightful laugh filled the halls of Darcy House, putting a smile on the face of any servant who heard the melodic sound.

As had been arranged earlier, they were alone in the master suite. Spying extra pillows on the settee, Elizabeth laughed again. Evidently Mrs. Reynolds had informed Mrs. Killion that the new Mrs. Darcy liked a few spare pillows on the settee in their private sitting room.

Her laugh was silenced as her husband gently placed his hands on either side of her head and drew her to himself. He leaned down and lightly brushed his lips against hers. His kisses became more and more ardent as she responded in kind, and soon their tongues were dancing the dance of love. Darcy pulled her sleeves down a little more so he could have unfettered access to her neck and shoulders as he reverently kissed each inch exposed. Soon he was suckling the exposed parts of her upper breasts and was almost undone when she purred with pleasure.

He took her hand and led her into his bedchamber, and she followed with no hesitation and much anticipation. They helped each other undress, revelling in being able to see the other as each part of them was revealed and was, something both had been dreaming about, albeit he a little longer than she. The last piece of his fantasy came to life as he removed the pins from her hair and the raven locks were freed from their restraints. As he drank in the sight of his naked wife, he was struck all over again at her beauty. Her breasts were ample, but not too large and her brown nipples were hard with anticipation. Her body was well formed with no excess, as would be expected for one who walked and rode as much as his wife did. He saw the triangle of dark hair between her legs and knew that he would soon be exploring that, and all of her body that had been forbidden until this moment. As he watched her, his desire for her was great.

For her part, Elizabeth was enthralled by the Adonis that was her husband as he stood naked in front of her. She had seen some statues that displayed the male form and a few plates in a book that her father kept in his study, but none of that prepared her for the sight that greeted her eyes. She had dreamed of seeing his neck exposed to her, and had imagined what the rest of his body would look like, but the reality far exceeded the dream. He had a broad, well defined muscular chest that she expected of a man who did not sit back and did nothing. He had a sparse covering of hair on his chest that tapered down as she followed it path over his flat stomach until it met a patch of dark hair around his appendage. What an appendage it was as it stood proudly to attention for her, none of the statues that she had seen had prepared her for the size that her husband sported. His legs were well muscled as expected from one who exercised often and rode as much as he did.

Darcy took is Elizabeth in his arms as he laid her down on his giant bed with their lips searching for the relief only their bodies could grant. His travelled down her neck, then her shoulders, until he finally had his whole mouth around her breast while he teased her nipple with his tongue. She arched her back in pleasure in a bid for more, which was granted when his hand caressed and teased the other. Soon his other hand slid down her stomach until it found the triangle of hair. He paused for a second and lifted his head to stare into her adorning eyes and found a clear invitation to continue his exploration.

His fingers found their way between her legs to her centre, he was delighted to find her very moist and welcoming. Slowly at first, he started to rub the spot that sent waves of pleasure through her body, the speed of his rubbing intensified as one of his fingers slipped into the place where no one had ever touched her before. She undulated her hips, helping him find the spot where she most needed his touch and she moaned, loudly as she achieved release.

"Make me your wife in every way!" the Duchess commanded, and the Duke obeyed her entreaty without delay.

~~~~~~~/~~~~~~~

As the Countess of Brookfield was relaxing with her husband prior to the wedding ball that night she let out an "Oooo."

Richard sat up, "Is everything well, my love?" asked the concerned Earl.

"Richard, I just felt it! I felt the quickening," Lady Jane said with excitement and tears of joy in her eyes. "It felt like a fluttering, like something was tickling me from inside, just like I have heard other women talk about."

"Does that mean that we can finally share our good news beyond Andrew and Marie, my love?" asked the very excited father-to-be.

"Yes, Richard, we can. Do you feel up to visiting Bennet House? Your parents and Aunts are there as well, so we can inform all of them together," she said and then with a look of determination she added, "We will make a stop at Bedford House before we come home. I want Aunt Rose and Uncle Sed to know today."

Soon after the couple were shown into the family sitting room at Bennet House, Jane sat while Richard looked to her and she nodded. "It is fortuitous that you are all together as Jane and I would like to inform you that my Jane is with child."

"Thank you for the news, Richard," Lady Sarah said with a huge smile on her face. "Just before you arrived, we were discussing that Jane looked like she was *enceinte,* and we were wondering when you would share the news with us."

"How did you know, Mama?" Jane asked.

"You have that glow about you, Jane, and when you think no one is watching your hand invariably goes to your belly," her mother informed her.

"Jane, Richard, I am so happy! Our first grandchild!" the Countess of Matlock gushed.

"My Jane felt the quickening just before we left the house," a very happy Richard Fitzwilliam added.

"First I gain many brothers and sisters, and now I am to be an Aunt," Georgiana bubbled in happiness, then looking at Mary and Kitty she corrected herself. "*We* are to be aunts!"

"Congratulations, Jane and Richard," Lord Thomas wished them, "Do you plan to share the news with Sed and Rose? I know that it would help brighten Rose's day as she is very concerned about my brother."

"Yes, Father Bennet," Lord Richard responded, "Bedford House is our next destination."

"Elaine you will be a grandmother before me," Lady Catherine sighed. "As far as my Anne knows, she has not become with child yet."

"Ian and Anne have been married for less time than Richard and Jane," Lady Anne reminded her sister, "and as far as we know, Marie has not achieved that state yet."

"I know that, Anne," Lady Catherine harrumphed. "You know how impatient I am to become a grandmother." Her eyes softened. "As long as my daughter is healthy, I care not when, or if we are so gifted whether it is a boy or a girl."

A quarter of an hour later, Bedford House's butler announced the Earl and Countess of Brookfield to his mistress. "Jane and Richard, what a welcome surprise. Are you here to inform me that I am to be a great Aunt?" Lady Rose asked with an impish smile.

"Not you too, Aunt!" Richard exclaimed. "Will we surprise no one with our news?"

"Your Uncle Sed will be surprised and most pleased," the Duchess said as she rose and led them into her husband's bedchamber.

They found his valet, Mr. Winters, fussing about his master, as usual. Richard and Jane were shocked at the deterioration of their Uncle's pallor from the start of the wedding ceremony earlier that day to this point.

"Do not...look...at...me...so," he rasped, hardly able to get a word or two out before he needed to take as deep a breath as he was able.

"Uncle Sed," Jane said as she wiped a tear from her eye, "Richard and I have very good news to share with you. I am with child, and the doctor estimates that our babe will be born in November or December."

The Duke of Bedford smiled at the good news. He had no

doubt that he would not get to meet his grandniece or grand-nephew. Truth be told, Sed Bennet doubted that he would see many more sunrises. He had a coughing spasm, and so the couple left their Uncle to be attended by his doctor and valet, they tried to make him more comfortable, that was all left for them to do. Jane and Richard visited with their aunt for another hour. She affirmed that she would hold to her oath to her beloved husband and attend the wedding ball.

~~~~~~~/~~~~~~~

Three hours later, the Duchess of Derbyshire reluctantly left her husband's bed for her own chambers to ring for her Abigail. Everything that her mother had told her was true, if anything it was even better than what she had been told. They had been able to enjoy their love four times, and if one added the other activities, with made her breathless with anticipation, it had been a truly pleasurable afternoon. If they had not already agreed to be at the wedding ball, they would have cried off and locked themselves in their chambers for a week. There had been a little blood, and she was somewhat sore just as her mother had said, but the thrill of feeling him deep within as he gave himself to her, as he attained his deepest pleasure only she had been gifted, was satisfying in a way she would never be able to explain, and understood why no one tried.

There was an ever-present, smouldering passion between them, and it took very little to ignite the flame. Selfishly, Lady Elizabeth never wanted her duke to leave the bed, but she knew that it was time. She pulled the bell for her maid and the housekeeper. Her maid was asked to see to her bath, and Mrs. Killion was requested to have a tray with a light repast sent up to their sitting room. Elizabeth sank into the steaming bath Jacqui had infused with the lavender water preferred by her mistress.

Carstens had never seen his master in such a state before. His normally stoic, at times even taciturn master seemed to be almost giddy. If the grin on his countenance was anything to go by, he was extremely happy with his duchess. Darcy stepped into his waiting bath, the aroma of sandalwood and spice wafting from the water. As he luxuriated, he felt a bliss that he could not remember ever feeling before. The reality of being with his Elizabeth far exceeded even his wildest dreams. She was even more passionate than he had hoped she would be. He knew for certain that his previous experience, limited though it was, was merely copulation and self-gratification. What he experienced with his wife that afternoon was physical expression of the love that they had one for the other, and soon expected it to be a celebration of the love they shared, which is what he had heard his mother once say to her sister when he was walking into a room. That was always what he had hoped to attain, and he had no doubts that he and Elizabeth would.

When they were both dressed, she in a hunter green silk gown and he with a waistcoat to match, they met in their sitting room and attacked the repast that Mrs. Killion had brought up. It was but cold meats, cheeses, and fresh bread, yet the newlyweds ate everything on the tray. Neither had realised how hungry they were until they took their first bite, washing down the small meal with a glass of madeira wine. Before they departed the sitting room, the Duke produced a velvet covered box from his inside pocket.

At his request, his duchess had not adorned herself with any jewellery when she had dressed, and he opened the box to reveal a magnificent set. The necklace he took out of the box and gently affixed to his beautiful wife was a series of alternating diamonds and emeralds culminating in a huge empire cut emerald in the centre. When he closed the clasp, the centre stone hung a few inches above her décolletage. Next were earrings that had a large diamond in the centre surrounded by four smaller emeralds. Lastly, he removed a bracelet made of white gold with alternating diamonds and emeralds. Placing it on her right wrist, he bestowed his wife with a kiss that promised the activities to follow the ball would ignite her imagination for weeks to follow. They were both relieved the ball would only be about half the length of a traditional ball held in the Ton. It was then that Lady Elizabeth noticed another box on the small table, her husband had signalled her abigail to join them. In the second box was a tiara. It was also made of white gold, and had rows of diamonds and emeralds with a large emerald on the apex. Her maid placed it on her head and her mistress then understood why her coiffure had not been completed in her dressing room. It was secured with emerald and diamond tipped pins.

Once they were alone again Darcy looked at his wife, truly in awe of the most beautiful lady he had ever seen. "These are not part of the Darcy jewels, my love," he said as he held his hand to her, the need to touch her too great to ignore. "When I noticed that you favoured diamonds and emeralds, I contacted the head jeweller at Harding, Howell, and Company and gave him this commission, hoping that one day I would be allowed to gift it to you." He lifted her hand, pride filling his chest when she blushed, not because of the gift of precious stones, but because she hoped he would kiss the hand he held, he did not make her wait long, though he took a moment to breathe her in, the scent of his wife thrilling him anew.

The Duke and Duchess of Derbyshire descended the main staircase to the foyer where the Killions and her grace's two footman guards were waiting. After donning their outerwear, and with Biggs and Johns trailing them, the couple made the short walk across Grosvenor Square to Bennet House. After divesting them of their coats, Mr. Thatcher informed them that the family was in the family sitting room.

When they entered, all conversation ceased as all eyes drank in the vision that was Elizabeth Darcy. At first Elizabeth thought that she had a blemish on her face, but was disabused when her mother recovered first. "Oh my, Lizzy," she said as she looked at the vision that was her middle daughter, "you are exquisite. That dress, your jewels, combined with the glow of love that is shining forth from you..." Her mother lost her words.

"Shows a contented woman who is besotted with her husband," Lady Anne completed for her friend. The rest of the family were shaken out of their stupor and the compliments for

Elizabeth were added to.

"You do not look like an unhappy man, brother," Lord Tom Bennet slapped his brother-in-law on the back.

"The same can be said of you and your foolish grin, Tom," James said in support of his new brother.

"Well, yes, I have nothing to repine…" Whatever the Marquess was about to say was lost as he scanned the room and his gaze fell upon his wife.

"Just make sure that you never make Lizzy unhappy," James admonished Darcy, "although based on the look I see on my sister's face, I think it is safe to assume that she is very happy."

The Ashby brothers walked up to Lord Tom and Stephen, and the Viscount reminded him of a similar admonition that he and Ian had issued with regards to their little sister Amy before the wedding. The warning was issued in jest as there was no doubt in any Ashby man's mind that the Marquess would move heaven and earth to make sure that Amy Bennet was always his priority.

Lord Thomas asked his sister how his brother was faring. She shook her head and opined that her brother-in-law should visit his brother after the ball concluded. Bennet nodded and said that he and Sarah would accompany Lady Rose back to Bedford House when it ended, all extremely fearful that Sed Bennet would have little time. They had all given him their oath that they would celebrate the weddings this night and not let maudlin thoughts spoil the evening, but no matter the oath he made to his big brother, Lord Thomas's thoughts were with him and he repeated his prayers that had proved futile so far.

The royals would be represented by Prince Edward and his sister Princess Elizabeth, who would arrive after the guests, but just before the first set. The plan was for the Duchess of Derbyshire to open the ball with his highness while her duke would dance with his new cousin, Princess Elizabeth. After a few minutes there would be a change of partners and the two royals would dance with Tom and Amy Bennet, and the Darcys would dance the rest of the first with each other. The royal cousins intended to leave after the first set.

Before the guests arrived, Lady Sarah intervened and noted that as it was a shortened ball, the new grooms could only dance two sets with their wives. Both men affected a pout, but as soon as each received a warning look from his wife, the expected complaints went unvoiced.

"Ha! Jane, I can dance all of mine with you. I am not a new groom." Richard grinned.

"I like this stipulation, mother Bennet. Lady Marie, may I have all your dances at the ball?" Andrew leaned down, his hand out for his wife's, her pleased laugh making him feel like he was the only man that mattered in the room.

Other than a minute or two, the grooms would dance the first with his wife and the full supper set. As there were only six sets total that night, there was no worry that their wives would be squired around the dance floor with anyone outside the family as there were fathers and brothers in abundance, though now two less in the pool of candidates, which meant they were still a dozen sets short of a second dance with any that were still available.

A few minutes before the expected start time, the receiving line was formed. At the head were the hosts, Lord Thomas and Lady Sarah with their sister, Lady Rose who was co-hosting the ball. They were followed by the newlywed Darcys, and Tom and Amy Bennet finished the line; including family, there were less that seventy guests expected.

Once all the guests had arrived and the royals received their bows and curtsies, a toast was offered to the newlyweds by each of the bride's fathers, and a further toast was raised to the health of the Duke of Bedford, and once the toasts were complete the first set formed. After less than two minutes Darcy found himself with the partner that he desired. It was his first dance with a royal, but the princess, in fact every other woman in the known world, paled in comparison to his duchess. They had discovered at the Netherfield ball when they had the pleasure of dancing for the first time that they both enjoyed dancing with each other far above anyone else.

"My Lizzy, can you believe that we are married after what seemed too long once you accepted my proposal," Darcy asked as they came together in a figure.

"After what we did this afternoon..." They separated as she circled another man and then returned to her husband and completed her thought with an arched eyebrow. "...and the number of times we did it, there is no doubt in my mind that we are married." The Duke of Derbyshire laughed, *in public,* in the middle of a ball room!

A countess almost swooned with surprise. Many had heard about the change in the dour, taciturn, and often-times arrogant man, but none had seen it outside of the family circle until that night, and there was much amazement at the changes so evidently on display. It also happened to be the first time that his Grace had attended an official public event after his Lizzy had said yes. Being that it was a private ball with a very select guest list, none of the mothers or daughters of the Ton who had tried to lay claim to Mr. Darcy of Pemberley were present to be vituperative. Many had lamented at failing to capture him when he was a plain gentleman, but now that he was a duke, there were many spleens that would be vented when the wedding announcement was printed in the Times on the morrow.

The Duke and Duchess of Derbyshire moved down the line and found themselves next to the younger Phillips'. "Lizzy, you look every part the duchess," Caroline Phillips offered and her cousin inclined her head at the compliment.

The second set Lady Elizabeth danced with another duke, her father, while the new marchioness danced with hers. "You look so very happy," Lord Thomas observed.

"Yes Papa," his middle daughter answered with meaning, "I could not be more contented if I tried. I know that William is the only one for me. It is almost as if we were formed for each other."

"I could not have parted with you, or any of you sisters, to one less worthy," her father said with much emotion.

Due to the shortened number of sets, it had been decided

that rather than dance full sets with only one partner, in the four sets between the first and last would dance change partners after each single dance. So it was that during the second set that Lord Thomas also danced with Amy while the Earl of Ashbury danced with Elizabeth.

After dancing the first with her beloved husband, Lady Sarah had joined her sister Pricilla, her sisters-in-law Lady Rose, Madeline Gardiner, Hattie Phillips, and Ladies Anne, Elaine, and Catherine. As they watched their married children dancing, they acknowledged that God had been very good to them. None knew it yet, but great joy was soon to be balanced with great sorrow that same night.

After the supper, the guests departed leaving only the family, and a footman from Bedford House approached his mistress and handed her a note. She read it quickly and then as calmly as she could she told the family what it said. "The letter is from Doctor Penrod; he urges us to return to Bedford House with all haste."

CHAPTER 11

Antonio Álvarez was in a quandary. The more he listened to his mother and Mrs. Younge venting their spleens, the more he continued to doubt the path on which his mother and the Younges were propelling them.

Tony had learnt to assimilate facts and then make a decision. Until he, his mother, and the Younges had come to Bundoran, he had never been exposed to everyday people as he was in Ireland. He had found that these people were the salt of the earth, and that money or possessions were not what made people truly happy. The contentment that he saw had nothing to do with material possession as the townspeople had very little in the way of money, but they seemed to have wealth in abundance.

He resolved that he would seek his future on his own, to set his own path rather than blindly follow his mother and her cohorts. He was becoming ever surer that their actions would lead them to the same fate as Karen Younge's Wickham and his own father. The only way that he could walk his own path without interference was to leave, so he decided that he would sneak aboard the Dennington Lines ship and stowaway. He knew that the *Coastal Trader* was due to arrive in the next sennight to ten days, and after they left port, he would reveal himself to the captain to work off his passage.

Once he had decided to chart his own future, he was deeply relieved. He had allowed the desire to avenge his father blind him to the fact that culpability for his fate was his father's alone and had naught to do with any other. He was decided to live a good and righteous life rather than to be swayed by the folly of others, not even his own mother.

~~~~~~~/~~~~~~~

The Duchess was met by her butler and before he spoke, she could tell from the sadness in his eyes that things with the duke were not good. "Is he gone?" Lady Rose asked, scared that she had missed being able to say goodbye to her beloved Sed. She felt a modicum of relief when the long serving butler shook his head, she instructed him to send a message to Buckingham House post haste, thus fulfilling her promise to the Regent.

The family sat in the family sitting room while Lady Rose and Lord Thomas went directly to Lord Sed's bedchamber. Both sets of newlyweds held each other tightly, the Darcys sitting with Lady Anne and Georgiana on one settee, while Tom and Amy sat with Lady Sarah and James on another. The older twins and their husbands sat near the younger Bennet twins, the tears too frequent to catch as all said their own silent goodbye to the man, the love of whom would never be allowed to fade.

When he entered his brother's chambers, Thomas Bennet was not sure who was supporting whom when he and his sister saw the grey pallor on Lord Sed. His breaths were crackling and rasping and there was no doubt that each one he drew, caused him pain. His wife knew that he had held on to see them and say goodbye, to not spoil the ball he had insisted should take place. The duchess gently let go of her brother-in-law and went to her husband's side.

"He forced himself to hold on to see us, did he not?" Lord Thomas asked Mr. Penrod who nodded in response.

"I believe so. I wish I could give you better news, your Grace," the doctor offered with quiet solemnity, "but it is the end. His Grace will not see another sunrise."

"Oh, Sed," his wife said as tears streamed freely, "I would have come home to be with you if you had summoned me." As it was too painful to talk, he shook his head as vigorously as he could in his state. "But of course, you wanted us to finish the ball, after which you knew you would see me, us, to say goodbye before you rest." She soothed and he relaxed, wondering to himself how he could have worried she wouldn't understand him better than he understood himself. "We are here now, Sed. We will all be here as you start your eternal slumber." She motioned her brother-in-law to the bedside.

"You were always a stubborn one, Sed," Thomas said as he cried quietly. "I could not have asked for a better brother than you, Sed. When I was a young boy, my *much* older brother always protected me. You taught me to have fun, to swim, to ride, and so much more. I will miss you, brother, but I cannot be selfish. I can see how you suffer, and as much as I hate to do it, I must let you go be with Mama and Papa. I love you, Sed, we all love you." Thomas Bennet kissed his brother on the cheek and felt a weak squeeze of his hand.

"Thomas, give me a few minutes and then bring the family in," Lady Rose requested, "You want your family with you as you go to sleep, do you not Sed?" She nodded when he gave a small nod of agreement. "I will send a footman when we are ready, brother," she told her brother-in-law. Lord Thomas, the doctor, and the valet left, the last man closing the door.

Once they were alone, Rose sat as close to her ailing husband as she was able, and took both of his listless hands in her own. "I do not regret one day that God has allowed me to have with you, Sed. At one time I was very angry with the Lord that He did not grant us children, but, as He always does, He had a plan. He allowed us to be a second set of parents to Sarah's and Thomas's children, and we could not have loved them more if they had been born of my body.

"How I will miss you," she said with tenderness. His wife did not miss the tears that were running down her husband's cheeks. "You are the love of my life, Sed. I love you with my all heart, and always will. The pledge that I made to you that I will only mourn you for a year, and will live my life rather than pine away and force myself to join you before God calls me home, will be upheld. I will not be alone; I will be with our brother and sister and our three daughters still at home. My preference would be that God grant us the miracle that we have all prayed for, but it seems that He wants you in His Kingdom." Lady Rose leaned over the bed and embraced her husband, kissed his lips, then walked to the door to ask a footman to summon the family. She returned and sat next to her beloved, taking one of his hands and clasping it tightly.

"I...love...you...Rose," Sed rasped out. His declaration caused her tears to fall anew, both because she was about to lose the love of her, and knowing how much speaking must have pained him.

A few minutes later the family respectfully entered the bedchamber. Each of the former and current Bennets kissed their uncle and said a tearful goodbye, followed by the rest of the family that had come to say their final farewell. His breathing became more and more laboured, there was a distinct crackling sound as he fought for his shallow breathes, he then passed into an unconscious state, and a few minutes after the final goodbye, Lord Sedgewick Bennet, the tenth Duke of Bedford, drew his final breath; all movement ceased and he was at peace. Mr. Penrod confirmed that he had passed, and so it was, Lord Tom Bennet was then the eleventh Duke of Bedford.

Not long after the Duke of Bedford passed, the Regent arrived at Bedford House with his contingent of royal guards and retinue. He was shown into the family room and as the occupants stood to honour him, no one had to say a word. The tears flowing freely was all he needed to see to know that he was too late, he missed saying a final goodbye to Cousin Sed. Prince George was relieved that at least he had spoken to his cousin the day of the wedding. The Regent understood that the Dowager Duchess of Bedford was with her husband and did not ask for her to be disturbed. He commiserated with the Duke of Hertfordshire and his family, with the promise that he and the other members of the royal family would see Lady Rose in a few days, at the late duke's funeral; he offered subdued congratulations the new Duke and Duchess of Bedford, and then left as quietly as the Regent could.

Tom Bennet, the newly minted Duke of Bedford, felt the weight of the world descend on his shoulders. He was grateful that he would have his duchess with him to lighten the burden and responsibilities that came with the dukedom, but was devastated at Uncle Sed's loss. A few short weeks ago he had accompanied his beloved Amy as they toured Birchington, now he was to move into Longfield Meadows in Yorkshire, the primary estate and jewel in the crown of the ducal properties entailed. He had gone from caring for one estate, and the servants and tenants who were dependent on it, to five estates, three of which were equal or larger in size to the Marquess of Birchington's estate. The number of dependents that he was responsible for had increased exponentially.

He sat next to his duchess as she leaned over to him. "Tom, please remind our aunt she never needs to leave her house if she does not want to, and that she could just visit with our Bennet parents as she chooses. I would be as glad to have her with us as you, possibly more I dare say, as you will be out riding the estate some days and I can have her teach me about her charities and works so we do not miss something so special." She asked softly, her eyes imploring him to remind her she was loved by many of her children.

"It will be Aunt Rose's choice, Amy," he agreed with absolute resolution. "I too would be glad she stayed for as long as Aunt Rose needs, and if it is the full year of mourning, then so much the better! However, with her understanding I would like us to take over management of the estates as we do not want to neglect them or those dependant on them due to Uncle Sed's passing."

"I hope that Aunt Rose comes to see me as another daughter as she sees you and your siblings as her sons and daughters," Lady Amy said.

"I know that she already does, my wife," her husband responded and kissed her lightly on the cheek. He had never doubted that Amy would love his family, but it was gratifying to have the fact reinforced again.

Lady Rose was alone in Lord Sed's chambers after the family, doctor, and servants had withdrawn to give her time to say her final farewell to her beloved Sed in private. She held her husband's now cold hand, she knew that his soul was no longer in this world and was sure that he had ascended to heaven and was looking down on her as she sat with his mortal remains.

"I will miss you for all of the days of the rest of my life Sed," she said as the tears flowed freely down her cheeks. She lifted his lifeless hand and bestowed a kiss on it. "I know that God made the heart with unlimited capacity to love, but I will never be able to bestow mine on another man after you, and I make this pledge now: until I leave this world and join you in God's Kingdom, there will never be another.

"When I met you in the middle of my first season, I was a bright-eyed debutant and you were a very handsome and eligible Marquess. It was love at first sight for me, and I never thought that the son of the Duke of Bedford and Hertfordshire would give notice to Miss Rosamond Davies, the daughter of an insignificant baronet, but I was wrong. You did notice me, and it was not long after that you requested permission from my late papa to call on his only daughter.

"Do you remember, my love, that I asked you if you were sure that you wanted to call on one as low as I when you could have the pick of the daughters of the first circles with far larger portions than mine? I told you that I only had ten thousand and you made me understand, in no uncertain terms, that the things I mentioned held no importance to you. I fell even more in love with you when I found out what an estimable man you were.

"Before I knew it you had requested a courtship and then you asked for my hand. Oh, Sed, I felt like it was a dream. Do you remember that before I accepted you, I requested that you pinch me so that I could make sure that it was not a dream? Rather than a pinch you bestowed my first kiss on me, and I knew that it was no dream and accepted you without reservation. The reaction of the jealous harpies, hoping to be the next Marchioness of Birchington was so vituperative, the insults that they flung about the 'nobody that had used her arts and allurements' to trap you, the snide remarks and digs made to me or within my hearing all ceased when your parents made it known that any who dared to insult or snub me was doing the same to them and their royal cousins.

"Our marriage made me blissfully happy, and my love for you grew each day. Just when I thought that I could not love you more, I would find another reason to do so. When I did not fall with child after three years, I began to believe that God would not bless us with children. It was not for lack of trying," Lady Rose said with a half-smile as she thought about their many attempts for her to become *enceinte.* "It was a great regret that we did not have children, and I felt as if I failed. But you were so warm and understanding, telling me that if it was God's will that we not have children, that we should accept it."

"I cried for Thomas when he was entrapped by *that woman.* He could have tried to buy her off, but his honour would not allow that. God had a plan even for that. He allowed her to give us Jane and Marie before He sent the despicable person to hell where she belonged! How happy we were when our brother and sister married, and then a year later, Tom was born and the line of succession was extended. When Lizzy was born I had not a doubt that she would be exactly as she turned out to be, and then they were gifted with James so that Tom would not carry the weight of both titles as your late father did. We did not have children born of my body, but we were gifted with the love of seven nieces and nephews that accepted us as a second set of parents. And we are even luckier still as by the end of this year Jane will gift us our first grandchild.

"First my mama was taken, and within a year Papa followed her, and I was the only by blood Davies left. We all believed that my father died of a broken heart giving up after Mama passed. That is why you extracted the pledge from me about the mourning period, ensuring that I would continue to live, did you not, my love? Even as you lay dying you wanted to protect me, even from myself. I swear this oath to you, Sed, I will live! There is much to live for, with four of our surrogate children marrying, there will be more than just one grandchild, and I know that I will have the love of family to support me for the rest of the days that God grants me on the mortal coil. Living with Sarah and Thomas, I will not be on my own, so I will not be left to brood in my sorrow like my father was.

The Dowager Duchess of Bedford stood, still holding her husband's hand, "You are and will always be the love of my life," she said as she leaned over and bestowed a light kiss on his cold lips. "Rest in peace, Sed." Lady Rose relinquished her dead husband's hand and slowly made her way to the sitting room where the family were awaiting her.

CHAPTER 12

Aweek after the death of the former Duke of Bedford, the train of carriages, which included more than one royal coach, arrived at Longfield Meadows to deliver Lord Sedgwick Bennet to his final resting place with his parents and the previous dukes before him. It was a drab, June day when the multitude of mourners descended on the estate.

The housekeeper and butler, Mr. and Mrs. Dudley, who themselves were adorned with black armbands, waited to farewell their previous master and welcome the new Duke and Duchess to their estate. Benedict Dudley had started as a footman for Lord Sed and had quickly risen through the ranks until he was promoted to under butler some eight years previously, and three years after that, when the butler retired, Dudley was promoted again. His wife Matilda had started as an upper maid then too had steadily risen. When her predecessor was felled by an attack of the heart four years previous, Lady Rose and Lord Sed had agreed that she be offered the post. Mrs. Dudley wore her darkest dress in addition to her armband out of respect to both the late master and the former mistress of the estate. The late Duke and his Duchess treated the servants with respect and paid better than most, which engendered deep and abiding loyalty.

When Lady Rose, in full mourning dress with a black lace veil, was assisted out of the first carriage behind the undertaker's conveyance bringing her husband on his last journey from London to his estate that he loved, she wordlessly walked to her housekeeper and fell into her arms, and the two cried unashamedly together.

"I miss him so much, Mrs. Dudley," the Dowager Duchess wailed plaintively.

"We all miss him, your Grace," Mrs. Dudley responded as she wiped her tears away. "Let me help you to your chambers, your Grace. I will have cook send up a tray with some relaxing tea."

"No thank you, Mrs. Dudley," Lady Rose said as she lifted her chin as she focused on her husband's coffin as it was carried into the house. "I will be sitting with my husband so please send my regular tea to me in the blue parlour," she said with determination. Lady Sarah took one arm and Lady Priscilla the other as they supported their sister on her walk into the house. The new Duchess of Bedford walked next to Lady Sarah to be near to her mother-in-law. The rest of the ladies followed the four after the royals. The four royals who had come stood back respectfully and allowed Lady Rose to proceed them into the house behind her husband. Princes Edward and Adolphus and Princesses Elizabeth and Mary and their spouses represented the Queen and Regent.

Lord Sed's body had been lifted onto the shoulders of his brothers and nephews to be carried into the parlour where it would lay until the funeral on the morrow. At the front was Lord Thomas on one side with his brother Lord Cyril on the other. Behind their father were Tom and James Bennet and William Darcy, behind the Earl were Richard and Andrew Fitzwilliam and Wes De Melville. Once the deceased and the ladies had moved on, the rest of the family followed them into the house.

The housekeeper directed footmen to escort each to their chambers. Lady Rose had insisted that her belongings be moved to the dower suite in the family wing, no matter how much her nephew and his wife insisted that she did not need to do so. The Dowager Duchess insisted as she explained that it was necessary to her moving on with the grieving process. Eventually they had reached a compromise as they would not hear of their uncle's chambers being packed up without his valet Mr. Winters performing the service himself. No one had dared suggest that the valet go on ahead to Longfield as he would have surely mutinied at the suggestion that he leave his master on his ultimate journey. He had ridden in the undertaker's carriage and no one tried to convince him otherwise. After conferring with Lady Rose about what she wanted set aside to keep in her chambers at Bennet House and Longbourn, Winters would start the task of sorting through his master's possessions after the funeral.

Winters would never need to work again; his master had left him a legacy of fifteen thousand pounds which, with prudent investments by Edward Gardiner, would bring in a little more than one thousand per annum, many times the loyal retainer's yearly pay. The Bennets believed in rewarding loyalty, and Winters had served his master for almost thirty years. He would live with his late brother's son and with his income he would be able to help the family improve their standard of living. He would also find out when the will was read that both of his nephews would be able to study at the university of their choice if they so desired, thus being able to rise above the family's roots in service.

After washing the dust from the road, all of the older ladies joined Lady Rose as she sat in the blue parlour. Lady Anne sat next to her and held her hand. "You will eventually start living again, Rose," one dowager duchess offered to the other. "When my George was murdered, I thought that my world had come to an end, and he did not get me to promise that I would only mourn for a year like your Sed had you promise."

"How long did you mourn, Anne?" Lady Sarah asked.

"For two years," Lady Anne said sorrowfully as she invariably got when she thought about the passing, no the *murder* of her beloved husband. "It was my children that made me realise I had much to live for."

"But I have no..." Lady Rose did not finish the sentence before Lady Catherine interjected.

"Stuff and nonsense, Rose," she said pointedly. "you may not have birthed them, but you have many children, and you know it!"

"Catherine has the right of it, sister," Lady Sarah said. "They are not *my* children; they are *our* children!"

"I do know that," Lady Rose said while a tear rolled down her cheek as she looked at the coffin holding her beloved next to her. "When I said my farewell to Sed, I said the same myself, but in my grief, I have allowed my maudlin thoughts to overwhelm me."

"That is bound to happen, Rose," Lady Elaine empathised with her friend. "As you grieve you will have many emotions and thoughts, but just remember that we will all be here for you."

The ladies all rose as they were joined by Princesses Elizabeth and Mary. "Please rest, cousins, we are all family and we are here to support you," Princess Elizabeth stated as she walked to her Cousin Rose and gave her a hug. "George is not happy that matters of state kept him in Town and will not able to be here on the morrow when Cousin Sed is laid to rest. Mother also wished to be here, but, like my brother, she was unable to leave London. She felt that the least that she could do was send The Most Reverend Willowmere, by Divine Providence Lord Archbishop of Canterbury, to accompany the remains of our cousin to his final resting place and perform the service." After the princesses spent a few minutes with their cousins they retired to their chambers.

Lord Thomas Bennet loved spending time at his childhood home, but he wished that they were not there for the reason that they were. No amount of wishing or praying would change the fact that his brother Sed was gone. As the men sat in the green drawing room with the younger ladies having subdued conversation, the Duke of Hertfordshire was heart-sore. His brother had always been his rock, the one that he would turn to in times of uncertainty. Sed had loved his sport, riding his horses above all; he had ridden in the rain many times previously, so why had God taken Sed this time? Lord Thomas knew that it was very arrogant of him to question God's plan, but he could not help the way he felt. His brother-in-law, the Earl of Jersey, was sitting quietly to his right sipping his port slowly, while Matlock and the princes talked quietly closer to the fire.

Across the room, Lord Tom was thinking about his new duties. '*I know Uncle Sed trained me, but how can I ever replace him?*' he asked himself, his grief overpowering his confidence in his abilities. '*My uncle made it look so easy and now I must replace him, here, at the other Bedford Estates, in the Lords...*' Tom Bennet halted his unproductive thoughts, the whirl of his thoughts stopped when he felt his Uncle Sed was standing next to him with a hand on his shoulder as he had been wont to do, reassuring him.

'*You know what to do, Tom,*' the new Duke of Bedford heard his uncle's voice clearly in his thoughts. '*You knew I would die at some point, Nephew, and that is why I taught you all I did even believing there would be ample time before you would need to take over these duties. Just remember my lessons and all will be well. You are a very smart man with a sharp wit; so, use your God given talents and all will be well. I have every confidence in you, Tom...*'

The Duke of Bedford was sure that he had imagined hearing his uncle's voice, but he still was comforted by the assurance, even were it from within himself. His wife and three married sisters joined him; Amy, and Lizzy on the settee, and Jane and Marie in chairs facing them. Being a duchess had not stopped Elizabeth from observing those around her and trying to divine their thoughts and motivations.

"Tom, your expressions have changed so much as to be confusing, is there anything we or I can assist with?" his middle sister asked.

"I allowed myself to forget that Uncle Sed prepared me to assume this role one day, and then I swear that I heard Uncle's voice telling me not to doubt my knowledge," Lord Tom offered quietly.

"If I know Uncle Sed," Jane said with a half-smile, the first sign of one that she had displayed since his passing, "he found a way to reach from heaven to remind you, Little Brother."

"I agree with Jane, Tom," Marie added. "There was a reason that Uncle Sed made us all promise that we would not mourn him for longer than three months. He wanted us, and especially you and Amy, to get on with the task of living."

"It is daunting to be a duchess, much earlier than any of us would have wanted," Amy admitted. "However, I believe that God does not place a burden on our shoulders that we are not able to carry, Tom. The prospect of becoming a duchess before I was used to being a marchioness intimidated me, until Mother Sarah, my mother, and our aunts all pointed out that they would be here to help me learn. With the support they and the rest of the family provide, we will be well, my husband." His duchess took his hand as she spoke and leaned her head on his shoulder.

"My wife and my *much* older sisters are all wise," the Duke teased half-heartedly. He felt more assured of the future, but it would take longer for the weight of sadness that he felt for his second father to lift.

Longfield Meadows' clergyman, Mr. Adgar Chadwick, was sitting in the parsonage's sitting room with the head of the Church of England as they planned the service for the late Lord Sedgwick Bennet. Mr. Chadwick had only received the living from Lord Bennet three years previously when his predecessor retired after over thirty years of serving both the parishioners who resided on the estate and those who lived in the nearby town of Bedford. He had been the curate serving the Bedford All Saints church before and had been very honoured when the Duke had tapped him for the livings. The dukedom had a third living within its purview in the town of Hemmingdale, on the other side of the estate. The incumbent there would retire in the next year or two and the late duke had intimated that he would offer the living to Mr. Chadwick. Now he would see what the new duke decided to do with the living.

The two clergymen agreed that they would honour the late duke's wishes to keep the service short and simple. It would be held in All Saints as it had more than double the capacity of Longfield's church. With the royal presence, the number already present at the estate, and the number of expected mourners, they had cause to believe that the church would be filled to overflowing. Tenants and servants would be as welcome to say their final goodbye to the deceased duke as those of royalty and peers. With the service laid out, the two men settled into a theological discussion. When the local pastor extended an invitation for the Most Reverend Archibald Willowmere to share their dinner, he fully expected the Archbishop to politely refuse but was surprised and most pleased when the head clergyman accepted.

Dinner at the manor house was a sombre and subdued affair. Lady Rose, for the first time since her beloved husband passed, had joined the family that evening. All of the ladies were wearing mourning dresses and the men with their dark clothing and black armbands, which contributed to the overall mood. No one sat at the head of the table in the late Duke's seat nor the mistress's as his wife had refused stating that she was, in fact, no longer the mistress of Longfield Meadows or any other Bedford property. In deference to their late uncle and their aunt, the new Duke and Duchess would not sit in their places until after the funeral.

After dinner the ladies departed for a drawing room and Lady Rose, Lady Anne, and the two new duchesses went to relieve Winters who had sat with his master during dinner. As the men smoked and had drinks with hushed conversation around him, Lord Tom thought about the day when Mr. Gilroy Abernathy Esq, Uncle Sed's solicitor, had read the will. He had been aware of the contents of the will, or so he thought. Everything was as expected until the solicitor read the last section with regards to the ownership of Dennington Lines and the shipyards.

"My fifty percent stake in Dennington Lines and the shipyards," Mr. Abernathy read, *"is to be awarded as follows: ten percent to each of my nephews, Thomas Bennet Junior and James Bennet, the remaining thirty percent is to be split evenly and gifted to my five nieces, daughters by blood of my brother Thomas Bennet, Duke of Hertfordshire."*

So far, the final piece of the will had gone as Tom expected until the solicitor read the final paragraph. "The funds that have been earned from my share in the shipping line and shipyards which had been saved and invested, after ten percent is set aside for the benefit of the Haven House project, is to be split in the same percentages among the same individuals as laid out in the above paragraph. I charge my nieces and nephews to invest these funds for the dowries of their daughters and to be able to give legacies to second sons and beyond. As of the writing of this final will and testament there is a little over three million pounds in holding."

The solicitor informed them that the reading of the will was complete and was asked how such a sum was set aside, or if it was part of the assets that belonged to the dukedom. *"Your great grandfather started setting all profits from the shipping line aside as, like your grandfather, he had no brothers and carried both titles just like your grandfather,"* Abernathy had explained. *"When your father was born, his father started putting fifty percent of the profits into an account designated for Lord Thomas. The balance was added to the investment as it had been done for three generations.*

"When it became clear that Lord and Lady Bennet would not have any children of their own, your uncle decided that the funds would benefit the future children born to his nieces and nephews. These funds are not in any way tied to the title as they were a separate venture. He was free to will those funds as he saw fit. Knowing that I would be reading the will, I checked the balances a few days ago and there was an additional one hundred and twenty thousand pounds that have accrued since the late duke had me write this will five years ago."

The Duke of Bedford was snapped out of his reverie when he heard the scraping of chairs as the men stood to re-join the ladies for tea and coffee in the drawing room.

Lady Rose Bennet was vastly appreciative of the outpouring of love for her husband demonstrated when the house had been opened for servants and tenants to file past the coffin that afternoon. There was a nonstop sea of humanity for the full three hours set aside for the viewing. It was now the last night that they would ever share the same room, the family had gone to bed and it was herself and her brother-in-law sitting with her beloved.

"It has only been a sennight and I miss him so much it aches, Thomas," Lady Rose said as the ever-present tears began to fall again.

"I too miss him very much, Rose," he rose and handed her his handkerchief.

"He knew what he was about when he made us swear that we would not mourn beyond the periods that he stipulated." Lady Rose dabbed her eyes as she looked off into the distance. "He wanted to make sure that we all carry on living our lives and looked to the future, not live in the past."

"He was the best of brothers and I will miss him until God calls me home and I see him again, but until then I will do what he wants, I will live. We have so much to live for Rose," Bennet offered gently.

"It will be hard, but I will do the same, Thomas. Four of our children are married, Jane will present us with our first grandchild this year, and unless my sister Sarah is wrong, Marie is with child as well."

"You were so good for him, Rose. I knew from the very first time that he introduced us while I was still in my final year at Eton that he was in love with you," her brother-in-law reminisced. "At fifteen I did not know anything about love between a man and woman, but I did not miss the way that the two of you looked at each other. I had seen the same between my mother and father and knew that they were deeply in love, so I deduced that it was the same for you two."

"My Sed cut a dashing figure," Lady Rose remembered, "he was such a handsome man right up until God took him home, and the best man that I knew." She paused. "I remember when we were first seen in London together. I was unknown and when the jealous harpies of the Ton found out that Papa was a nobody country baronet and we were neither connected nor wealthy they started sniping. My Sed and his parents stopped it so very quickly. I was telling the ladies earlier how he silenced them and made it known what would happen, as anyone who disrespected me disrespected him and the *whole* family."

"Sed told me about that, and even though I was still at school, I was willing to do anything that I could to support him. Our mother was sick at the time, so father was not able to assist, but he let it be known through his friends that when Sed spoke, he spoke for all of us." Bennet gave her a slight smile.

"It was very fortuitous that we married before mother Bennet and my parents were taken from us. We had only been married a year when she succumbed to her cancer. My dear mama passed the following year from a fever and Papa followed her to heaven before a twelve month was complete. It was so hard to lose both of my parents within that short of a time, but Sed supported me in every way and was my rock." Lady Rose kissed her hand and then placed it on the lid of the coffin to send the kiss to her Sed.

Winters cleared his throat to let her Grace know that he was present. Brother and sister-in-law said goodnight to each other and went to their chambers to get as much sleep as they could before the late duke was laid to rest in the morning.

"How is Rose?" Lady Sarah asked when her husband climbed into bed next to her.

"She is as well as can be expected," he answered. "We were talking about remembrances of Sed, I think that it helped both of us."

"He will be missed, Thomas," his wife said as she kissed him. After nearly a quarter century of marriage the passion between the two was as strong as when they married, but as much as they loved each other, the grief was too great just this night for even such comfort. As they grieved and moved forward, things would return to a semblance of normalcy, but not yet.

After dismissing her lady's maid, Lady Rose was sitting in her bed. The hardest thing that she had to get used to at night was sleeping alone. From the day that they had married until her Sed got so sick, they had spent every night that they were under the same roof in the same bed. Her husband was downstairs and would never be able to join her in bed again in the mortal world. It took her more than an hour, but she eventually fell into a fitful sleep.

"Hello Rose," Sed said as he took his wife's hands.

"Sed, you passed away, so how is it that you are here with me?" Lady Rose asked, her tone conveying she was bewildered.

"I am no longer part of the mortal world, Rose, but I will always be with you, here," he touched her heart and when he did, she felt all of the love that he had for her fill the hole his loss had created. "Whenever you want to talk to me, I will be with you here in your dreams, my beloved wife."

"Oh, Sed, I miss you so very much. I want to be able to hold and touch you, can we do that in my dreams?" she asked hopefully.

"We can do anything in your dreams, my love. Can you not feel my hands holding yours?"

"I can, Sed, but it is not enough, I wish that God had not taken you home!" she finally said what she had been choking back for days.

"It will never be enough, my beautiful Rose, but it is better than nothing." He soothed.

"Have you seen Heaven, Sed?" she asked softly.

"Yes, Rose, it is beyond the comprehension of mortal man. I have seen my parents and yours, and we will all be waiting for you many years from now when you join us, although in the time of heaven it will be a blink of an eye. Tom and Amy will do well, as will the rest of the family. My little brother is the head of the family now, and I know that he will do me proud. I love you, Rose, and please honour your pledge to me to live your life to the fullest."

The dream faded into the background leaving a restful slumber for Lady Rose as she felt more at peace that she had since her beloved husband had died.

CHAPTER 13

That morning, before the coffin was moved to the church, Lady Rose relieved Winters from his vigil so she could say a final goodbye to her love before he was carried out on the shoulders of his family to the undertaker's carriage which would transport him to the church. The women all stood in support of the Dowager Duchess as she farewelled her husband when the carriages departed the front of the house.

The funeral was understandably very well attended. All Saints church was packed with men from royalty down to servants. Mr. Winters was given a place of honour behind the family, the only servant to have a seat in the pews. The Archbishop, assisted by Mr. Chadwick, had kept the service short with a sermon that extoled the exemplary life lived by his Grace, Sedgwick Aaron Bennet, Duke of Bedford.

After the service, the cortège slowly made its way to the graveyard behind the church at Longfield Meadows where all of the previous Dukes of Bedford had been laid to rest. The route was lined with tenants, servants, and citizens of Bedford all with heads bowed and hats in hand. There were not a few tears shed by the mourners as the coffin was lowered into the ground and then covered up as Lord Sedgewick Bennet was entombed in his resting place. The Archbishop deferred to Mr. Chadwick who read Psalm nine and thirty from the Book of Common Prayer:

"I said, I will take heed to my ways, that I sin not with my tongue: I will keep my mouth with a bridle, while the wicked is before me.

I was dumb with silence, I held my peace, even from good; and my sorrow was stirred.

My heart was hot within me, while I was musing the fire burned: then spake I with my tongue,

LORD, make me to know mine end, and the measure of my days, what it is: that I may know how frail I am.

Behold, thou hast made my days as an handbreadth; and mine age is as nothing before thee: verily every man at his best state is altogether vanity. Selah.

Surely every man walketh in a vain shew: surely they are disquieted in vain: he heapeth up riches, and knoweth not who shall gather them.

And now, Lord, what wait I for? My hope is in thee.

Deliver me from all my transgressions: make me not the reproach of the foolish.

I was dumb, I opened not my mouth; because thou didst it.

Remove thy stroke away from me: I am consumed by the blow of thine hand.

When thou with rebukes dost correct man for iniquity, thou makest his beauty to consume away like a moth: surely every man is vanity. Selah.

Hear my prayer, O LORD, and give ear unto my cry; hold not thy peace at my tears: for I am a stranger with thee, and a sojourner, as all my fathers were.

O spare me, that I may recover strength, before I go hence, and be no more."

When he completed the reading, he intoned a final prayer, asking God to accept Sedgwick Aaron Bennet's eternal soul into His care. After the clergyman had concluded, the vast crowd dispersed, leaving Lord Thomas, his brother, his sons, and his sons-in-law alone to say their own silent goodbyes. When they were done, all but Lord Thomas withdrew from the graveside to wait some paces away in an offer of both respect and privacy.

"My big brother is with you now, Mama and Papa," he said as a single tear rolled down his cheek. "Look after him until we join you. I love you, Brother." Thomas Bennet touched the headstone and then joined the other men for the sombre walk back to the manner house.

~~~~~~~~/~~~~~~~~

The *Coastal Trader*, sailed into the harbour at Bundoran as the sun started to rise on the morning of the tenth of June. The ships doctor and surgeon, Mr. Clive Tetley, who was at his leisure, was standing on the starboard side when he looked up and noticed a sloop at anchor as they glided toward the dock. At first, he thought that he was projecting, so he rubbed his eyes and read the name again to find that he was not mistaken. It was the very one the entire fleet was on the lookout for, the *Stealthy Runner*! Mr. Tetley walked as fast as he could to the quarterdeck.

"You cum' ta' learn ta' be a real sailor?" the first mate, John Cox, teased the doctor.

"No, Mr. Cox. Captain, I need to speak to you most urgently," Tetley said and simply pointed at the sloop that they were passing. The captain read the name and nodded once that he understood.

"Jones," he beckoned a seaman on the port side of the deck.

"Yes Cap'an" Jones snapped to attention.

"Go summon Mr. Clements. Now!" Captain Beauclerk barked.

"Aye, aye Cap'an." Jones nodded once and headed to the forecastle where Jack Clements was standing to supervise the men with the lines that would secure the ship to the quay. After a brief conversation, Clements told Jones to take his place and made his way to the quarterdeck.

"Reporting as ordered, Captain," the ex-royal marine reported in, almost saluting before he remembered that he was no long in the King's navy. Captain Beauclerk inclined his head toward the sloop at anchor. The captain did not miss the man's look of pure rage when he saw the ship.

"Why the anger, Clements?" the Captain asked. Clements explained that the murdered Sergeant Hamms had been a mate of his, so he was itching to repay the debt. He begged to be able to find those responsible and 'deal' with them. "As much as I would love to give you that satisfaction, we will be back in Dublin in five days and I will make sure that the ship that departs for Liverpool the day after we dock will have a missive for his Grace. By the time we return in a month we will have our orders.

"What if they move before we return?" Clements asked reasonably.

"We are carrying six of your men, are we not?" The captain asked and his head guard nodded.

"In that case, let us make a show of 'dismissing' three of your men for pilfering. That way their remaining here after we sail will not raise any suspicion, then if the ship seems like she is getting ready to put to sea, they can find a way to join the crew, even if they are the *cause* of why the *Stealthy Runner* needs replacement crew members." Clements agreed with the plan; he knew exactly who to choose and was equally sure that they would relish the assignment as one of the three had also served with Hamms.

The Captain was not worried that the activity on board the *Coastal Trader* would rouse any suspicion on the other vessel, as any sailor would know that the ship's crew would be running hither and yon as they docked. He assigned a group of three seamen to watch the ship at all times. The man who took the first watch reported that there was no activity on board, surmising that the crew was sleeping off a night of revelry at the Happy Leprechaun.

Clements summoned Greg Jones, Julius Forester, and Mark Tibbson to meet him on the crew's mess deck. The three accepted the assignment with anticipation, and Forester was most gratified to be included in the group as Hamms had been a good friend of his. The three were instructed to remain below decks until the ship was docked, and the rest of the crew was informed about the 'pilferage' and 'dismissal' so that if they met any crew members of the *Runner* at the inn, the story would not be contradicted.

Tony Álvarez felt his excitement mount as he watched the Dennington Line vessel dock. He was more convinced than ever that the decision that he had made was the only choice he had, unless he wanted to waste his life as his father had, and like the three schemers most certainly would if they did not change course, which he had no cause to believe they might. He had no intention to stay with them for the next two to three months as they had planned, their expectation was that the search for them would be over and it would be safe for them to return to England to act.

He observed that the *Trader* was quite a lot larger that the *Runner*. Even though they were both classed as sloops, they were on opposite ends of the scale of sizes for that class of vessel. Tony had a plan; he had got himself employed with the crew of locals that would unload and then reload the ship. He would help unload and then when the ship was half again loaded, he would hide himself in the hold and wait until the ship sailed with the tide on the morrow before revealing himself.

He knew that his mother and her cohorts would not start to seek him for a day or two. Since he had decided to leave, he had started to 'explore' the surrounding area, setting out for one or two days at a time. His mother had accepted his excuse of learning about the area in case they had to make an escape and the seaward side was cut off, had lauded it even.

The three schemers had planned to keep out of sight while the ship was in port just in case, so Tony was sure that none of them would notice he was part of the work crew, but just to make certain he had 'borrowed' a blonde wig from Karen Younge which hid his jet-black hair. With his hat pulled down over his eyes, even his mother would walk past him without recognising him as her son.

Before any of the unloaders he was waiting with were allowed on board, the crew of the ship assembled on deck, and three men were led onto it with their hands initially tied, though they were untied when they stood before the assembly. Anyone close to the ship heard the captain dismiss the men without pay for attempted pilferage. While the crew jeered them, the disgraced men were roughly dragged off the ship, and they and their clothing were thrown onto the dock. The three slunk away in the direction of the inn, their disgrace making all who had witnessed the scene give them a wide birth.

Clay Younge had been watching the *Coastal Trader* with both interest and envy as she docked. He was a sailor so any ship interested him, but it did not take an expert to see that the *Trader* was superior to the *Runner* in every way. He was envious of the way that the crew worked as a cohesive unit to accomplish their tasks, unlike his band of miscreants. Then he saw something that piqued his interest. Three men were tossed off the ship for attempted theft and slunk away toward the inn. His first mate was sitting with him playing cards, so Younge told the man to join the three in the bar and to find out as much as he could. The man grunted his agreement and headed down to comply, especially since the ales would not be at his own expense.

As much as she disliked the delusional woman, Johanna Álvarez had agreed to sit with Karen Younge to have some company for the day. She hated having to stay in her room, but it was only for that one day. Tony had gone on one of his rambles that morning and had said that he would return no later than the morning of the third day hence. Her son had been distant for the last few weeks, but she had experienced distancing from him before as it was just part of his growing up and did not let it concern her overly much. He would soon remember that she was his primary source of company and his responsibility.

It did not take very long before Karen Younge started babbling about her *dear George* again. If she was not sure that Younge would set his crew on her if she harmed his sister, she would happily cut the annoying woman's throat. As it was, she was seriously thinking about having the insane woman 'fall' overboard when they finally sailed from this nowhere town they were holed up in.

~~~~~~~/~~~~~~~

The visits from friends and neighbours were long, but the family appreciated that it was a needed part of the grieving process. The new Duke of Bedford had known that Lord Sed had been much loved in the area, but until he saw the outpouring of genuine love and sorrow for his uncle, he had not realised the depth and breadth of the love and esteem the tenants, servants, and townspeople had held for his late uncle. That night he had discussed his observations with his wife, and they had both pledged to continue the legacy of benevolence that their uncle and all the Dukes of Bedford preceding him had set.

Lord Tom was no longer overwhelmed by his new position; yes, it would take him some time to grow into his role as duke, but thanks to his training and the confidence of his wife and family, he did not doubt that he would follow the tradition set by his father and Uncle Sed, and those who came before, and be fair in his dealings with those who depended on his estates for their livelihood. His wife was growing into her role, gaining confidence with the support she was receiving from all of the ladies in the family. Each day that passed found Lady Amy Bennet becoming more comfortable in her role as mistress of the estate. Tom and Amy Bennet had finally moved into the master suite.

Lady Rose said that she was happy in her new suite. No one would hear of her moving to the dower house, even though it was less than a mile from the great house. An additional change for those in residence was that Mr. Winters, who had been overwhelmed when his legacy was revealed to him, had taken his leave to go live with his family and relax and enjoy his sunset years in retirement only the day before. It had been hard for him to leave the Bennet's employ, but he felt that with his master no longer alive that it was time to retire.

The royals and their spouses had departed following the funeral after conveying theirs and the rest of the royal family's condolences once again. The family, excepting the Duke and Duchess of Bedford, would depart for Town in three days. They would take their time on the return trip, the first stop at Pemberley where the Darcys and Lady Catherine would remain for a few days. They had also planned for there to be at least one day spent at Brookfield to see Jane's and Richard's estate. Next would be Snowhaven to take leave of the Fitzwilliam parents, and finally Hilldale as Marie and Andrew returned to their estate. From the Viscount's estate, the Bennets, Phillips, Bingleys, and Gardiners would travel to Longbourn. The older Phillips would return to their home in Meryton, their married children and the Gardiners were to be hosted with the Bennets. After a day or two, the three families would travel to their own homes in London.

The first order of business on arriving at Longbourn would be to move Lady Rose and her belongings into her suite. As hard as it was to contemplate life without her Sed in it, she had to proceed; the living had a responsibility to live for those they lost, and with the honour of both those alive and lost, she would live her life to the fullest. Now that Bingley's lease had ended, James Bennet would move into Netherfield and take the reins of his estate, he glad to take the burden of the daily running of it from his father who had taken it on while James had attended to his schooling.

~~~~~~~/~~~~~~~

The unloading of the *Coastal Trader* had gone as smoothly as Tony had hoped it would. The local men were resting as they waited for the wagons to pull up on the quay so the goods that were to be transported to Dublin could be loaded. The young man was almost shaky as his excitement grew to an almost fever pitch as the point of no return closed in, preparing to execute his plan. The first of the carts pulled up and was ready to be unloaded, and once that process was completed the goods to be loaded would be carried on board.

At the bar in the Happy Leprechaun, the three 'disgraced' men were bitterly complaining about the 'unfair' treatment that the captain had meted out. Some of their former shipmates had arrived at the inn and had jeered and yelled at the disgraced men until they had left the inn when they were threatened with more than verbal obscenities. Amos Laraby sat and watched the scene unfold with interest. After the three left, themselves yelling obscenities and threats of vengeance back at the crewmembers, Laraby approached one of crew to ask if he could buy him a tankard of ale.

"I's never one to say no to grog, thank ye kindly," the seaman said. After the briefing he knew what to say to keep a consistent tale if asked about the three thieves.

"Ow come your cap'an kicked 'em there men off your ship?" Laraby asked, certain he was being subtle.

"Cause they tried to steal fr'm us, thas why! Let 'em rot in 'ell, tries to thieve from us!" the seaman said with what convincing disdain.

"Where do ya' sail to fr'm 'ere?" Laraby asked.

"To Dublin with us," the seaman said with genuine glee, "we's gets us a week shore leave before we sail agin." he sighed. "Gre't 'ity tho', them 'as some o' da best sail'rs we 'ad." Laraby felt that he had learnt enough and said his farewell to his new friend by wishing him a safe trip back to Dublin, then went back upstairs. After verifying he was alone, he knocked on his captain's door and was bade enter.

"T'is what we thought, Cap'n," Laraby reported. "Them three tried to steal and gots caught so the Cap'n tossed 'em off 'is ship. I 'eard the crew talking about it at the bar and I spokes to one. 'e spilled that they be kicked off but 'tis gonna be 'arder fer de rest as they's some o' the best sailors they 'ad. I 'ad a man follow 'em, 'n they went ta the ol' wider's 'ouse an rented out a room for all three of 'em."

"Well done, Laraby. If we needs more crew members we knows where to find them!" The men watched as the labourers loaded the vessel. As Younge watched, aside from it going slow because the longer it took, the longer they had to stay inside, he scanned the group. He started when he thought he saw Alvarez, but the lad was blonde and at this distance many had the same features, so he dismissed it with a chuckle, many young men look the same at that age.

On his third trip loading sacks, Tony decided that with the cargo already in the hold, and what they had added, there were more than enough places to hide. He made sure that he was not in anyone's line of sight and deftly slipped behind some crates, finding a little void between two large crates that had others on top of them. There was just enough space for him to lie down between them. What he could not have known was that Mr. Clements and his three remaining men kept a count of who boarded and disembarked their vessel.

It was after seven in the evening before the cargo was all loaded. Some of the *Trader's* crew who had stayed aboard to work and were not part of those lucky enough to have liberty, went through the hold to make sure that the cargo was all secure. Clements knew that there was one left hidden on board somewhere. The four blended in with the crew as they secured the hold for sailing early in the morning. One of the guards heard a sound coming from a void between some crates and signalled Clement and his fellow guards. Once his men were stationed to cut off any possible avenue of escape, Mr. Clements stood next to the void.

"Out with you," he commanded. "You do not want me to have one of my men drag you out, now do you?"

"I am coming out," came the muffled, wary response. Tony Álvarez stood and could see that even if he so desired, the men had all possible escape routes blocked. He was placed between two of the large men and marched up to the captain's day cabin. Clements knocked on the cabin door, and when bade enter, was followed in by one of his guards with the lad proceeding him.

"What have we here, Clements?" Captain Beauclerk asked as he turned from the ship's log that he had been working on.

"We caught ourselves a stowaway, Captain," the head of security answered.

"He is a young lad; how do you think he will enjoy being keel-hauled?" the Captain asked with a half-smile. His crew members knew that their captain would never partake of that barbaric cruelty, but Tony did not and he was quaking with fear.

Beauclerk was not a brutal man so he put the lad at ease right away. "None of the Bennet's employees would ever do anything against the law, and keelhauling is very much illegal. We were just having some sport at your expense. Now what are you running from, lad?" the Captain asked calmly.

"How do you know that I-I am running away, sir?" Tony asked, calming somewhat but still nervous, fearing that the Captain would throw him off his ship as he had the three sailors earlier.

"That is usually why someone stows away, in my experience. What is your name, lad?" the captain asked in an attempt to get him talking.

"My name i-is Tony, captain," Tony took a deep breath and decided that he had a better chance of being allowed to remain on board if he was completely honest. "I am not running away from something that I have done, but from something that others plan to do and want me to participate in their schemes."

"Well, Tony, tell us the whole tale and we will see if we are willing to help you." Beauclerk looked past Tony to the guard. "Smithers, ask one of the men outside to request that cook send us some food, I have an idea that we will be here a while." Then he looked back at Tony as he stood. "Sit with us, Tony, and while we eat you can share all with us."

Fifteen minutes later the Captain's steward brought up a plate of cheese and cold roast beef sandwiches with ale to drink. As they started to eat, the Captain nodded toward Tony in a signal for him to commence.

"It started when my late father let greed overrule his good sense, and he participated in a scheme to..." Tony told them all, how they planned to kidnap the Duke's daughter, Elizabeth Bennet. Lost in his recounting, he did not notice the Dennington Line employees sitting up straighter or that they leaned forward to listen more keenly after he mentioned the lady's name. He told them the perspective from his side of the attempt, how it had gone very wrong with the mastermind's death and his father's arrest and subsequent hanging.

He related all from Fowey and the precipitous escape once Younge realised that they were being watched, and the order to make sure that the man following Karen Younge was dispatched. He described how they came to be in Bundoran and the plans his mother and the Younges were making to exact their revenge with all of their combined wrath focused on the lady who, in Tony's opinion, had done nothing to earn their enmity. Lastly, he told them how they planned to ransom her for two hundred fifty thousand pounds and that he had heard Karen Younge rant about what she would do to the lady.

"Who killed the man in Fowey," Clements asked, keeping his voice regulated to the situation even when he wanted to demand an answer.

"There were three, two held him and McLamb did the deed," Tony offered, praying it was enough to keep him on board.

"Did you know what they planned to do ahead of time?" the Captain asked.

"No, sir, I did not," Tony denied emphatically. "It was after we sailed that the three boasted about what they had done."

Clements leaned over to his man and told him to make sure that their 'friends' received the names of the murders. Once the guard left the cabin to follow his orders, the captain resumed the questioning.

"You know that this ship belongs to the Dennington Lines do you not, Tony?" The captain was not surprised when the lad nodded that he did. "Do you know who owns the company?" This time Tony shook his head. "The father and family that is the target of your mother and her accomplices. In fact, Lady Elizabeth is the Duchess of Derbyshire and is one of the owners." Tony's mouth hung open as the reality started to sink in. "Not only that," the captain continued, "did you or any of the schemers know that the Bennets are not only cousins to the royals, but close to them and that any move against *any* of them is treason? You do know the punishment for treason, do you not, lad?"

"I do, captain," Tony said dejectedly. "Will you clap me in irons now and send me to the tower to be beheaded, or shall I work for you for the trip then be beheaded?"

"No, Tony," the Captain laughed, "just the opposite. I believe his Grace would very much like to meet you, son. You have already proven that you are a young man with honour, even if you did swear revenge for your father. You had enough character to see the error of your ways and make the hard choice to change. You took a great chance sneaking on board my ship, but it just so happens that you could not have found a safer place to be. Every ship in the Dennington Line has been on the lookout for the *Stealthy Runner*. We were sending a letter to his Grace as soon as we arrive in Dublin. Now we will send a letter and you." He looked at Clements. "Mr. Clements, give young Tony one of the three open births and assign him some tasks to help you." The Captain turned back to the young man. "Everyone on my ship works, Tony, from the captain down."

"Hard work does not frighten me, Captain. Thank you, sir. I will not let you down!" Tony vowed, feeling better that he had in a long while.

"No, I do not believe you will, young man," the Captain agreed as he dismissed the two that remained in his cabin.

The next morning, just before sunrise, the *Coastal Trader* slipped her moorings and sailed with the tide with a very pleased Tony Álvarez still on board. He stood on the deck and watched as Bundoran shrank until he could no longer see it as they made a heading for Dublin.

CHAPTER 14

Johanna Álvarez was beside herself with worry. None of the searches by Younge's men had produced any sign of her son. They had even hired the three men who had been thrown off the *Coastal Trader* who had searched for long hours along with the rest of the crew, but no trace was discovered. Finally, it dawned on her to search her son's room, and in it she found a letter.

5 June 1812

Dear Mother,

I am sorry if I have caused you worry, but I cannot follow the path that both you and my father set for me. The only valuable lesson he imparted was to think for myself and evaluate situations, and to then make decisions based on facts not emotions.

The facts are these, Mama; you want to exact revenge on an innocent lady for choices that my father made freely. It is not her fault that Mr. Wickham's plan failed. I know that Mrs. Younge will never be able to assimilate the information, but everything that happened that led to her 'beloved's' death was by his design, not his intended victim's failure to be his victim.

What did those involved in the plot think? That the victim and her family would just sit by and allow them to do what they wanted because they willed it? If my father was not driven by greed, he would not have been blind to the possible pitfalls in the plan.

If you want to blame someone for Papa's death, Mama, then it must be Withers. He is the one that told the runners all and wrote the missive that led to his capture. Lady Elizabeth did none of that, she was the target of the plan for no other reason than men and women driven by avarice wanted what was not their due.

While we have been in Bundoran I have watched the locals, observing how they live and how happy they are. It taught me that there are many things in life that can make one happy, and I want to point out that stealing, kidnapping, and hurting others for one's own gain are not among them.

I intend to live a good and honourable life, Mama, and I pray to God on High that you cease your scheming and go on with your own. By the time you read this I will be many days ahead of you, and do remember that Ireland is a very big country.

With all my love,

Tony

Johanna was furious. How could her son turn on her in such a way? She missed everything her son was trying to tell her and added his defection to the list of sins that she laid at the Bennet chit's feet. When she returned to her room, she cast the letter into the grate and watched as it burned to ashes.

She made the critical error in judgement of not mentioning the letter to the Younge siblings so they had no idea that Tony had left and was out in the world with knowledge of where they were and all of their plans. Without the pertinent information, no decision was made to find a new port in which to disappear.

~~~~~~~/~~~~~~~

The Dennington ship, the *June Bell*, arrived at Liverpool and was met by the Line's manager of the Liverpool office, a Mr. Lloyd Wrightfield, as soon as she docked. He was handed an express for the Duke of Hertfordshire who, the manager knew according to his Grace's schedule he had received, would be at Pemberley in Derbyshire for another two days. He summoned his best courier and charged him to get the missive into his Grace's hands by the next morning at the very latest. The courier was told to spare no expense and to change horses as many times as needed to arrive at Pemberley as soon as humanly possible. It was just after eight in the morning when the determined man started his headlong dash toward Derbyshire.

Not long after the courier was away, Mr. Wrightfield was introduced to young Mr. Tony Álvarez. After reading the message from Captain Beauclerk, the manager ordered a carriage and six and eight of his best ex-marines to act as outriders. Within the hour the young man was seated in a very comfortable carriage and was on his way to Pemberley.

It was just before ten o'clock that night as the family at Pemberley was about to retire when Douglas knocked on the music room door to inform the master that an express rider from Liverpool had just arrived with an urgent message for his Grace, the Duke of Hertfordshire, so Lord William offered his father-in-law his study. Before exiting the room, Lord Thomas requested that all of his sons and the two earls join him as he suspected that the news pertained to the *Stealthy Runner* being sighted. He could not imagine another reason that Wrightfield would dispatch a rider with an express to thim, the urgency was obvious when he saw the rider, he was shown into the study with hat in one hand and the sealed missive in the other.

"When did you depart Liverpool?" Lord Thomas asked.

"After eight in the mornin' your Grace," the man answered, having recognised the Duke from his visits to the Liverpool office.

"You rode twelve hours to get here? How often did you change horses?" Lord Thomas asked, impressed by the dedication to duty the man demonstrated.

"Every two 'ours, your Grace." The express was handed over and the master of Pemberley instructed Douglas to make sure that the man be fed and had a place to rest for the night with the grooms. The courier was told to see the Duke of Hertfordshire in the morning in case there was a response to be sent to Liverpool. After the man followed the butler out of the study and the door was closed, Lord Thomas decided to read the letter aloud so he could satisfy the obvious curiosity all of them had.

10 June 1812
The Coastal Trader
Docked at Bundoran, Ireland

His Grace the Duke of Hertfordshire,

On the way to the quay this morning, the doctor spotted the Stealthy Runner at anchor.

Your order to observe and report was clear, your Grace, and no action will be taken without your order, but I decided that I had to leave some men behind to keep an eye on things in case the ship departed. Three of Mr. Clements's marines were 'sacked' for pilfering, and in a very public way were 'thrown off' the ship. One of the men was a good friend to the murdered former sergeant Hamms, and he and his shipmates volunteered for the mission.

Once we had taken on the cargo to transport to Dublin, Clements discovered a stowaway in the hold. His name is Antonio Álvarez

There was a mumbling of recognition as the men in the study heard the name and correctly assumed that the stowaway was somehow connected to the *Spaniard*. Once the men quieted again, Lord Thomas continued.

I allowed the young man, he is just eighteen, to remain on board and he will work for his passage, but he had a very interesting tale to tell. I have sent a letter to Mr. Wrightfield so he will know to send Tony to you right away so you can hear the story from his own lips. He did impart the names of Hamms's murderer and his accomplices. They will take no action until we receive your instruction, your Grace.

With respect,

Hugh Beauclerk, Captain

"We have them," Richard whistled.

"If they do not up and sail away," Darcy pointed out.

"Do you think that they will run once they realise that young Álvarez has defected?" Andrew asked.

"No way of knowing, son," his father pointed out.

"How should we proceed?" James asked.

"You are the military man here, Richard," his father-in-law stated. "What strategy would you employ?"

"How often does Captain Beauclerk's ship visit the town?" Richard asked thoughtfully.

"If memory serves once a month, somewhere around the middle of the month," Lord Thomas shared.

"If that is the case, I would have the captain contact his men ashore, I am sure they set up a way to contact each other if need be," Richard began, the plan in his head forming but he needed more details. "A few days before the *Coastal Trader* returns, the murderer and his accomplices should disappear. I assume that it is expected for your ship to unload and then take on new cargo?" Richard received a nod from his father-in-law. "In that case, they should be drugged and placed in a crate, or crates if needed, to be loaded with the rest of the cargo.

"That way even if the ship is being watched, the miscreants will see naught out of the ordinary. It sounds like the three will be good 'replacements' for the men that go missing from Younge's ship. This will ensure that we will always know where the conspirators are, and we will be able to catch them as soon as they set whatever ill-advised plan they have hatched into action." Seeing the indignant look from his cousin William, Richard took a moment to reassure him. "Lizzy will never be anywhere near them, William. I swear to you, to all of you, that she will never be placed in harms way. You have my word of honour."

Darcy relaxed and nodded. There was agreement among the men, so Lord Thomas wrote a detailed missive to Captain Beau-clerk that he sealed inside one for his manager in Liverpool.

~~~~~~~/~~~~~~~

Luckily Johanna was a reasonably good actress so the Younge's and the rest of the crew bought her act as she 'mourned' her son who she claimed was obviously dead after meeting with some foul play or drowning in the sea as he some-times liked to go sea bathing. Her pride would not allow her to admit that not only had her son left her, but that he had censured her for her desire to avenge his father. She was already wearing mourning garb for her late husband so there was lit-tle she had to change besides lamenting her 'dear' Tony's death when in company with her cohorts.

Younge was impressed with the three men who had been kicked off the ship. They were big and strong, which is always a bonus, and they had been dedicated to their tasks during the search for the Álvarez whelp. It was a pity that he had no openings in his crew, but occasionally men would take off without letting anyone know so it could be that a spot or spots would open up. One never knew.

~~~~~~~/~~~~~~~

It was midday of the second day of travelling from Liverpool when the carriage conveying Tony to the Duke of Hertfordshire turned off the road and passed through the gates of an estate. The young man surmised that the estate must be very grand as it took them close to an hour to arrive at the biggest house that he had ever seen. Waiting for him were a group of serious looking men in very high-quality clothing, far better than worn by anyone that he had known up to that point. He noticed that all of the men wore black arm-bands similar to the one that he wore for his father. Once the conveyance halted, a footman placed the steps and young Álvarez climbed out feeling rather stiff after so many hours sitting in the same position.

He was approached by the men who were led by an older gentleman who had sandy blonde hair with streaks of grey in it. "You must be young Tony Álvarez," Lord Thomas Bennet stated.

"Y-yes, sir, I am," Tony answered nervously.

"I am Lord Thomas Bennet, the Duke of Hertfordshire," Bennet informed the young man.

"Your Grace," Tony said as he bowed to the Duke.

"This tall fellow is Lord Fitzwilliam Darcy, the Duke of Derbyshire. Next to him is Lord Reginald Fitzwilliam, the Earl of Matlock. These two," he pointed at the Fitzwilliam brothers, "are Lords Richard and Andrew Fitzwilliam, the Earl of Brookfield and Viscount Hilldale. This," Lord Thomas indicated to his right, "is my son Lord James Bennet, Marquess of Netherfield, and behind him is Lord Maxwell Ashby, Earl of Ashbury." Tony was cowed like he had never been before; he had never met a knight of the realm never mind dukes, earls, or a viscount, which is exactly what Bennet had intended.

"When last did you eat, Mr. Álvarez?" the master of the estate asked.

"Some hours ago, your Grace." Tony managed to answer, remembering just in time that he was being addressed by the other duke. Darcy indicated for Douglas, who had been standing in the background, to approach. "This is my butler, Mr. Douglas. He will show you to your bedchamber and have a footman bring up some sandwiches and something to drink. Would you like ale?" Darcy asked.

"Yes, thank you, your Grace, that would be most welcome," Tony answered quietly. Lord William inclined his head and his butler indicated that the young man follow him, the peers amused when the lad's mouth fell open wide as he was led into the mansion, the signs of obvious wealth stunning his senses.

"He did not do too badly, considering everything that boy has been through and then to be confronted by all of us," Richard said with amusement. "I will request that Douglas show him to your study in an hour, if that meets with your approval William, Father Bennet?" Both men nodded. The men decided that in order to help put young Tony at ease, he would initially only meet with Lords Thomas, William, and Richard.

Before he arrived, the plan was to put the young man in a servant's room, but Lady Elizabeth wisely suggested that he be assigned a guest chamber. From the little that the Captain of the *Coastal Trader* had written, the boy had broken with his only family to follow his conviction that there was a better way. Thanks to the mistress of the estate, Tony was shown into a single guest chamber. It had a bedchamber, bathing-changing room, and a large walk-in closet. Comparatively, the rooms were on the smaller side, but they were the biggest, and nicest Tony had ever stayed in. A footman deposited his meagre belongings on a dresser and left. Not long after, another brought him a plate with cold meat and cheese sandwiches and a tankard of ale. Until he took the first bite, he had not realised how hungry he was, and it was not long before there was naught but crumbs left on the plate.

Tony sat in a very comfortable armchair looking out over the back gardens and the forested hill beyond them as he drank his ale. He started when there was a knock at the door and the butler informed him that he was to follow him to the master's study. Not many minutes later Tony was shown within where two dukes, a duchess, and an earl were waiting for him.

Before Douglas went to summon the young man, Lady Elizabeth had strenuously requested as the target of the plot being hatched, she wanted to be in the meeting. After half-hearted argument from the three men, they had acquiesced. Subsequently she was sitting next to her husband on the settee below the windows while her father and brother Richard were sitting on the one opposite. Darcy pointed to a chair between the two settees for Tony to sit.

"This," Darcy inclined his head toward his Elizabeth, "is my wife, Lady Elizabeth, Duchess of Derbyshire."

"The one that first Wickham, and now it seems the Younges, are determined to kidnap and worse," said Lady Elizabeth said.

"My mother too, your Grace," Tony admitted with shame.

"I think you had better tell us all, Mr. Álvarez," Lord Thomas instructed.

Tony told them about his life at home and how his mother had run some of his father's houses of ill repute. He related how, after his father was arrested and all of his assets seized by the crown, he and his mother had left London for Fowey as Wickham had told his father about Clay Younge. His mother had a few thousand pounds that were hidden in their home and that was all that she managed to leave with from all of the money that his father had amassed. He described how angry she was when she tried to enter the house where the bulk of the funds were hidden, only to witness soldiers and runners exiting the house with all of the chests.

Young Álvarez believed that it was the loss of the fortune that was driving his mother's quest for revenge, rather than the hanging of his father. He told them how McLamb and his helpers had boasted about taking care of the spy in Fowey as they sailed away. He was honest and admitted that there was a time when he was committed to vengeance for his father, then detailed how his opinion changed because of his father's single gift of worth, learning to think for himself.

Tony gave them a detailed account of the plans to kidnap and ransom Lady Elizabeth by the criminals she now had focused on her. The listeners were chilled when they learned what he had heard Karen Younge had planned, how she would slowly kill her victim as payback for her lover being killed. He began to tell them about Wickham's plans for Mrs. Younge, but Lord Thomas informed him that they knew that piece from Withers.

After Tony was done with his recitation, there was quiet for a few minutes as each assessed what they had learned. "Do you know why they are obsessed with me? What have I ever done to any of them? I have no idea who your mother or the Younges are," Lady Elizabeth asked with no little exasperation.

"It all stems from George Wickham targeting you, your Grace..." Tony was cut off as Lord William cut in.

"Wickham!" he spat the name out, "from beyond the grave he is a thorn in our side!"

"If he were not dead already, I would do the deed myself," Lord Richard growled. No one who knew him doubted that he would have done exactly what he said.

"Once my father and mother were fixated on the ransom, they started to believe it was due to them, just like Wickham had," Tony continued. "You already know that my father was planning to dispatch both Wickham and Karen Younge, notwithstanding Wickham's plans for his paramour." The three men nodded. "I am convinced that Mrs. Younge is insane. I have heard her blame her Grace for Wickham's death a multitude of times, completely ignoring that he brought it all on himself." Tony concluded.

"All of them must be insane to place the blame on the intended victim," Lord Thomas opined and none in the room disagreed with him.

"I hope I am right and that you are having them watched as we speak, your Graces, and your Lordship," the young man stated.

"What makes you think we may be watching them, Tony?" Lord Thomas asked.

"The three that were dismissed, I overheard Mr. Clements's men talking one night as we sailed home. I did not mean to eavesdrop," he assured them, "but from what I heard, the casting out of the three was theatre for Younge to see or hear about." He organised his thoughts and then added, "If it was me, I would find a way to get them into the crew of the *Stealthy Runner*."

"You are a very smart young man," the Duke of Hertfordshire noted then changed the subject "Have you thought about what you want to do with your life, Tony?"

"If I could get the required education, I think that I would like to read the law, your Grace." Tony blushed.

"We will just have to see what happens," Lord Thomas said with a half-smile. It was the first time that he had almost smiled since his big brother had passed.

"Your Graces, your Lordship, I have one request regarding my mother," Tony asked with some trepidation.

"What is it, lad?" Lord Thomas asked.

"Will you allow me to write to my mother so I can try one more time to divert her from her path and beseech her to give up this madness. I will not mention anything about any of you, your knowledge, or plans. In fact," he added to assure them, "once I have written my letter you will be free to read it to make sure that I have not written anything that you would not desire me to write." After looking to his sons and daughter, Lord Thomas agreed.

"There will be no direction on the letter. It will be sent to Liverpool to be placed in Captain Beauclerk's hands. When they dock in Bundoran next month, he will deliver it to the inn. What did you say its name was, Tony?" Lord Thomas asked.

"The Happy Leprechaun, your Grace." Tony was relieved they had accepted his request.

"Yes, well, he will deliver the letter telling the landlord that he can claim that a boy handed it to him in Portrush, Ballycastle, or even Belfast to avoid anyone knowing your real location," Lord Thomas said, thus laying out a way that Tony could communicate with his mother safely. "If she chooses to write back to whichever location that the captain says he was given the letter, which is doubtful as she will have no direction but the town, we will have the Dennington agent at the location he chooses have the postmaster direct any letters addressed to you to be held and passed onto our agent." Lord Thomas offered the kindness of hope with the tempering of his expectations.

The meeting then concluded. Tony returned to his spacious chambers to bathe and change into the one halfway decent suit that he owned for dinner. Lord Thomas and the three who had been in the meeting repaired to the drawing room to relay what they had learnt to the rest of the family.

CHAPTER 15

Sitting on the huge bed that she shared with her husband every night in her bedchambers at Hilldale, Lady Marie Fitzwilliam was overjoyed. Not only was she hosting her younger brother and unmarried sisters at Hilldale, but she had missed her courses for the second month. She had felt a tinge of envy when Jane had revealed her state, but now she had nothing to be jealous of as she was sure that she too was *enceinte.* She had not experienced any of the sickness that Jane had in the early months of her being with child and was very thankful that, so far, she seemed to have been spared that particular malady.

Andrew could not but notice the glow emanating from his wife, almost like she was surrounded by an angel's halo. He had not missed that it had been at least two months that they were able to join without interruption of her monthly indisposition. "Is there something that you would like to inform me of Marie?" His brow quirked in inquisition

"Oh Andrew, I think that I am with child!" she exclaimed in happiness. "I have missed my courses for two months and my breasts have lately become much more tender..." she let her words fade away embarrassed that she was about to refer to the size of her assets.

"... and larger," Andrew finished the thought for his wife. "I had noticed *that* particular occurrence," he agreed with a rakish grin, "and I highly approve and enjoy the extra bounty it has provided," he teased.

"Andrew!" she admonished playfully as she swatted at his arm. "You are embarrassing me." As if to prove the point she was blushing a deep scarlet.

"Should we ask Mr. Granger to come see you, my love, so he may confirm your state?" asked the hopeful father to be.

"Do you mind if we wait a day?" Seeing his questioning look, Marie clarified, "Mama, Papa, Aunt Rose, and the rest of the family depart on the morrow. If they see that the doctor has come to see me, Mama will know why. If it is agreeable to you, my loving husband, I would like to keep this between us until I feel the quickening. We can revel in becoming new parents before we allow others to share our joy. I know it sounds selfish..." Marie was cut off by her husband kissing her soundly.

"It is not selfish, my love," he said as his wife tried to recover her equanimity. "If you had not suggested that we wait, I would have done so for the same reason now that the surprise has worn off. It is prudent to wait until the quickening, not selfish." Lord Andrew returned to his chambers so that his valet could help prepare him for the day while Lady Marie used the bellpull to summon her lady's maid.

~~~~~~~/~~~~~~~

Life at Longfield Meadows was slowly returning to normalcy. The new duke regularly met with his steward, Mr. Brian Mason, about estate matters and any issues that needed to be addressed. Mason had been involved in helping the late Lord Sed train his heir and had seen then that Lord Tom Bennet seemed to be of the same ilk as his uncle. Now that Lord Tom was the new Duke of Bedford, the steward was very happy to see that his estimation of the young man had been on point.

The new duchess met daily with Mrs. Matilda Dudley, her housekeeper. Mrs. Dudley and her husband had been in service with the Bennets for over twenty years, both having risen through the ranks of the servants to attain their current positions of most senior servants that serviced the house. The housekeeper was most impressed with the young duchess. She was very intelligent and she treated all with respect from the lowest scullery maid on up. One would make a big mistake if they assumed that the way that she treated her servants indicted an easily led woman; the opposite was indeed true. She would listen to advice when asked for, however she would make the decision that she felt best suited the situation, only changing her mind if there was good, factual information that warranted said change. She was proving to be very fair, but firm.

Before the family departed for Pemberley, Aunt Rose had spent as much time as Amy required to educate her on the running of the house and the needs of the tenants. Lady Rose had visited all of the tenants at least once a month while she was in residence and shared with her daughter-in-law that she insisted that the housekeeper inform her of any emergent needs while she had been away from the estate. Given the large number of tenants and the large area that Longfield Meadows covered, Aunt Rose informed Amy that she would visit a different group who lived close to one another each week, thus making sure that she was able to stand by her self-imposed schedule for her visits.

At least once a week the Duke and Duchess would walk to the family cemetery to visit Uncle Sed and talk to him as if he was there to let him know that all was well with his beloved estate. On this particular day, his Amy was indisposed so Tom made the walk to visit Uncle Sed on his own.

"How I miss you, Uncle Sed," Tom opened his one-sided conversation with his loved, late uncle. "I pray that it is many years before God calls my father home. The loss of you, my second father, is not something that I want to feel again. I consider it one of the best gifts to our family, having you and mother-aunt Rose, but there is a thorn in this gift, although it is the way of the mortal world and, I will eventually be forced to face this kind of pain again. All I can do is beseech God to make it a very long time in the future.

"My hope is that you knew how loved you were, still are, Uncle Sed." Tom lifted his eyes to the heavens. "One day we will all be together again, but while Amy and I are still here we will continue on with your and Papa's examples to guide us. I can only hope that we garner a fraction of the love and respect that the servants and tenants have for you and Aunt Rose, we will endeavour to do so. You taught me well, Uncle, and I was prepared for what you left me, if only it could have been many more years before I inherited." A single tear rolled down Lord Tom's cheek.

"Amy sends her regrets. She is not able to visit today, but will join me on the next one. How grateful I am that you were able to witness our wedding, and I know that Lizzy and William feel exactly the same. We understand why you would not allow for us to be summoned to your side before the end of the wedding ball, but you have to know that all of us would have forgone the celebration to have more time with you, Uncle Sed." Tom placed his hands on his late uncle's headstone as if to have some tactile contact with him. "I love you, Uncle Sed." As he spoke the last Tom felt a chill, but it was not a cool day and it almost felt like there was a presence that he could not see. Mayhap his Uncle was telling him that he was loved by him as well.

<div align="center">~~~~~~~/~~~~~~~</div>

The Duke and Duchess of Derbyshire were settling into married life very comfortably. In a little over two month's time, they would take their wedding trip to Seaview Cottage, near Brighton, and spend three weeks in seclusion. In the meanwhile, Elizabeth quickly found out that her jest about getting lost in the vast expanse that was Pemberley's manor house did not come to pass. Besides the fact that the way that the house was laid out was easy for her to get her bearings, there was never a footman or maid far from any point that she happened to be.

Lady Anne spent as much time as Elizabeth felt she needed to help her assume her duties of mistress. With a new mistress at the estate, Lady Anne had more time to dedicate to her music, and would often be found playing duets with her young daughter. Just as she had suspected, having Elizabeth as part of the family made them all happier. Elizabeth was not the cause of the felicity; it was that she was a piece of the puzzle that had been missing. Now that it was complete, it was as if all of Pemberley breathed a sigh of relief.

Young Tony Álvarez was to stay at Pemberley until all of the conspirators were either in captivity or had decided to scrap the ill-advised scheme and move on. Clay Young would be held to account for ordering the murder of Sergeant Hamms, regardless of whether or not he put his kidnapping plan into action. Tony had written his letter which had been sent to Liverpool with the same courier, this time instructed to make the return after a night's sleep as the letters were not urgent. The *Coastal Trader* would not depart Dublin for almost ten days, so the letters would be in the captain's hands long before it sailed. In his letter to his mother, Tony used the coastal town of Ballycastle as the location from which he would 'hand' his letter to the postmaster, who would pass it onto the Captain with the 'request' that it be delivered to the Happy Leprechaun.

While he was at Pemberley, Tony had been told to shadow the steward, Mr. Edwin Chalmers, who, like Tony, had once wanted to read the law but had decided to become a steward rather than practice as a solicitor. It had only been a few days, but Tony very much enjoyed his work and Chalmers was impressed as no matter how much was asked of the young man, he accomplished his tasks without complaint.

Lady Elizabeth knocked softly on her husband's study door and entered when she heard his deep baritone voice call "Come."

"I was missing you, William," she said seductively. "How much longer is required to respond to your correspondence?" she asked as she gave him an inviting look. Her husband stood and put his head out of his study door instructing the footman on duty to make sure that unless it were a life-or-death emergency no one was to disturb them. He then locked the door and turned to his beautiful duchess.

"How I love you," he growled as he became fully aroused, "I think that it is time we discovered how strong my desk is, my Lizzy." Darcy swept his arm across his desk pushing his papers to one side. Luckily his ink pot was not sent flying and he moved it to a shelf then took his wife in his arms and perched her on the edge.

"Love me, William!" she instructed, and her husband complied with relish.

~~~~~~~/~~~~~~~

Lord James Bennet sat in the coach with his parents and younger sisters, his eyes closed as the largest and most comfortable of the Hertfordshire carriages bore them south toward Meryton. He was a very happy young man as he had learnt that a year would be cut off his waiting time to declare himself to the woman that he loved above all others; the *only* one he had ever had tender feelings for as a man does a woman, Lady Georgiana Darcy. He remembered with pleasure their conversation in the drawing room at Pemberley which still filled him with joy.

"Mama," Georgiana said, "Mary, Kitty, and I have been talking."

"This cannot be good," Lizzy teased.

"What is it, Sweetling?" Lady Anne asked.

"As you know, Mary and Kitty turned eighteen in March of this year." Lady Anne nodded that she did. "Loretta will be the same age in August, and they had planned to have their come out together during the little season."

"Yes, we know all of this," her mother stated, "pray tell me what are you getting at, Georgie?"

"As I will be seventeen in November, would you, William, and Richard allow me to have my come out in the season of 1813?" Fearing that her courage may fail her with all eyes on her now, Georgiana proceeded at all speed. "Would you allow me to have my come out with Kitty, Mary, and Retta?"

"Mary and Kitty, you know that this will mean that your come out will be delayed by two to three months, do you not?" Lady Sarah asked her youngest offspring.

"We do, Mama," Kitty responded. "Georgie asked us before Uncle Sed passed and we discussed it with Retta, and the three of us decided to wait for Georgie so we could all come out together. Retta asked Aunt Priscilla and she has no objection as long as everyone else agrees. We decided that before Uncle's funeral was not a time to bring the request to you."

"Please Mama, William, Richard?" Georgiana requested, her blue

eyes wide and beseeching as she looked at each in turn.

"Let us confer, Georgie," her brother said kindly. The three had a quiet conversation where they agreed that with the maturity and self-confidence that Georgie now exhibited, and the vast changes to the positive in her, that there was no reason to make her wait an extra year.

"As long as Sarah and Priscilla agree, you have our permission, Georgie." Lady Anne had barely got the words out when to belie her maturity she squealed like a school girl and threw herself into her brother's arms. Three very happy young girls departed to Georgiana's sitting room to start making plans.

Darcy asked James to join him in the corner, having not missed the pleasure on his brother-in-law's face when permission was granted to bring her come out forward by one year.

"None of us have missed the clear preference that you and Georgie have for one another, James," Darcy said quietly. "Richard, my mother, and I all agree that we want her to experience a season before anyone declares for her." James nodded as he understood what his brother was saying and why. "If at the end of her first season you both feel as you do now, then you may request a courtship from her, which I will consider after I have you and your family investigated to make sure that you would be appropriate and deserving of my sister!" Darcy joked, producing a huge grin from James. They shook hands as the restriction was understood and accepted.

James again smiled to himself. In less than a year he would be allowed to request a courtship. He would use the time to learn all of his present and future duties, and prepare Netherfield for the woman that he prayed would be its mistress in the not too far distant future.

~~~~~~~/~~~~~~~

The courier had slowed per his Grace's instruction, spending the night at an Inn about halfway between Pemberley and Liverpool thus he arrived early in the morning the following day, having left the inn before sun up. As soon as he dismounted, he handed the pouch containing his Grace's instructions to Mr. Wrightfield.

After reading the Duke's instructions, the manager made his way to one of the line's ships that was to sail for Dublin with the tide. He handed the packet of missives to the captain with expressed instructions to get them into the hands of Captain Beauclerk on the *Coastal Trader* as she was set to depart Dublin the day after the *Wander* docked. Wrightfield noted the urgency in the missives that went both directions and remembered well his instruction to make sure that young Tony was sent to his Grace post haste. Were he a truly compassionate man he would feel sorry for those who had attempted to hurt the Duke's daughter, but his compassion was reserved for those who led a life without crime. These particular individuals had no idea what was going to befall them at some point in the not too distant future, and he would be glad to assist in any way that was asked.

~~~~~~~/~~~~~~~

The three cohorts were sitting around a table at the Happy Leprechaun in Bundoran. Johanna Álvarez was maintaining her façade as the 'grieving mother' while in company with others.

"Why must we wait longer, Clay?" Karen Younge whined with her oft repeated complaint.

"We 'ave bin 'ere for jus longer than a month, we need to be patient sister," he said with no small amount of exasperation. "I knows that you want to avenge your 'dear' George, but if we depart too soon and are caught? Then what vengeance will you 'ave?"

"Listen to your brother, Mrs. Younge," Johanna soothed. As much as she disliked the woman and knew that she was as much a 'Mrs.' as Johanna was the Queen, she was needed. Possibly only as a diversion, but needed none the less.

"I suppose that you are right," she said petulantly. "I just miss my dear..." Her brother and Johanna both ignored her speech as they had heard the same from her many times over.

'Oh, to see your face if you learned the truth,' Johanna thought to herself. 'I know, I will tell her right before I have her killed and tossed into the sea!' The thought of dispatching the delusional woman engendered warm feelings in Mrs. Álvarez, ones that likened to happiness, even.

"Those three who were kicked off that ship have proved to be very useful," Johanna opined as she changed the subject.

"They 'ave," Younge agreed, "Pity I have no room on my crew for them. 'O knows, could be we will find a use for them anyway even if we'll be cramped when we leave. Them three would be very 'andy with what we need to do." He mused. "From what me sister 'as told us, the woman may 'ave some large footmen with 'er, and they's would be able to get rid of them." he said as if killing someone in his way was just a matter of course, again showing his lack of any decent feelings.

"So we will take her from the Prig's estate in Derbyshire," Karen Younge stated. "That will accomplish two aims, we will have the whore and the prig will be hurt. If my George could have been with us to witness our triumph, it would have filled him with pride." Johanna turned her head and coughed so that the delusional woman would not see her roll her eyes at her ridiculous speech.

"Yes, as we have discussed many times," Johanna responded, trying her best to keep the exasperation out of her voice, "that is the last place that they will expect the woman to be harmed. They are toffs and will be nice, soft targets thinking that they are safe in their homes."

"You know this is best, sister," Younge added. Karen Younge nodded her agreement, like she had every other time they had discussed their plans. She smiled as she thought of the pleasure that she would take when she slowly killed the woman that killed her George.

~~~~~~~/~~~~~~~

A few days later a company messenger delivered the packet of missives to Captain Beauclerk on the day before he was to set sail for his normal run along the Irish coast. He saw there was one letter for him and another one sealed and directed to '*Mrs. Johanna Álvarez, the Happy Leprechaun, Bundoran.*' He broke the seal on the missive for himself and scanned to the signature,

SHANA GRANDERSON A LADY

starting when he saw that it was from his Grace the Duke of Hertfordshire. he quickly returned to the top of the missive to ensure he read it in the proper order in case there were tasks with dependencies.

23 June 1812
Pemberley, Derbyshire

Captain Beauclerk,
Your missive and the young Mr. Álvarez are much appreciated. I laud you for the quick thinking in the way that you handled leaving three of Mr. Clements's for surveillance.

From your report and what young Tony has told us, we have a good idea what the misanthropes are planning, but we do not want to leave anything to chance. To that end we ask the following:

You will notice that there is a letter addressed to Mrs. Álvarez. Please have one of your officers take it to the inn after you dock in Bundoran and let it be known that you were handed the missive during your stop in Ballycastle and requested to deliver it.

Next, I am sure that Clements set up a way to communicate with his men. We want our men to capture this McLamb and his two accomplices a day or two before your ship docks. They are to be delivered, alive, *in individual crates when the outgoing cargo is loaded. They should be well drugged with laudanum so that they will not draw any attention or move around when they are brought on board. My son-in-law, Lord Richard Fitzwilliam, would like to 'talk' to the men that murdered his man. There will be no objection if they are not in perfect condition when they arrive. They are to be 'shipped' to the former colonel's estate, Brookfield, in Derbyshire in the custody of a contingent of guards to make sure that they do not have an opportunity to escape.*

Please have me notified at my estate, Longbourn, in Hertfordshire, once they arrive in Liverpool.

My family and I wish to thank Mr. Tetley for his observation of the criminals' ship. We also thank you and your crew members who are helping us in this matter.

Lord Thomas Bennet

Duke of Hertfordshire

The captain whistled. If the band of criminals did not deserve everything that was coming their way, then he did not know who would.

~~~~~~~/~~~~~~~

Lady Marie Fitzwilliam was beyond happy. The previous day Dr. Granger had confirmed her state. It had been a day of both joy and sorrow. She and Andrew had said goodbye to the Bennets as they left for Longbourn, which had made Marie a little sad as it would be some months before she saw all of them again. After the doctor examined her and confirmed her state, she was ecstatic. She and Jane would birth their children within two to three months of each other and the cousins would all grow up near one another. Once Lizzy and Amy were in the family way, the group of cousins would expand rapidly.

Marie and Jane could never keep secrets from one another, so when Marie told Andrew that she wanted to inform Jane, was in fact impatient to, she sat at her escritoire in her chambers and wrote her sister a note. They would see each other at Pemberley in a week, but Marie wanted to send a footman that very day. Once she had completed her missive, she descended the main stairs to request that Mr. Payton have a footman or groom take it to Brookfield and hand it to her sister.

Mayhap she was dreaming of her babe or sharing her joy with her sister, but she missed the eighth step from the bottom and tumbled down the remaining steps landing forcefully directly on her belly as the butler and footmen stood frozen in horror for a moment before they sprang into action. A footman was dispatched to summon the master who was meeting with his steward and stablemaster in the stables. Another was sent to inform Mr. Granger that his services were required urgently.

In a matter of minutes Andrew sprinted into the foyer where a chilling sight greeted him, his unconscious wife lying prostrate on her front, seemed to be bleeding from two places. One where her head had hit the marble floor and a second from the area of her most private area. Her husband was sure that Marie had just had a miscarriage and he had no idea how he was going to break the news to her.

CHAPTER 16

Lady Anne Darcy felt a sense of contentment that she had not felt since her beloved husband was taken from them. Pemberley was no longer just a house; it was a home again. The undeniable love between the master and the mistress seemed to permeate every corner of the great house. She felt that the atmosphere at Pemberley was so very much lighter, it was as if the whole estate had woken up from a five-year slumber. The tenants that had the pleasure of meeting the new mistress had sung her praises to their friends. In a few days, Elizabeth would join her mother-in-law to visit the tenants so that Lady Anne could formally introduce the new mistress of Pemberley.

The Dowager Duchess chuckled to herself as she remembered how Pemberley's clergyman and friend of William's from Cambridge, Mr. Patrick Elliot, and his beloved wife Emily had stood and stared at the happy and ebullient Duke of Derbyshire with mouths gaping. Their little daughter Grace, just two, and the cutest imp of a young girl with auburn ringlets, had giggled at her mama and papa's funny reactions.

The Elliots did not join them in London for the wedding as Emily Elliot was heavy with child, and Mr. Elliot did not want to risk his wife or new babe with almost three days of travel each way. Pemberley's doctor, Mr. Ulysses Jamison had concurred with the worried husband and added his recommendation that they not travel. Their son, Timothy, or Tom as they called him, had been born six weeks previously.

Patrick Elliot was one of the few people in Darcy's life that had always been honest with him. Lady Anne knew from conversations that she had both with William and the clergyman, that on the master's return in December of the previous year after his setdown by his now wife, Mr. Elliot had not minced words as he had pointed out that it was high time that someone had taken him to task. He had talked to his friend about his behaviour on prior occasions but as he was then, Darcy had dismissed his friend's council.

Lady Anne was certain that the reason that her son valued the rector's friendship so highly was that he did not defer to her son; he told him the truth as he saw it, not what he felt that William wanted to hear. In addition to the Pemberley living, Elliot had also been gifted with the Lambton and Kympton parishes. Unlike most clergy in similar positions, his income from three lucrative livings brought him close to two thousand a year. He was actively involved with the parishioners in all three parishes, to make sure that there was always a clergyman in each parish, he employed two curates. He and them rotated each Sunday so that as the living holder, he would perform the services at each church once every three weeks. The curates were paid in excess of the norm for those in a curator position, and despite the objections of his friend, Darcy insisted on paying half of their salaries.

Elliot was the third son of Sir Everett Elliot, a baronet, and his mother was Lady Ilene. The pastor owned a small estate, Riverdale, in Shropshire that brought in a further two thousand a year. Money was not a motivator; Patrick felt a true calling for his vocation. The Elliots had been effusive in their well wishes over both the elevation and the marriage, and already loved the new Duchess. Emily and Lady Elizabeth were already well on their way to being friends.

Elizabeth woke to find her husband still in bed and staring at her with an adorably loving expression. "Do I have a blemish, husband?" she teased. "What are you thinking of, William?"

"You are my first thought when I wake in the morning, and my last thought before I fall asleep at night," he told her as he took her hand and kissed it then leant over and kissed her lips lovingly. "My heart beats only for you, my greatest joy is having you as my wife and sharing all that the future holds for me with you, my Lizzy." He leaned over and kissed her more deeply than before. "You, my Lizzy, fill my thoughts and I am still in amazement that I get to fall asleep and wake up next to you each and every day, and," he added with a rakish grin as he waggled his eyebrows, "I get to do all the things that we do before we fall asleep, my love."

"Fitzwilliam Darcy!" his duchess scolded him playfully as she blushed deeply, "it is most indecorous to talk of such things to a lady." She swatted his arm in jest. "I too think of you all the time, William. As grateful as you are to be married to me, I am as grateful that you are my husband. Not even death will stop me loving you, William." She leaned over and trailed kisses down his chest and was able to prove her words truth as he responded to ministrations with needs he wanted only her assuaging, however she chose to that morning.

Afterward, her husband exited the bed to use the necessary and his wife leaned on her elbow as she admired him. "You are better to look at than any statue or painting I have ever before viewed," she said saucily as she appreciated his naked body. "I always considered you handsome, but as I watch your muscles ripple beneath your skin, it is fascinating." She soaked him in, her words no more than a breathy whisper by the end of her speech.

Darcy stopped and turned to look down at his beloved wife, "As I am your husband, you are welcome to look at me and admire what you see any time you wish," the Duke agreed, displaying his dimpled smile that would have made her weak at the knees had she been standing. "As happy as I am that you find my body pleasing, I know that what we have goes far beyond physical beauty as you, my dearest loveliest Elizabeth, are the most beautiful woman in the world. For the longest time I have dreamt about loving you, but I have to tell you that not even my wildest dreams came close to the reality of you. Having you with me every night and day since we married has met and far exceeded any of my hopes and dreams of what it would be like to be married to you my love."

"My feelings mirror yours, William. It is not only you who dreamed about us before we married," Elizabeth admitted. "Even before I allowed my head to acknowledge what my heart was screaming out to it; I would dream of you. Even only being married to you for this short a time, I too can say that the reality far exceeds anything that I dreamt, my grace," she teased trying out a new pet name for her husband as she reluctantly arose from the warm bed and they rang for their personal servants to prepare for the day.

They joined their mother and sister to break their fasts, and had just taken their seats when Mr. Douglas brought in a missive on the silver salver. Darcy saw that the message was from Andrew, broke the seal, and read the short and to the point note.

"Oh no!" he exclaimed.

"What is it, William?" asked his concerned wife.

"Marie fell while descending the stairs and has been injured," he reported with much worry for his sister-in-law. The missive did not specify what the injury was.

"I am sure that Jane and Richard are on their way to Hilldale, we…" Elizabeth said with tears in her eye for her sister's pain.

"The carriage will be ready to take us thither in an hour, my love," he said, pre-empting his wife's request.

"Georgie and I will stay here," Lady Anne said. "If we are needed, let us know. We are close enough that we can be there in three hours."

"We will, Mother Anne," Elizabeth replied distractedly. As she walked away from her mother-in-law, she requested that a footman tell her maid to pack a few things and to pass the same information onto the master's valet. After a hurried meal, the Duke and Duchess of Derbyshire headed to Hilldale with all speed.

~~~~~~~/~~~~~~~

The *Coastal Trader* arrived in Ballycastle on schedule. The Captain of the ship went ashore to visit Mr. Liam O'Connor, the postmaster who was an acquaintance due to his monthly visits to the small coastal town. As a favour, and without questioning why Captain Beauclerk needed it, he franked the letter showing that it originated from his post office. He was given the direction of the Dennington Lines office in Liverpool and agreed to forward any letter that arrived addressed to Mr. Anthony or Tony Álvarez to Mr. Wrightfield at that direction.

With his task accomplished, the Captain returned to his vessel to relieve the first mate and supervise the loading of the new cargo as was his wont. They would arrive in Bundoran in a sennight and he hoped that Clements had been successful in his attempt to contact his men.

~~~~~~~/~~~~~~~

Jones returned to the boarding house with a letter that the postmaster had handed to him when he went to check if there had been any post for him, Forester, or Tibbson. Once he had closed the door to their room, he broke the seal.

"What 'ave you there, Jonesy?" Tibbson asked.

"A latter from Mr. Clements," was the terse reply. "Ere, let me read it to you two layabouts," he joked with his brothers-in-arms.

June 24 1812
Dublin Docks

We have orders from his Grace.

A day or two afore we dock in Bundoran, you are to capture McLamb and his two cronies. Make it look like they scarpered. Get a crate or crates large enough to put them in, and make sure that they are drugged and sleeping on the day that we load our cargo.

They will be loaded into the hold for transport to see his Grace's son-in-law, an ex-colonel in the Royal Dragoons and a hero of more than one battle, the very one who employed Sergeant Hamms. He is right keen to acquaint himself with Hamms's murderers.

They must be alive when you deliver them, but no one will repine if they are not in 'pristine' condition. His Grace and his family are aware of their plans and wants you three to infiltrate Younge's crew, keep us informed of their movements.

The sooner this assignment is over the sooner you will be back where you belong, where I can keep you in line.

Clements

"At last," Forester exclaimed, "we get to pay 'em murderers back for what they did to Hamms." Forester had been a friend of Hamms and had served with him. He was especially glad that the missive gave leave for the three bastards to feel a little...*discomfort* before they were put in the crates. The three made their plans and went to see the Dennington agent in the town to ask for the crates that would accommodate their needs.

~~~~~~~/~~~~~~~

When the Darcys arrived at Hilldale they could not miss the looks of sadness that they saw around them. The butler met them, informing them that Lord and Lady Brookfield had arrived an hour earlier and that an express had just arrived informing the master that their graces the Duke and Duchess of Bedford were on the way.

Elizabeth felt a sense of foreboding. "Have expresses been dispatched to Snowhaven and Longbourn?" she asked the butler.

"They have, your Grace," he answered with all due deference, "Lord and Lady Matlock were visiting a neighbouring estate and will be here by this evening."

The Darcys rushed up the stairs to the master suite where they found Andrew being comforted by his younger brother. "Andrew, how is my sister," Elizabeth asked with concern, "is she badly injured?"

"Other than a lump on her head, she is physically well, Lizzy," he said emphasising the one word, "We had just..." he paused as he was overcome with emotion, "found out that Marie was *enceinte* that morning. When she fell, she landed on her belly and she lost..."

Elizabeth bit back a sob as she understood that her older sister had lost her babe. She kissed and hugged both brothers-in-law and then proceeded into Marie's chambers. The sight that greeted her almost broke her heart. Here they were mourning the loss of a most beloved uncle, and now this tragedy on top of that was more than she could imagine, and she was not the one who lost a babe.

Jane, whose expanding belly was easily seen now, was comforting her sister who was crying in despair and repeating over and over again, "It was my fault! It was my fault!" Jane was trying to console her and was relieved to see Lizzy enter the chambers.

"Look Marie, Lizzy is here," Jane said, hoping that seeing their younger sister would lift her spirits somewhat.

"Lizzy, I am so ashamed," Marie sobbed, "God punished me for feeling envy when Jane became with child and I was not. I broke the commandment 'Thou shalt not covert' and I received what I deserved." Marie collapsed into her younger sister's arms as her body was wracked with sobs. Elizabeth and Jane exchanged a distressed look. Marie was always the strong one, they hardly recognised the lady full of guilt before them.

"MARIE ROSE FITZWILLIAM!" Elizabeth's voice cut through the room to make sure that her sister would look at her. She was still crying, and her head was down so Elizabeth placed her fingers under sister's chin and gently lifted her head. "You are not being punished for anything, and how can you think that God would do something so...so evil?" Before Marie could formulate an answer, her younger sister proceeded. "You were envious of the state that Jane was in, not that Jane was with child. Did you ever wish any ill on Jane and her pregnancy?" Marie shook her head tearfully.

"O-of c-c-course not," she stammered between sobs.

"You never showed anything but joy for Richard and me," Jane said softly. "We always did everything together, it was only normal that you would feel sad that I became with child before you, Marie," she soothed. "As Lizzy said, you did not resent me for my blessing, your envy was at you not attaining the same state, but then you did."

"You had an accident, Marie," Elizabeth said as she hugged her sister. "Andrew told me that you missed the edge of step and fell, something that could have happened to any of us. I am sure that as the doctor had just confirmed your state that you were feeling blissful, unfortunately you were not near the banister and did not see what you were about to do. That is all it was Marie, bad luck, no more and no less."

"Marie, look at me and at Lizzy. Do you see any disapprobation?" Jane asked her twin sister. After looking at both sisters through her tear-filled eyes, Marie shook her head. "There is naught that you have done that God needs to punish you for! Lizzy has the right of it, it was an accident that had a very unfortunate consequence due to your injury." Marie wiped her eyes as she started to see the truth in her sister's words. "Do not forget, sister dear, that all of us women have to live with the risk of a miscarriage, with or without falling, so this may have happened whether you fell or not. It is one of things that we have no control over," Jane added to point out to her sister that her guilt was misplaced.

"Amy and Tom and the Matlocks will arrive later this afternoon and I am sure that Mama and Papa will be here in a day or two at the latest," Lizzy informed her sister. "All of us love you and will be here to support you as long as possible. It is very hard, and no one will tell you that you should not grieve your babe that will not be. Many women have to go through the same thing, survive, and go on to have more children after.

"Look at Mother Anne. I am sure that when you see her, she will tell you the same thing. Between William and Georgie, she had three miscarriages and a still birth, but then God blessed her with Georgie. She said that she would come if you need her, but she did not want to overwhelm, you."

"Will you," Marie paused to blow her red nose and wipe her eyes, "send her a note and ask her to come? I think that it would help me to speak to her."

"Of course, I will, my dear Marie," Elizabeth said as she squeezed her sister's hand. "Never forget that you know that you were able to fall pregnant and there are others like Aunt Rose, who are not able to."

While their wives were consoling Marie, the husbands were

helping Andrew. He blamed himself that he was not there to protect his wife. Both Richard and William put paid to his self-pity in short order. They pointed out that a miscarriage was just one of the many risks of pregnancy and that what had happened to Marie was an accident. Richard even semi-joked with his older brother asking him if he was so arrogant to think that he was omnipotent like God, that he could always be everywhere.

Andrew informed his brother that Mr. Granger had seen Marie soon after the fall and found no broken bones. He did not believe that she had a concussion, but recommended vigilance just in case. He was not sure if the accident would preclude the Viscountess from having a child, but given where she had fallen from, he believed that she would be able to still bear children.

One of the brothers placed a snifter of brandy in Andrew's hand, which he gulped down in one swig as he felt the brown liquid burn its way down his throat. "Lizzy and my Jane will help Marie, Andrew," his younger brother opined. "You have to remember that it just happened, and so close after Uncle Sed's death, I am sure only magnified the grief that my sister was already feeling."

"You are going to have to be strong for your wife, Andrew," Darcy told him. "It is a miracle that Marie did not suffer any more serious injuries to her person, God must have been looking out for her, as it could have been so very much worse."

"Mayhap you are right, William," Andrew stated as he stiffened his back. "I will do whatever Marie needs to help her," he said with absolute conviction.

"Do not forget to grieve yourself as well, Brother," Richard said as he gave his brother a hug.

Just then the butler announced the Fitzwilliam parents. They were without Lady Catherine who had left a few days earlier to go visit her daughter and son-in-law on their estate, Sherwood Park in Surrey. After Andrew informed them what had happened, his mother kissed both of his cheeks then proceeded into Marie's chambers. She was pleased to see Jane and Lizzy with Marie. She noticed that Jane's pregnancy seemed to be progressing apace but given what Marie had just lost, she made no comment to Jane in Marie's presence. She gave her grieving daughter-in-law a hug and kiss and then hugged her other daughter and her niece.

"We would have been here this morning, but we were visiting the Holders, so we only received the message after it was sent on from Snowhaven," Lady Elaine said as she replaced her niece next to Marie's bed.

"Mother Elaine," Marie said, much calmer now thanks to her sisters, "just like I could not predict that I would have this accident, you had no way of knowing that your presence would be needed at Hilldale. As my much wiser sisters," she looked at both Jane and Lizzy, "have ably pointed out, sometimes things happen, and we have no control over them. You are here now, that is all that counts."

The Countess was informed that the Longfield Meadows Bennets were on their way, and were expected in an hour or two, and that everyone expected the family from Longbourn to arrive in a few days. There was a knock on the door answered by Marie's maid, who allowed the three men to enter after she made sure that her mistress's modesty was preserved.

Andrew was much relieved to see that her sisters had calmed his wife considerably. It was expected that she would be sad for some time, but he felt somewhat better now that she seemed to have stopped blaming herself for what happened.

"I have a suggestion," Lord Reginal Fitzwilliam said after he made sure that his daughter was as well as could be expected. When he had the attention of all he continued. "Gardiner told me of an accoucheur, Sir Fredrick Gillingham, that has a sterling reputation who had seen his wife for her confinements. If you are worried that the fall has precluded your ability to have children, it could be worth your while to hie to Town once Marie is able to travel so that she may be examined by him."

"What do you think, Marie?" her husband asked. He had seated himself on the bed on her other side so he could hold her free hand.

"I like Father Reggie's suggestion, Andrew," she said softly. "If nothing else it will give me peace of mind."

"Then I will write to Sir Frederick and request an appointment, my love," he said as he placed an affectionate kiss on her wrist.

Marie indicated that she was weary, so the family wished her a good rest and withdrew from her chambers after requesting that her maid, who would sit with her mistress, inform the master as soon as his wife woke.

The Duke and Duchess of Bedford arrived while Marie was sleeping. They were filled in on the facts and commiserated with their brother-in-law while at the same time they were most grateful that Marie did not seem to have any permanent physical injury. When dinner was announced there was no formality observed and the conversation was subdued as Marie's empty chair reminded them that she was not able to join them. There was no separation of the sexes, and not long after dinner a footman notified them that the mistress was awake, and that Doctor Granger had arrived to check on the patient.

~~~~~~~/~~~~~~~

Lady Sarah was beside herself with worry. They had set off north within two hours of receiving the note from her son-in-law. The note was not too explicit, but he did let them know that Marie had an accident and it had caused a miscarriage. She had suspected that her daughter was with child before they had departed Hilldale to return to Longbourn, but Lady Sarah knew that Marie would share her news when she felt that the time was right. Mary and Kitty were left at Longbourn with their companions and guards. In addition, Charlotte Pierce was there if need be and she had promised to look in on the girls a few times a day.

Lord Thomas and Lady Rose had been much worried when they first read the note from Andrew, but were somewhat mollified that if it had been worse, the note from Andrew would have indicted thus.

Lady Rose still had her dreams where she spoke to her beloved Sed, but she had come to accept that they were dreams and not her talking to her dead husband's ghost. She thought about her Sed all the time, and the pain from his passing was still palpable and most probably would be until God took her home to join her husband in His kingdom. As much as she hated the reason, Lady Rose could not repine seeing her nephews and nieces again. How she loved all of her children and she drew strength from that love as she grieved her Sed.

The following morning, Lord Andrew Fitzwilliam received the express from Hertfordshire and calculated that his in-laws would arrive late that evening or the next day in the early morning. Knowing how her parents would want to be assured that his wife was well, he expected that they would arrive that night rather than spend another night in an inn. Luckily the moon would be full to aid them in their travels.

He shared the news with the rest of the family, none of whom were surprised that Marie's parents would arrive as soon as they were able. It was just before ten that night, a mere four days since the accident, when the Bennet carriages pulled up in front of Hilldale. After greeting everyone and being assured that their daughter was safe, the Bennet parents and Lady Rose went directly to Marie's chambers before their own chambers to change and wash from the road.

As soon as she saw her mother, father, and Aunt Rose, Marie burst into tears all over again. After kissing his daughter, Lord Thomas retreated to allow his wife and sister to talk to her and went to his chambers to change.

"My darling girl," Lady Sarah said with tears in her eyes, "I am so sorry that this happened to you. How are you feeling?"

"There is pain from the miscarriage, Mama," Marie said as she looked to both her beloved Aunt and her mother. "According to our physician, no more than to be expected after losing..." Marie could not complete the sentence.

"We know, my dear niece," Aunt Rose said as she looked lovingly at her surrogate daughter. "How is your head, Marie?"

"It is far better than the first day," Marie informed her two mothers.

"James is so sorry that he could not come. He had some issues that urgently needed his attention at Netherfield," Lady Sarah informed her second daughter. "He said to send him an express if he is needed."

"I miss James, Mama, but with all of the family here there is no need for him to come as well," Marie said with a wan smile.

When her mother asked if the local doctor could tell if the fall had affected her ability to become with child again, Marie told them what Father Reggie had suggested and that Andrew send a letter to the accoucheur and was waiting for his reply. Lady Sarah told her daughter that they would remain at Hilldale until the answer was received and Marie felt well enough to travel and would then accompany them back to London. It made Marie feel much better that she and Andrew would not be alone when they travelled to Town.

Later, after Lord Thomas had agreed to the plan, Sarah had told Elaine what they planned to do and after a short conference with her husband, Elaine informed her friend that they too would be travelling to London with Andrew and Marie.

CHAPTER 17

The *Coastal Trader* docked in Bundoran on schedule. Once all of her fore and aft lines were secured, and the gangway put in place, the unloading of freight destined for the town began. The Captain decided to walk to the Happy Leprechaun himself, and on arriving, he greeted the landlord, Rory O'Rourke, who he had met on his first run some five years previously. He informed the landlord that he had a letter for a Mrs. Johanna Álvarez, and that he had been charged with placing the missive into her hands personally.

O'Rourke sent one of his young sons up to Mrs. Álvarez's room to request that she come down to meet with the Captain. When Johanna descended, she was most inquisitive as to why the handsome man would seek her out, taken aback that he was the captain of the very ship she was avoiding. She adopted a coquettish manner which directly contradicted her mourning garb, and was somewhat miffed when she realized that Captain Beauclerk was not impressed or interested in her in the least. After all, her skills of attracting a man had been honed in gambling halls and brothels, so it was upsetting to not get any reaction from the tall, well-built man.

"Would you join me in the corner so we can talk in private?" Beauclerk asked. She nodded curtly letting all pretence fall since he could not be persuaded by her charms.

"What is it that I can do for you, Captain?" she asked, her annoyance conveyed in her tone.

"I have a letter that the postmaster in Ballycastle requested that I personally put into your hands," he told her as he held out the letter.

"There is no one that ..." The protest died in her throat as she saw the writing and recognised it as her son's hand. "Did you meet with the writer?" she asked softly.

"No, madam, I did not. The postmaster handed it to me with the charge to put it into your hands; which presumably is what the writer asked for." Seeing that she was about to quiz him further he added. "No, I did not see or meet the writer in Ballycastle, the postmaster handed me the missive to deliver. I apologise, but now that I have fulfilled my charge, I must return to my vessel and supervise the unloading and loading." He gave her a curt bow and left the inn before she could ask any more questions.

Johanna quickly made her way to her room, and as soon as the lock on her door clicked, she hungrily broke the seal and read.

2 July 1812
In the area of Ballycastle

Dear Mama,
I pray that you took what I said to heart in my previous letter and that this letter has not found you still in Bundoran. If it did reach you there, then I must make an appeal to you once again.

Please stop this madness, Mama! I have done some checking in a copy of Debretts that I found. Not only is the lady married to a duke and is the daughter of another, but the family are cousins to the royals! Close cousins, Mother. Any move against them is treason and your chances of success are no better than Wickham's were.

*Please do not make the mistakes that my father made and let greed rule your good sense. I know that you are an intelligent woman, Mother, so please use your God given faculties and stop this scheme before it is too late. If you try anything against the lady or a member of her family, it will be treason, Mama, and there is **only one** penalty for that. Please do not make me have to read about you meeting the same fate that my father met.*

I beseech you, Mother. If I did not love you or care about you, I would not write this letter to you, taking a chance that you will in-

form Younge where I am and have him search for me again. The post-master does not know my actual location, but I will check from time to time in case you wish to write to me. I still hope against hope that you will not tell Younge, and that you come to your senses and leave.

With much love and hope,

Your son, Tony

Johanna Álvarez was furious. How dare her son turn on her in this fashion. She was angry, and angry people seldom make wise decisions, so rather than think clearly about what her son wrote, she consigned his epistle to the fire, just like his first letter, and chose to again hide the information from the Younges.

Jones, Forester, and Tibbson watched from the shadows as the three particular crates were carried onto the *Coastal Trader* and taken below to the hold. Inside each was a drugged and very securely bound and gagged criminal. Forester thought back to the pleasure that he and his friends had had in their capturing.

Two days before the sloop was scheduled to arrive, they saw their opportunity. McLamb and his two cohorts had been drinking until the landlord stopped serving at the Happy Leprechaun. When they left, they had staggered towards the docks and went behind a ware-house to relive themselves and woke up bound, gagged, and in foul moods as they each had a headache for the ages as one would nat-urally receive after a blow to the head. They glared at their captives, the attempt to intimidate even when at such a disadvantage quickly changed to expressions of fear because the murderous looks in the eyes of the men standing over them was one no man did not innately fear.

"It aint' so easy when you are the one taken unawares, now is it?" Jones asked menacingly, though it was clear that the three captives did not understand the reference.

"The man ya murdered in Fowey was me mate!" Forester growled; his burning malice unmistakable in his voice. The three blanched, real fear overtaking their expressions. "He was a sergeant in the Royal Dragoons, an' 'is former Colonel, is real keen to 'ave a talk with you three!"

Jones stood in front of McLamb. "I am gonna take your gag off. Scream and you will lose your teeth! Do ya understand me?" The bound man nodded his head, so Jones inclined his head toward Tibbson who removed the gag.

McLamb hoped he could talk himself out of the very tough spot that he was in. "It wer'n't me that offed that man. If you let me free, I will bring the man to yous," he blustered.

"Do we looks like we be simpletons?" Jonesy asked menacingly. "We know exactly 'oo did the deed," his brown eyes burned holed into the murderer who turned away, "an' we know which despicable men 'elped you." Jones turned and glanced at the two men still gagged.

"It wern't me, I tell ya," McLamb said trying to sound convincing and received a hard punch to his gut for his trouble. As he doubled over in pain he started to yell and was silenced with a hard punch from Forester. Two teeth broke and two more were loosed, the broken ones spat out with blood.

"You be wastin' your time, we 'ave young Álvarez and he done tol' us everything," Jones said nonchalantly. He allowed his words to sink in, amused when their captives realised that lies would be a waste of time. "You two wanna lie to us?" Jones asked McLamb's cohorts who both shook their heads emphatically.

"Ya three be very lucky that 'is Grace wants ya alive," Tibbson told the three. "If it were up to us, ya three would be in Davy Jones's Locker by now!"

"His Grace?" McLamb murmured through the pain.

"Yeah, cousins to the royals they be. You and your capt'n 'ave no idea 'oo you bin messing wif!" Forester informed them and was not unhappy when he saw their captives' blanch as McLamb was again gagged.

Forester smiled as he thought of the pleasure that he felt when he hit McLamb in the mouth, he would have liked to end is miserable life, but they were charged to deliver the captive alive. All three watched with pleasure as the last of the crates disappeared below deck. They made their way to the Happy Leprechaun for their midday meal as they did every day; the last thing they wanted to do was change their routine to give

Younge and his cronies reason to question them.

The next morning the *Coastal Trader* sailed for Dublin with the tide just as she did every month. The Dennington men had succeeded spectacularly as no one was the wiser. As the sloop sailed on her way toward her destination that evening, the three ex-marines sat at their table eating their meal when Younge approached. As he had the last time that the sloop was at Bundoran, he had kept himself out of the public eye until she sailed.

"You three be sailors, aint ya?" he asked without preamble and the three men nodded. "Ow would ya like to get outa 'ere in a month or so men?"

"We would at that, Capt'n," Jones answered for the group.

"I 'appen to 'ave an opening in me crew, and I needs three good men; is ya three up fir it?" The three looked suitably surprised and grateful as they discussed terms with Younge. Later, Jones dropped a missive off with the postmaster to an address in Dublin. It was very short and simply read: *'Success, we be in the crew, Jones.'*

On the *Coastal Trader*, once the town was no longer visible, the three men were extracted from their crates, and when they awoke, they were shocked to find themselves chained to the bulkhead in the brig on a ship.

~~~~~~~/~~~~~~~

Lady Anne arrived a day after the Duke and Duchess of Hertfordshire and the Dowager Duchess of Bedford at Hilldale. After washing and changing, she met Elizabeth and William in their suite's sitting room. "Is Marie doing any better, Lizzy?" she asked her daughter-in-law with concern.

"Yes, Mother Anne, she is," Elizabeth allayed Lady Anne's fears. "With Jane and me helping her see that this was nothing more than a terrible accident, followed by the arrival of Aunt Elaine and Amy who talked with her as well, she was already starting to feel a little better. Mama, Aunt Rose, and Papa being here had helped a lot, but she really wants to talk to you, Mother Anne."

"Of course, I will assist her in any way that I am able," Lady Anne said firmly. "Has she had much bleeding since the event?"

"Not much at all," Elizabeth said, "In fact, Doctor Granger said that the fact that since her accident she has had little bleeding is a very good indicator for a full recovery."

"I remember after your one miscarriage how concerned my father was that there was so much bleeding, mother," Darcy said. "He tried to keep it from me, but I heard him talking to the doctor."

"Yes, William, I remember how concerned George was. God spared me then as He did after I birthed Georgie, and I am still here with by beloved family now so much larger than it used to be," she smiled. "Is Marie resting, or may I go to see her?"

"Let us go to her directly. Mama and Aunt Elaine are with her, but she made me promise that I would bring you to see her as soon as you arrived," Elizabeth told her mother-in-law as she stood, and the two ladies walked to the master suite while Darcy went to go join the others in the family sitting room.

When Lady Anne entered the viscountess's chambers with her younger sister, Marie came as close to smiling as she had since her fall. She was very keen to be able to talk to one who had experienced what she just had. Ladies Sarah and Elaine greeted Elizabeth and Lady Anne, then both kissed Marie and went to join the rest of the family. Elizbeth kissed Marie's cheek and told her that she would see her a little later as she was sure that it would be best to leave her sister and mother-in-law to talk in private.

"Thank you for coming, Aunt Anne," Marie said as she started to cry again. "Oh, I am such a watering pot lately," she chided herself.

"Do you believe that I was any different the times that I miscarried? I was even worse after my Colin was stillborn," Lady Anne told her niece as she held her hand tightly. "I thought that part of me died each time, and I had three of them."

"That is just how I feel," Marie said with relief at knowing that she was not mad for feeling as she did. "Will the pain ever go away fully?"

"It will with time, and when God gifts you with a babe, this will be a distant memory that you will have difficulty remembering ever happened," Lady Anne shared and was happy to see the look of relief on Marie's face.

"Lizzy and Jane both told me it was not my fault, but it was hard for me to accept," Marie said through her tears. "Jane reminded me that miscarriage is a risk that all woman face. I realised that it was self-indulgent of me to believe that I am the only one to suffer like this. You did not fall or have any other injury that caused your three events, did you Aunt Anne?"

"No, Marie dear, I did not," Lady Anne said. It was not easy talking about her disappointments, but if some good for Marie could come out of her past experiences then she was more than willing to canvass the difficult subject for as long as her niece required her to do so.

"Your late husband was not disappointed by your..." Marie still had a hard time saying the word too often.

"No Marie, not at all," Lady Anne answered vehemently. It dawned on her that the biggest part of Marie's guilt was a feeling that she failed her husband. Lady Anne had thought the same at the time but had quickly learnt that all her husband cared about was her wellbeing and did not blame her for that over which she had no control. She took both of her niece's hands in her own. "Look at me, Marie!" she instructed.

Marie lifted her head and wiped the tears from her eyes and looked into her aunt's eyes. "I want to say this plainly so there is no room for misunderstanding," Lady Anne said firmly but with sympathy, "Not for one moment did my dear George blame me. Just like Andrew loves you, he loved me and his *only* worry, as I know is the case with Andrew, was my health and wellbeing. The love that you share with Andrew would be a shallow and sad kind of love if he were to blame you for something in which you have no blame. Is that the kind of love that you and Andrew share Marie?"

"No, we have the deepest love..." Marie's mouth formed a

perfect 'O' as it dawned on her that her aunt's question had been designed to break through her malaise and force her to face the truth. There was only one person who was blaming her...herself. As the realisation washed over her, she felt the weight of the self-imposed guilt lift. She would grieve for the child that she would never have, which was only natural, but she would no longer indulge in misplaced guilt, and she knew that her love would be there to support her without any recriminations. She thanked her aunt for helping her see the truth and requested that she tell Andrew that his wife would like to see him.

"Aunt Anne said that you wanted to see me, my love," Andrew said as he closed the bedchamber door.

"Yes, my dear Andrew. I need to offer a very big apology to you..." He cut her off, presuming that she was going to take the blame for what happened on herself.

"Marie, we have all told you it was not your..." His wife's fingers on his lips silenced him.

"I understand and accept that, my husband," she assured him as she removed her hand from his lips and took his large hand in her smaller one. "My apology is that I did not trust our love as I should have. I was worried that you would blame me until Aunt Anne made me see that was the furthest thing from the truth; that the love that we share is strong enough to overcome any of life's trials that we face, together.

"You are my heart, Andrew, and I will never allow churlish thoughts to make me forget that we will always support one another no matter what." Andrew was overjoyed that his wife had come to accept that she bore no blame for the miscarriage and leaned over to kiss his wife soundly.

"All of the family members' lives would be so different if God had not returned Aunt Anne to us after she birthed Georgie," Andrew said as he lifted his eyes to the heavens to thank the Lord for sparing his Aunt. He looked at his wife with love and adoration, relived that she had moved past her misplaced feelings of guilt. "Did Mr. Granger say when you would be able to travel to London, my love?"

"When he examined me earlier, he said that as soon as I felt well enough, Andrew," she offered her first genuine smile since her loss. "Would you ring for my maid? I think that I would like to join the family. How does departing in two days sound?"

"That will be perfect, my love," he agreed happily. "I received a note back from Sir Frederick, and he said to contact him as soon as we are in Town and he will be able to see us."

"Once I am checked by him and he says that all is well then, we will just have to start again, and I am very much looking forward to the attempts," she said with an almost seductive smile. Andrew rang for her maid with glee and went back to the family to first kiss and thank Aunt Anne, and let the rest of the family know about their travel plans.

~~~~~~~/~~~~~~~

McLamb and his crewmates were very uncomfortable; they were in a brig and in chains. On the second day of sailing toward Dublin they were visited by the ship's captain.

"Why be you doin' some toff's dirty work?" McLamb spat out.

"Because, that "toff," as you call him," Beauclerk answered calmly, "is the Duke that *owns* the Dennington Lines, and I work for him." All three men shrunk back. Not only had they made an enemy of a close relation of the royals, but of one that seemed to have unlimited resources.

"Whots' gonna 'appen to us," asked one of the others, the fear threading in his voice making it quiver.

"Tomorrow when we dock in Dublin, you three will be transferred to one of our ships headed for Liverpool, from there you will be escorted to Brookfield where an ex-colonel will meet you," the men looked in question and then all three men turned white. "From what I understand he is very much looking forward to meeting you and properly giving his appreciation for your deeds in Fowey."

Any fight that may have been left in the three was gone. They had no doubt that in the very near future they would be paying for all of their crimes. Beauclerk left and the door in the bulkhead that led to the brig was locked, leaving three men to contemplate the remaining duration of their miserable lives.

~~~~~~~/~~~~~~~

Tony Álvarez was revelling on his work with Pemberley's steward. He found it very fulfilling to see the results of his labours, and to be able to help others at the same time. He had met a good number of the estate's tenants and had seen in them the same contentment that had first led him to question his and his mother's choices in Bundoran. They did not have much, but they had enough and were happy, not looking to others to provide them with that which they did not earn.

What impressed Tony further was the reverence with which both the tenants and servants held the master and the new mistress. He had seen for himself that the Duke and Duchess were always fair toward those who dependent them, even went out of their way to help, when and if needed. He did not miss the genuine loyalty that he saw towards the Darcy's from all on the estate, and when he contrasted that to Younge and his crew, he saw a vast difference. Younge's men were afraid of him, but were loyal to their own self-interest. Young Álvarez had been invited to share a dinner with Pemberley's vicar, Mr. Elliot, and his wife. As he rode the cob that had been provided for his use while at Pemberley toward the parsonage, he remembered his riding lessons when he first arrived at the state.

His Grace, Lord Darcy, had asked Tony if he could ride, to which the young man answered in the negative. Given the size of the estate and the plan to have Tony work with the steward, he was told to go see the stablemaster who would teach him to ride.

Mr. Toby Carlson had started as a groom fifteen years previously. The former master had recognised his talent with horses and the respect that the men that worked with him held him in; and Carson had risen fast, becoming the under-stablemaster after three years. When his predecessor and mentor retired five years later, George Darcy promoted him knowing that there was not a better man for the position. He was a gruff man, but was always fair, and he was an excellent riding instructor.

It had taken a week of intensive lessons from Carlson before Tony was allowed to ride outside of the training ring. A week after that he was introduced to the cob that he now rode and told that it would be his for as long as he remained at Pemberley.

Tony smiled as he thought back on his lessons and all the other kindnesses that had been shown him since his arrival. He tied the cob with a long line so it could reach the grass and water easily then knocked on the door.

"Welcome, young Álvarez," the parson said as he extended his hand. "Do you need to wash before we sit down?" Tony indicated that he did and was directed to the kitchen where a basin of warm water was prepared for him. After he dried his face and hands, he returned to the drawing room, and a few minutes later the housekeeper informed them that dinner was ready.

It was a very convivial atmosphere in the Elliots' house, proving once again to Tony where true happiness was to be found. "Have you heard back from Oxford?" Mrs. Elliot asked her guest.

"I have Mrs. Elliot," Tony replied with pride. "With the backing of their Graces and the Duke of Derbyshire willing to fund my studies, I have been accepted to Oxford to begin my studies when the school year commences in September."

"Do you still want to read the law?" Elliot asked.

"No sir," Tony stated emphatically. Seeing the questioning looks form his hosts he explained. "These weeks that I have worked with Mr. Chalmers have shown me a path that piques my interest more than the law. My intention is to get a gentleman's education, then I will return to work as an under-steward under Mr. Chalmers One day I hope that I will be ready to become a steward in my own right," he stated with pride.

"Will you be happy working for others, Tony?" Elliot asked. "I have no doubt that you have the intelligence and drive for the path that you have chosen, as long it is the true calling for you."

"Once I realised that very little of that which my parents taught me was correct, and I finally understood from where true happiness is derived," Tony explained what he only recently himself had come to understand, "it was as if I was starting my life again, and from this point on the past influences were removed completely.

"It is fulfilling work that I find I enjoy immensely. I had considered the law as it was as far removed from my parents as possible, but I had an epiphany and now know that it is not for me to atone for their crimes and my life is my own. I want to live a good life, a life of service, and I believe the path I have chosen is the one for me."

"Will you not feel resentment toward the Darcys and the Bennets if your mother does not change her path and meets her end?" Elliot asked a penetrating question.

Tony considered his answer carefully before responding. "No sir. Her choices are hers alone," he answered sombrely. "I have written her two letters beseeching her to change her path, but I realize I have no control over her decision more than that. Just like I made my choice to live a righteous life, she can do so as well. Just like it was no one but my father's fault that he met his end at the end of the hangman's noose, If that is my mother's fate, it will be her decisions that lead her there. I refuse to blame the victims as she and her cohorts do for the ills that they themselves have wrought.

"If she does not choose a different path, and he meets her end, I will be sad as I will always love her, but I know that I have done everything in my power, and the decision is hers to make."

"You are wise beyond your eighteen years," Emily Elliot offered with pride for the young man she saw maturing day by day before her eyes.

CHAPTER 18

No matter how much Marie had protested that they did not need to join them, all of the family that had been at Hilldale, excepting Tom and Amy Bennet, made the trip with them to town. The new Duke and Duchess of Bedford still had a lot that they needed to accomplish at Longfield Meadows before they took a longer break from the estate. The day before the departure, Darcy had collected his sister and her companion from Pemberley, and the caravan made a detour to Longbourn where Georgie and Mrs. Annesley joined Mary and Kitty and their companions.

The groups decided that they would open only two of their houses, so the younger set would reside at Darcy House while the parents would be at Bennet House. On their arrival, Andrew sent a note to Sir Frederick and received a prompt reply that the accoucheur would see Marie at ten the following morning. By ten minutes before the hour, Lord Andrew Fitzwilliam presented his card to the butler at Gillingham House and he and his wife were shown into a parlour used as a waiting room.

A few minutes before ten, a nurse asked the Viscountess to follow her to the examination room. Andrew wanted to go with her, but the nurse told him that husbands waited while their wives were examined, and Marie assured him that she would be well. More than a half hour later, Marie returned to her husband and they were shown into Sir Frederick's study.

"Please sit," the accoucheur indicated two chairs facing his desk. "Welcome Lord Fitzwilliam." He started, then without preamble the physician explained his findings. "Her ladyship explained what happened and how she fell. I cannot be sure, but I believe that had Lady Hilldale not fallen her state would have continued to the natural conclusion. During my examination I found nothing that would indicate that your wife will not be able to become with child again.

"My theory is that because you fell on your belly with force, it caused damage to the foetus and the body's way of protecting itself was to miscarry. Had you landed in your posterior, or just about anywhere else other than right on your belly, I believe that this would not have happened. Based on what I observed, Lady Hilldale is healthy and can return to a full level of activity as soon as she feels able," the man concluded, his short and concise manner.

"When can we...er..." Marie was not sure how to ask the question.

"Are you asking when you may have marital relations again?" Sir Frederick asked and both nodded sheepishly. "My answer is the same as I told you for normal activity. As soon as Lady Hilldale feels no more pain and there is no more spotting, then you are free to resume *all* of your normal routines."

"Thank you, Sir Frederick, you have relieved much stress with your advice today," Andrew said as he stood and shook the accoucheur's hand. "May I ask you an unrelated question?"

"You may ask whatever you wish, my lord," Sir Frederick responded with an incline of his head.

"Do you travel out of the environs of London to attend ladies for their lying in?" Andrew asked hopefully. "I think that we," he looked to his wife for confirmation and she nodded as she had a very good idea what her husband was asking, "would feel more comfortable if you were able to be with Marie when we are so blessed."

"Your estate is in Staffordshire, correct my Lord?" Andrew nodded that it was so. "That unfortunately is too far for me to travel as I would not be able to attend to my patients in London. However, if the Viscountess were in London for her eventual lying in, then I would be happy to attend her," the accoucheur said in apology for not being able to attend them at Hilldale.

"Let me become with child again first before we worry where

I will be for my confinement, Andrew," Marie said as she placed her hand lightly on her husband's arm.

"I find that I must defer to my very wise wife," Andrew said with a half-smile, "she is correct. I was putting the cart before the horse."

As they had no more questions, the Fitzwilliams thanked Sir Frederick for his time and departed his study. As they left Gillingham House, Andrew placed the expected gratuity in the box for that purpose. They returned to Darcy House where they knew that the family was anxiously awaiting their news.

<center>~~~~~~~/~~~~~~~</center>

Clay Younge was very happy with his three new crew members. Not only did they know what they were about as sailors, but they were all big men who he felt had skills that would be very useful if they were ever in a fight. He gave no further thought to McLamb and his two cronies disappearing, he instead thought how providence had smiled on him to make an opening in his crew and gift him three of the best crewmembers that he had ever had aboard.

Johanna Álvarez was still seething at the temerity of her son for lecturing her. Who was *he* to tell *her* what to do? She did not want to admit it to herself or anyone else, but she was having doubts about the chances of success of their plan. However, as quickly as the doubts were considered, she dismissed them because revenge would be had.

Johanna could clearly see that Karen Younge was delusional, but she could not see the same weakness in her own person. She was aware that they were attempting to harm a member of one of the most powerful families in the realm, after the royals, and that if they were caught after the attempt to kidnap Lady Elizabeth, that there was only one punishment, hanging. There would be no chance of mercy or transportation. Unfortunately for Johanna Álvarez, her avarice overrode her good sense as she told herself that they would succeed for her husband where Wickham had failed them all.

The prior evening the three conspirators had decided that

they would sail a day after the *Coastal Trader* departed in August, in less than a month's time. All were most relieved to finally have decided on a date for their plan. It had been pleasant enough in Bundoran, but other than the inn there was no entertainment. For many months now there had been no wenches or ladies of ill repute. Having no one with which they could slake their needs, the information had been especially welcome to the members of the crew. The barmaids at the Happy Leprechaun had been friendly, but had never permitted any liberties, and the captain had made it clear what would happen to anyone who caused trouble while they were waiting to return to England.

The three new crew members were also very pleased, but not for the reasons that their shipmates assumed. As soon as the date of departure was set and the destination confirmed, Jones wrote a letter and handed it to the postmaster to send to the Dennington offices in Liverpool. The three could not wait to be away from the group of miscreants and return to their own ship, but they would see their duty through until the conclusion.

~~~~~~~~/~~~~~~~~

McLamb and his two accomplices looked around nervously as they were pulled from the back of the cart that had transported them from Liverpool. Originally, they were headed for Brookfield in Derbyshire, but then the destination changed and rather than one day, they had travelled three. McLamb had heard one of the twelve outriders mention 'Hertfordshire' and 'Longbourn.'

The Liverpool manager for the lines had received an express telling him to send the prisoners to the Duke's estate near Meryton as Lord Brookfield would be there and not at his estate. The man in charge of making sure that the three arrived at the correct destination was Mr. Standish, he was the fifth son of a minor country squire, and had been a major in the army, he was employed by the company after he resigned his commission three years ago.

The head guard was met by Longbourn's butler, Mr. Hill, who

had instructions from his Grace on how to 'accommodate' the criminals until the family returned from London on the morrow. "There is a room with no windows and a very solid oak door in that barn," Mr. Hill pointed it out to the guard. "You are to place these," Mr. Hill pointed to the captives with disdain, "there. You will find a sufficient number of irons for their hands and legs waiting, and we will get more should you want to make it more unpleasant."

"Thank you, Mr. Hill. We will make sure that this trash is secure in the barn, then my men and I will do eight hour shifts, four of us at a time, to make sure that no one," he looked at the three frightened men malevolently, "tries anything unadvisable."

The three were secured in the room in the barn. There were three pallets of straw on the floor, a bucket of water with a ladle for them to drink from, and another bucket for them to use as needed to relieve themselves. Once the three were secured in the manacles, some bread and cheese was brought in for their meal and the door was securely locked.

~~~~~~~/~~~~~~~

With the news that Marie and Andrew had shared with them after the examination by Sir Frederick, the following day a much-relieved family departed London for Longbourn. None returned to their own estates as all of the men wanted to be present for the three criminals' interrogation. James Bennet had received an express from his father instructing him to leave the men be until the party arrived from Town. Lord Thomas did not want to take a chance that James would take his displeasure out on them before Richard had made sure that all information had been extracted.

The Marquess of Netherfield, along with his three sisters who were in residence at Longbourn and the Hills, met the carriages that arrived from Town. James went directly to his sister Marie and enfolded her in a hug, asking for himself if she was feeling better. He was very pleased to take note that there did not seem to be any outward physical signs of the trauma that Marie had endured. She assured him that while she still grieved for the babe that would not be, she was as well as could be expected.

As keen as the men were to start the interrogation, they agreed that they should wash, change, join their wives for tea, and share what they knew so far with them. One angry Bennet lady, more than any of them, wanted to face the men. Angering multiple Bennet ladies was not something any of the men were willing to do, so they complied knowing that the prisoners would not be going anywhere.

At the summation of the tea and treats from Longbourn's kitchens, Lord Thomas requested that his butler summon the head guard to the drawing room. When the man entered, he bowed to those within.

"Standish, is it not?" Lord Thomas asked.

"Yes, your Grace, that is correct," Standish responded, impressed that the owner of the shipping line knew who he was.

"I trust that all three are well enough for my son-in-law to *talk* to them?" Lord Thomas asked with a sardonic smile.

"They are, your Grace," the head guard smirked. "None too happy, but that was not our concern."

"Did they say anything on the journey that you think useful?" Bennet asked.

"Not that I noted, your Grace," Standish said as he searched his memory. "Not that I heard, and if they had said something to one of my men it would have been reported to me right away."

"Have you met my son-in-law the Earl of Brookfield, the former Colonel Richard Fitzwilliam?" Lord Thomas asked as he inclined his head toward Richard.

"I have not had the pleasure, your Grace, but like so many other officers, I do know of his exploits," Standish said as he gave Richard a half bow which was returned with an incline of the head.

"What do you say that we move this conversation into the barn, gentlemen," Richard suggested, and none present disagreed.

Lady Elizabeth tried to use the same logic she did when she

asked to be in the meeting with young Tony, but in this instance both her father and husband said no and were supported by her brothers. She begrudgingly understood the reasoning for her not being present, and was mollified when her husband promised that he would tell her all when they had time to themselves later.

~~~~~~~/~~~~~~~

The three prisoners were unshackled from the chains that connected to the wall and unceremoniously dragged by the manacles to stand in front of men who would decide their fate. Their interrogators were sitting on chairs facing them with looks of disgust from all. Richard, who the three were intimidated the most by, because of the fury in his visage, did not speak right away as he gave them time to contemplate their futures, or lack thereof.

"Which one of you is McLamb?" Richard demanded. The offender raised his hand slowly. More than anything Richard wished that he had his sabre; he would have liked nothing more than to run the dastard through. He brought himself under regulation after a short time as he breathed deeply. "Why did you murder my man?"

McLamb mumbled something that none of the men could hear. One of the guards moved toward him menacingly so he repeated it loud enough for all to understand, "Me cap'n ordered it."

"So Clay Younge is God? When he gives and order, you have to obey and do not have the ability to ask yourself what is right or wrong? Before you give me all sorts of excuses," Richard growled, "you could have knocked him out or bound and gagged him, yet you and your band of misfits would have been long gone before he was discovered," Richard spat at the man. "I will wager that you are one of those bullies who likes to inflict pain on helpless people.

"You big, brave man," Richard drove his fist into the man's stomach causing him to double over gasping for air. McLamb would have fallen to the floor if it were not for the two guards holding his arms. "You had these two wasted human beings," he pointed angrily at the accomplices, "hold sergeant Hamms down while you did the deed; showing him mercy never entered that evil mind of yours.

"Hamms served with me on the continent and survived untold hell, returned to his wife and children whole, only to have his life stolen by the likes of you in a most cowardly fashion. The rope is too good for you. If I had my way, I would use you to sharpen my skills with my sabre."

"I can...tell ya...about the...cap'n's plans if...you spare me," McLamb said as he tried to regain his breath in a vain attempt to save his neck.

"There is nothing that you can tell us that we do not already know," Lord Thomas glowered at the prisoners as he stepped forward. "My men who captured you are the crew members that your captain took on to replace you, so we will know everything that we need to know, and from a source that we can trust."

"We also have the advantage of young Tony Álvarez, who was most forthcoming and told us about all of the half-witted plans that were made before he left Bundoran," Lord William added, relishing their shocked looks at the mention of Tony.

"The yung-uns not dead?" one of the men blurted out.

"No. Unlike any of you, he has a *conscience* and could not sit idly by and do nothing. If you had one, then you would not have a date with the hangman in the next week or two," Lord William informed the criminals who only now fully understood that they had no leverage and their lives would be in the hands of a judge and jury at the Old Bailey. The accomplices had a sliver of hope at transportation rather than being hung, but it was fifty-fifty at best.

Richard turned to his family, "There is nothing to be learned here, so much for an interrogation. We know much more than they could tell us as we have our own men in the crew. We could have gone home as we have learnt nothing new from these snivelling weasels. At the very least, I had hoped to see some expression of remorse for what was done, but I do not believe the man is capable. Do any of you want to ask them anything?" The five shook their heads. "That being the case, Standish," Richard called the man over.

"Yes, my Lord," Standish offered.

Richard whispered in his father-in-law's ear and received a nod of agreement from the man, and then turned to the head guard, "Could I impose on you and your men to escort this trash to the Old Bailey?" he requested.

"That will not be an imposition, Lord Brookfield," Standish replied snapping a smart salute to the ex-colonel, "it will be our pleasure to serve you."

"You have all of the statements from the witnesses as well as their confessions, correct?" Richard confirmed. Standish nodded allowing that the Earl was correct. "One more thing, Standish. Make sure that none of the three are allowed contact with any but yourselves and that they are not, under any circumstances, allowed to send letters to *anyone*."

"It will be so, your Lordship," Standish replied.

"There is a way to make sure that they have no chance to repeat what they heard today," Lord Thomas offered. He saw the comprehension on William's face, but the others looked at him, quizzically.

"What do you mean Thomas?" Reggie asked.

"I will write an express to our cousins," he offered, watching as understanding dawned. "In it I will explain that these men are part of the plot to harm Lizzy. The Regent will order them to the Tower to pay the price for treason."

There was quick agreement that it was for the best. Richard called Standish over to supply him with the new destination. The two accomplices would soon find out that there would be no transportation, and the sentence would be carried out in a few days, rather than weeks.

With their remaining future decided, the three were dragged back into the room and the chains on the wall were reattached to their manacles. On the morrow as the sun rose, they would be back in the open cart that had transported them to Longbourn for one last journey.

As they walked back toward the manor house, Lord Matlock put his hand on his younger son's shoulder. "I know that you wanted to do the deed yourself, Richard," his father condoled. "Remember, we never want to be like these men, we follow the law, and you did that today no matter what your own desires were. If one of them had been stupid enough to try something, I would have handed you the sabre myself son. I am very proud of you my son. Do not forget that within a few days they will lose their heads."

"Any one of us would have happily performed the task, father," Andrew said seriously, "even though none of us served with the late Sergeant Hamms in the army like Richard did."

"It will be up to the Tower's executioner to make them pay the price for their crimes," Lord Thomas pointed out.

"If any of these schemers get near my sister…" James spat out with anger.

"No one with malevolent intentions will be allowed near my wife, James," William said with certainty. "As soon as we receive the group's final plans from our men, we will know how and when to act."

"At the very least I can inform Mrs. Hamms that her husband's murderers will face justice," Richard said with resignation. "Some men just do not have honour and it has nothing to do with their class. I have seen the lowliest privates display bravery and honour and Lords with none."

"Let us return to the women who love us, brother," Andrew offered as he placed his hand on Richard's shoulder. "Do not waste any more thoughts or energy on men who deserve none."

When the men entered the drawing room, Lord Thomas requested that the three younger women excuse themselves. Once they had departed for the music room, he informed the remaining ladies what had decided. With the fate of the three sealed, it left only the group in Bundoran to deal with.

As they would depart for Pemberley the following day, Elizabeth asked her husband to accompany her on a walk to Long-bourn village's parsonage to visit her friend Charlotte. When Charlotte's housekeeper answered the knock, Lady Elizabeth quietly asked her to allow her to surprise her friend. The lady agreed and informed her Grace that the mistress was in the day parlour. Charlotte Pierce looked up expecting to see her husband or the housekeeper, and instead their stood the Duke and Duchess of Derbyshire!

"Eliza, beg your pardon, *your* Grace," Charlotte teased as she knew from their letters that her friend did not desire any formality between them. "I did not know that you would be here, what a good surprise." She looked to her friend's husband. "Welcome to our home, your Grace. Mr. Pierce is in the study if you would like to join him while Eliza and I catch up."

"I am happy to see you as well, Charlotte," Elizabeth said as they hugged. "Is there something that you have forgotten to mention in your letters to me, Mrs. Pierce," Elizabeth asked as she arched an eyebrow and looked at her friend's belly after they had hugged.

"My intention was to inform you in my next letter Eliza, it was but a few days ago that I felt the quickening," Charlotte shared her happiness.

"Before this conversation proceeds any further," William said, "I think that I would enjoy talking to your husband, Mrs. Pierce. If it will not be an imposition." Charlotte rang for the housekeeper and asked her to show his Grace to Mr. Pierce's study.

Once the door closed the two friends sat on the settee close to one another. "How are Emma and Paul taking the news that there will be a baby in the house soon, Charlotte?" Elizabeth enquired.

"They are both most excited, Paul demands a brother, while Emma wants a sister," Charlotte smiled as she thought about her children, currently on a walk with their nursemaid.

"I am certain that Sir William and Lady Lucas are happy at becoming grandparents again," Elizabeth stated with surety.

"Did Frank pluck up the courage to ask Miss Poole for a courtship?"

"Yes, he did," Charlotte nodded, "and she happily accepted. My Christopher told me about some criminals being held in one of the barns, what did they do?" Charlotte asked her friend.

Elizabeth told her the story of the murder, and then about the plans that the blackguards were trying to make to kidnap her. Charlotte was mollified when Elizabeth explained that they were, and would continue to be, aware of all plans, and that those still conspiring would never be allowed to hurt anyone.

The two filled each other in on the happenings since their last exchange of letters, and Elizabeth was saddened that due to Charlotte's being with child she and her family would not be able to visit Pemberley later that year. When the ladies had completed their *tête-à-tête,* Charlotte rang for the housekeeper and ordered tea, asking that their husbands be summoned to join them. The men entered the drawing room just before the refreshments arrived. Little Miss Pierce and young Master Pierce came down to greet the guests after they had washed and changed after their walk. They both loved 'Aunt Eliza', and begged her to tell them a story. Their aunt explained that there was not time on this visit, but the next time they visited each other, she would tell them a very long story.

After tea, the Darcys returned to the manor house and enjoyed the evening among family very well indeed. There was no talk of plans, criminals, or accidents, they simply enjoyed being in company with loved ones. On the morrow the four families travelling north left Longbourn in convoy.

CHAPTER 19

Once the Regent agreed that the three men had committed treason, it was only two days later that they met the executioner at the Tower. By the time that the families traveling north reached their estates, the deed was done. The Duke of Hertfordshire wrote to both the Liverpool manager and the *Coastal Trader's* captain instructing them to communicate directly with the Earl of Brookfield, who would coordinate efforts once the conspirator's final plans were known.

The day after all four Darcys returned to Pemberley they met with Tony to see how he was enjoying his time on the estate. The original plan had been for him to stay on Pemberley until the criminals were all in custody, but before they departed Longbourn it was agreed that if the group in Bundoran did not execute their doomed to fail plan by the time that the new school year commenced at Oxford, that young Álvarez should not miss out because of it.

"Has any post been forwarded to you from Ballycastle, Tony?" Elizabeth asked.

"No, your Grace, nothing as of yet," Tony said, the disappointment evident in his voice. "I hoped against hope that my mother would be moved by my letter, but in my heart, I knew she would not be."

"You never know," Darcy said, trying to give the young man some hope even though he agreed with Tony's assessment. "Sometimes people surprise us," he stated as he looked at his duchess.

"I am afraid that she is too set in her ways," Tony replied

dejectedly, "Like her cohorts, she has come to believe that it is her due. There is no doubt in my mind that somehow she had blamed her Grace for my decision to make my own way and seek an honest life."

"Sad as it may be," Elizabeth said as she commiserated with the young man, "just look at where you have come, all by the honourable decisions that you have made. You have to know that we and the rest of the family will always support you."

"I thank you for your kind words, your Grace," he said with a bow of his head to both Darcys. "It is good to know that I have support if I need it, but I am determined to succeed on my own merits."

Both husband and wife lauded his resolve, and after him telling them what he had been doing on the estate he was invited to dinner in two days hence when the Elliots would be guests as well.

~~~~~~~/~~~~~~~

Lady Marie Fitzwilliam woke up and for the first morning since her accident she had no pain at all. She rolled over and watched her Andrew sleep, drinking in his handsome features. She willed him to wake wanting to resume all aspects of their married life now that she was no longer experiencing any discomfort. As if his heart heard hers calling out to him, Lord Andrew began to stir. As he slowly opened his eyes, he thought he was dreaming that his beautiful wife was lying propped up on her elbow watching him. As Marie's hand rested on his cheek, he was assured that this was no dream.

"Marie, my love, how do you feel this morning?" he asked hopefully. He wanted nothing more than to resume marital relations with his wife, but would not push her, and had promised himself to wait for a clear signal from her.

"I am well, Andrew," she smiled seductively. "In fact, I feel *better* than I have even before my fall," she said as her hand started to trail down his body until it rested on his tumescent organ.

"A-are you sure, Marie?" he asked, his breath hitching when

her answer came in the form of his wife stroking him. He pulled her into his arms, kissing her soundly.

When the master and mistress eventually rang for their personal servants, much later than was their wont, he was grinning from ear to ear with satisfaction, and she, with happiness after being soundly loved. After they assisted their employers to bathe and dress, her Abigail and his valet gave each other knowing looks but said not a word as they would never discuss any private information that they were privy to with a single soul.

No one needed to inform the servants that something had shifted to as it was before the accident with the viscount and his viscountess. They could once again see the happiness that radiated from the two. The two in question had a lightness to their step, similar to when the master had first brought the mistress home after their wedding trip. Both members of the couple were ruminating on the pleasure of the many times they would make love and hopefully return Marie to the state that she had been in before her fall.

~~~~~~~/~~~~~~~

Other than his wife, the rest of the family had transitioned to wearing half mourning six weeks after Uncle Sed's passing. At the end of August, they would end their formal mourning of their beloved brother and uncle, but he would forever be in their thoughts. At Longfield Meadows, the Duke and Duchess of Bedford had grown much more comfortable in their new roles.

Amy now knew that although her duties as duchess were many, with her own abilities and the support of her large family, she had fully embraced her new role. She continued Aunt Rose's tradition of visits to the tenants. By now she had visited each family in person and had learnt about each of the families and their needs.

Her loving husband was happy to see how relaxed his wife was and the seamless way that she had taken over her duties. Once he had owned that his initial doubts and fears were irrational, Lord Tom never looked back. Working closely with Mr. Mason, Tom had reviewed all aspects of the running of the estate and planned the upcoming harvest. He felt it was time for him and his wife to tour the other four estates that they had gained with the ascension to the title. The largest of the secondary estates, Nine Oaks, was in Yorkshire, so it was a logical place to start. The next estate in size was Dumfries Castle, near Dumfries in Scotland. The final two small estates were in Berkshire and would be visited last. The last two had the advantage of being close to Town and had been used for house parties during the season by his predecessors.

Uncle Sed was planning to purchase a small estate between the two and create one larger property as a single combined estate. Tom planned to consider the purchase when he and Amy visited, as the idea of having a decent sized estate that close to London was appealing to him. There would not be an issue with the entail on the properties under the Bedford dukedom as he would be adding land, not subtracting it. He summoned the butler and asked that he inform the Duchess he would like to see her. The man bowed to the master and went to fulfil his charge. Not two minutes later his Amy entered his study as he stood and came around his desk to welcome her with a hug.

"You wanted to see me, Husband?" she raised her eyebrows in question.

"I did, my Amy," Tom answered as he gently led her to the loveseat under the windows. "After thinking about a tour to see the other estates that we own for some time now, I feel that we are both confident enough in our duties to undertake a trip of about a month. Do you have any objection to our doping so?"

"No, my love. I can see no reason that would cause us to delay," his wife responded with a kiss to his cheek. She thought for a moment and then added, "What if the miscreants move against Lizzy while we are away?"

"We will make sure that the family knows where we will be and when," Tom informed his wife. "I am supremely confident that Lizzy will be well protected. Besides Biggs and Johns, who would sooner die that allow her to be harmed, William will move heaven and earth to protect our sister, not to mention the rest of the family."

"In that case, when should we depart?" Amy asked.

"Can you be ready in three days, my love?" Tom asked and received a nod of agreement from his wife. "We will start with Nine Oaks as it is the closest to us."

With their plans set, the housekeeper and butler were summoned and informed of the upcoming travel schedule.

~~~~~~~/~~~~~~~

Due to the fact that her daughter would have her come out with Ladies Mary, Kitty and Loretta, Lady Anne had suggested that the Longbourn Bennets and the De Melvilles be invited to Pemberley so that they could make their plans in one place. Neither William nor Elizabeth had any objection to her suggestion, so invitations were issued. The Fitzwilliams at Snowhaven too were invited and would bring Lady Catherine, who had recently returned from her sojourn with her daughter and son-in-law. The Bennets and De Melvilles responded positively and would arrive on the coming Friday.

The Fitzwilliam brothers and their brides had been invited to join the family and had responded that they would arrive on Saturday. Tom and Amy had sent regrets as they were about to embark on a tour of their estates. The Gardiners would collect Frank and Hattie Phillips in Meryton, and also arrive with the Bingleys, Hursts, and younger Phillipses on Saturday. What started out as a visit to plan a coming out ball had evolved into a full family visit.

Elizabeth knocked on her mother-in-law's sitting room door and was invited to come sit next to Lady Anne on the settee. Lady Anne could not but notice that her daughter-in-law looked sad. She knew that Elizabeth would talk to her about what ailed her when she felt ready.

"Is there something wrong with me, Mother Anne?" she asked as a tear rolled down her cheek.

"To what do you refer, Lizzy?" Lady Anne asked gently as she took Elizabeth's hands in her own.

"My courses started this morning," she said with a sob, "it had been almost three months since we wed, and I am not yet with child. William will regret..."

"Elizabeth Darcy! Do not even think such drivel," Lady Anne admonished her firmly. "Do you know how long I had been married to my dearest George before I was with child with William?" Elizabeth tearfully shook her head. "It was more than a year and a half!" Elizabeth's lips formed an 'O' as she assimilated to what her mother-in-law had said.

"I thought that all brides become *enceinte* soon after their marriage like Mama, Jane, and Marie did," Elizabeth stated as she began to understand that her perceived problem may not be anything more than her impatience.

"It is different for all, Lizzy," Lady Anne soothed. "Some are with child within weeks of the wedding and some take longer than it was for me. I have heard that sometimes stress can be a factor. While the uncertainty of the dastardly plans against you hangs over your head, it could be that God, in His wisdom, has decided that it is not a good time to gift you with that particular blessing."

"Thank you for reassuring me, Mother Anne," Elizabeth said as she dried her the residual tears on her cheeks. "Impatience has long been one of my faults, and even thought I have read on the subject and intellectually know that it can take longer, I suppose that I thought that I would become with child early in our marriage by sheer force of will."

Lady Anne squeezed Elizbeth's hands and smiled at her, "It is a hard lesson to learn, not everything happens when we want it to. Besides, it is not the worst thing for a couple to have time together without children for a while at the start of their marriage. In a few days Sarah and Rose will be here, I suggest you ask them for their perspectives, and I am sure that they will tell you something similar to what I have said." As she concluded her speech, Lady Anne relinquished her daughter's hands and gave her a warm hug. "You are the best thing that had ever happened to my William, so *never* let me hear you start to question whether he would be better off without you!" Lady Anne said firmly.

"I suppose that my disappointment led to illogical maudlin thoughts. You have my solemn oath that I will never allow it to happen again," Elizabeth promised Lady Anne.

The rest of their conversation was about happier topics, like the arrival of their family. Not long after, Georgie joined her mother and sister for tea and the discussion turned to her favourite topic, her come out.

~~~~~~~/~~~~~~~

The Earl and Countess of Matlock and Lady Catherine arrived on Thursday afternoon, and on Friday, a little after noon, the young groom jumped off his horse to inform the butler that a number of carriages had entered the estate. On hearing that the Bennet and De Melville carriages had been spotted; Lady Georgiana Darcy was particularly excited that she would presently see Lord James Bennet again.

The four Darcys waited on the broad stone steps in the courtyard for their guests to alight from their conveyances. Loretta, Mary, and Kitty, after quick greetings to their hosts, took Georgiana by the arms and walked into the house chattering away happily. None noticed the wistful look on their sister and cousin that she for not being able to greet James directly before the girls whisked her away. Elizabeth and the remaining Darcys greeted her parents, aunts, and uncle. The last to be greeted were Wes and James.

James gave his sister a bear hug after greeting her husband and mother-in-law. "You look very well big sister," He said after looking her over from head to toe. "Is my brother treating you well, or do I have to call him out?" he asked with a huge grin as he gave his brother-in-law a playful punch on the arm.

"If William allowed you to blind fold him and tie his right arm behind his back, you *may* have a chance against him, James," Wes teased.

"When you boys are finished talking nonsense, mayhap we can enter the house?" Elizabeth said with a wide smile. "If you would like to embarrass yourself again, James, I am sure that

William has a spare minute to fence against you," she teased her younger brother who looked away, chagrined at the memory of his drubbing by Darcy all those months ago.

"Boys do like to play with their toys," Aunt Rose opined, which garnered laughter from the party as they entered the house.

"Lizzy, you look so very happy," Lady Sarah said as she walked next to her middle daughter holding her arm. "I detected a sense of melancholy in your last letter, especially your comments about not being with child yet."

"I spoke to Mother Anne, and she reminded me that everything will happen in its own time," Elizabeth said with a half-smile, "You know me, Mama, always impatient. As I have learnt over the last year, not everything happens just because I want it to be so."

Lady Sarah squeezed her daughter's arm, happy to see her continued growth and maturation. "It is a great pity that we will not see Tom and Amy as they make their inspections of the Bedford estates," she said with a far off look in her eyes. The Bennet matriarch missed all of her children, and only had two left at home, although James was but three miles away. She was very happy that four of her children had made brilliant love matches, but that did not mitigate the loss that she naturally felt at times. Having Rose live with them filled some of the hole left by the majority of her children leaving home, but she relished the time that they came together as a family.

~~~~~~~/~~~~~~~

Jones, Forester, and Tibbson had never been part of such an incompatible crew. They followed Younge's orders begrudgingly. None were happy that they had not made a smuggling run for months so there were no profits to split. As much as they would have liked to force, if need be, their attentions on a local maiden, they had no doubt that the captain would make good on his threat of offing them and dumping their body at sea. The restlessness of the crew was somewhat pacified after the meeting was called for all and the plan going forward was explained.

The three Dennington employees met back in their room at the widow's house to compose a letter to the Earl of Brookfield, outlining the plan of which Younge had so proudly detailed. He promised each one of the ten crew members a bonus of one thousand pounds which more than made up for the months that they had not made any smuggling runs.

"They be countin' their chickens afore they 'atch," Forester said as he shook his head, "even 'ad we not known the plan, this lot woulda failed. They be delusional."

"That they are," Jones answered and Tibbson nodded his head in agreement. "You two agree that we wrote all the plan down proper?" Jones changed the subject back to their task at hand and both men nodded.

"Aye, Jonesy," Tibbson said, "you done covr'd all that 'e told us. An' if 'e lef' out some details whe 'e tol' us 'is plan, it aint a problem cause we will be there." The other two agreed with Tibbson as they had no doubt that if they needed to, they could put the miscreants down without much resistance.

The three had quietly rejoiced when the last message from Liverpool informed them that the men that murdered Hamms had met their end, so justice had been done. They were certain that any of the men, or women, that took part in the proposed plan would meet the same fate as those three. They would covertly sow some doubt among the crew so that when they reached their destination, they could cause some of the crew to scarper, making Younge's dependence on them grow. If the men did not leave willingly, there was always an option to have them meet with an 'accident' of sorts that would incapacitate them.

~~~~~~~/~~~~~~~

The Duke and Duchess of Bedford were most impressed when they arrived at the Nine Oaks estate in Yorkshire. They estimated that it was about the same size as Netherfield before any land had been annexed to it. The manor house was smaller than James's estate's house, but more than adequate. They had been welcomed by the long-serving couple that filled the roles of housekeeper and butler, and were very happy to see that the house was well maintained. It was easy to see that it received regular cleanings, speaking well of the servants that they took their duties seriously.

While the Duke met with his steward, the Duchess met with her housekeeper. Later that evening after a sumptuous meal, the couple sat in the sitting room attached to their bedchamber. "This is not your first visit here is it, Tom?" Amy asked.

"No, my love," her husband agreed as he remembered his prior visit. "I was here once, almost two years ago when Uncle Sed and I made an inspection tour of the four secondary estates," he said as the memory of his jovial uncle washed over him. "Uncle and I rode the entire estate and he introduced me to the tenants and servants as his heir. He was very diligent in his teachings, and it has stood me in good stead."

"You still miss him much, do you not, Tom?" Amy asked.

"Yes, my love, I do," he said with a hint of melancholy, knowing that even though they had entered the final month of mourning it would always be part of him. "However," he added as he visibly brightened. "I feel his presence with me, watching over me, us. He is gone from my sight, but never from my thoughts."

Amy hugged her husband tightly. "Take me to bed and love me, Tom." He lifted her in his arms and carried her into the bedchamber so he could most willingly comply with her command. Amy's tinkling laugh that he loved so very much rang out as he gently placed her on the coverlet. She had just missed her first courses but would not say anything to her husband until and unless she missed the next month's cycle.

Four days later the happy couple departed Yorkshire for Dumfries Castle in Scotland.

~~~~~~~/~~~~~~~

It had been resolved that the four young ladies having their come out together would take their curtsy before the Queen at the end of January, and that their combined ball would be at Hertfordshire House on Russell Square, which was rarely used by Lord Thomas and his family. It had the largest ball room of all of the family's properties, and it would be needed given the large number of the Ton that would be invited so as not to unintentionally snub anyone. Not surprisingly, while the numerous women were making plans for the coming out, the men elected to go hunting and enjoy other manly pursuits.

After the planning session that just concluded, where Lady Catherine offered her opinions most stridently, the younger married women retired to the veranda that overlooked the lake to have some of cook's freshly made lemonade and treats baked that morning by Pemberley's baker. The four young ladies who would be the recipients of the planning efforts had repaired to Georgie's sitting room to talk about their upcoming season and official entrance to the marriage mart.

"Lizzy," Caroline claimed her attention, "I see that you have made very few changes to your home."

"With Mother Anne's superb eye for decorating, there was very little that I felt needed changing," Elizabeth agreed. "The understated elegance of the house is exactly as I would have tried to decorate, were it required."

"There was very little that I had to change at either Hilldale or Hilldale House," Marie said happily.

"Little sister," a very pregnant Jane said, "you look so contented. Surely it is too soon for you to be with child again?"

"No, Janey," she replied with a dreamy look, one that the assembled ladies had seen many times from her since they had arrived, "I am a most satisfied wife as we are trying…a lot!" she exclaimed as she blushed a deep scarlet colour from her hairline down at her own audacity at verbalising her thoughts and her companions all smiled knowingly.

"Ooooh," Jane proclaimed, a hand pressing in on her belly. "She gave a very hard kick right then, mayhap she was not ready to hear about Marie's 'activities,'" Jane teased her twin as she explained her reaction.

"You know that you may have a boy, Janie," Elizabeth pointed out with arched eyebrow.

"I know, Lizzy. I just feel like this is a daughter. At least we are as sure as we can be that I am only carrying one." At the questioning looks from the ladies she informed them, "When we were in London, Richard took me to be examined by Sir Frederick after Marie saw him. He listened with his conical device and said that he could hear but one heartbeat."

"Well...I," Franny started to say. She saw the others waiting for her to continue. "This is the second month that I have missed my courses." She was relieved when she saw genuine happiness on all, especially Marie. "I did not want to make Marie feel badly so I was not going to reveal anything, but seeing you look so happy," Franny looked at her cousin, "told me that my news would not injure your sensibilities."

As the women were congratulating Franny, they saw an express rider come to a halt and hand a letter to Douglas who had stepped out to meet him. It was the letter from the three plants in Younge's crew addressed to Lord Richard Fitzwilliam.

CHAPTER 20

Early August 1812...

The excitement among the three co-conspirators was growing. The *Coastal Trader* was due to arrive in Bundoran in a matter of days and then the *Stealthy Runner* would finally put to sea four days after the Dennington Lines ship's departure. Once that ship sailed, Younge's ship would leave its anchorage dock to take on fresh supplies, then make ready for sea.

The three 'new crewmembers' worked as hard as any, and had fast become much liked by the other seven members of the crew, most especially Jones who was a natural leader. First mate Laraby was somewhat jealous that the rest of the crew gravitated toward the new man, but he was smart enough not to challenge Jones. Even he could see that he would come out on the losing end of any fight with the big man. Besides, the man and his mates would be good to have if there was trouble when they captured their prize.

Karen Younge was the happiest that she had been since the day that her George was 'murdered' by the whore. Very soon they would leave the Godforsaken place where they had sojourned for the last months and head toward her revenge. She had fantasized endlessly about all the ways that she would hurt the woman before finally ending her life. Nowhere in her delusions was there room for any outcome but complete success.

Johanna Álvarez was counting her share of the ransom already. As much as she was furious with her son for his defection, on some level her maternal instincts caused her to feel some sadness that Tony had left her, but not sad enough to reconsider his plea. She too believed that they had a plan which would not fail and that she would avenge the death of her husband, and those same persons would be punished for making, in her twisted logic, her Tony abandon her. She silently cursed her late husband for teaching their son to think for himself; the lessons were meant to keep him safe, not cause him to turn away from his mother!

Clay Younge was more than ready to leave Bundoran. He had been forced to increase the crew's take to one thousand pounds per man after his three crew members had absconded; he needed to quell the discontent that this waiting while not earning any money had engendered. Once he had his money, he could replace all the crew, excepting the three new ones, but until then, he needed them to be content and follow his plan. He was mollified by the thought that the men had no idea how huge his share of the prize would be, nor did they know the size of the ransom to be demanded. If they had, they would not have been content with just one thousand.

Luckily, he had not shared with them that the family was related to the royals and what it would mean if they were caught. Personally, he was rather attached to his head, which he knew would be separated from his body at the Tower of London if they were caught. Like his sister's late paramour, over confidence in his abilities was one of Younge's flaws, so he did not think about contingencies for the plan should something not go according to it.

Jones, Forester, and Tibbson were sure that the missive they had posted had reached the intended recipient by now, and that plans would be in place to stop the miscreants. One of the three would go see the postmaster of the small town where they expected to land in case a confirmation or even further instructions were awaiting them. The three were not unhappy that their time with the group of blackguards was drawing to a close, they were very much looking forward to seeing their families again, and being reunited with their own crewmembers.

~~~~~~~/~~~~~~~

The family gathering at Pemberley was a very pleasant affair except for the hours that the men had spent closeted in the master's study reviewing the letter from Jones. They spent some time composing a response to be sent to the town, which was mentioned as a waypoint. Darcy had sworn to his wife that he would tell her all so that she would not be kept in the dark about the plans to keep her safe, and away from the criminal conspirators. He had also promised that they would take decisive action to remove the threat once and for all. The rest of the young wives and older ladies had extracted promises that they too would be informed once the men had decided on a plan to defeat and capture the miscreants.

While the men had been busy, the ladies had not sat by idle. With the agreement of the four young ladies, a plan was set in motion for the joint coming out ball. With coaching from their older sisters and cousins who had made their curtseys before the Queen, the four had begun to practice so that when they made their actual curtsies, they would be fully comfortable with the procedure and the backing out of the reception hall without tripping over their feet. Luckily there had been foresight to bring the gowns that the sisters had used, and Lady Anne had someone retrieve hers from the attics so that there were enough for all four. As hideous as the young ladies considered the dresses with all of their hoops, frills and ruffles, they knew that there was no choice, so practice in the older dresses they did.

Notes had been sent to Madame Chambourg to start working on their presentation gowns, and the local dressmaker from Lambton had graciously come to Pemberley to take the four young ladies' measurements. When Mrs. Green arrived at Pemberley she was pleased to see her friend Maddy Gardiner, whom she grew up with in Lambton and had not seen for many years, although they did correspond occasionally.

When Mr. Gardiner was not found to be fishing in one of the estate's many locales for that sport, he and his wife had visited a number of their friends from Lambton, though they had not yet been able to visit with Miranda Green, so Mrs. Gardiner was most pleased to able to catch up with her friend after she had measured the four girls.

One afternoon while the men were fishing, the younger ladies took a ride up the bridle path to the point that overlooked Pemberley that had the best view of the Peaks in the distance. Jane, who could not ride, had stayed behind with the mothers and aunts, and so did Franny Bingley.

After the riding party had departed, escorted by a cadre of footmen and grooms led by Biggs and Johns, Hattie Phillips turned to her daughter. "I know how much you love to ride, Franny," she stated with raised brows. "Mayhap there is a special reason that you are not with the rest. Could it be the same reason that Jane cannot ride?"

"I had not planned to say anything yet," said Franny, as all eyes in the drawing room focused on her. "After I missed my second monthly cycle, I informed Charles and we decided that we would wait until I felt the quickening in a month or two before we shared our news with the family."

"Good luck hiding that state in *this* family," Lady Catherine said with a smile, "Most here can spot a lady in that state easily, so trying to hide the news is an exercise in futility."

"My sister has the right of it," Lady Elaine agreed. "Both Anne and I suspected but decided it was not for us to say anything."

"I did also," Lady Sarah and Aunt Maddy added at almost the same time.

"Have you seen a doctor to confirm your suspicions as of yet?" Hattie asked her daughter as she filled with the joy of becoming a grandmama.

"Yes, Mama," she said, long knowing that with the assembled group there was no way to hide anything. "Charles took me into Lambton to go see Mr. Jamison. He confirmed my state and says that if all goes well, I should enter my confinement in January or February of next year."

"How wonderful that we will be grandmothers soon, Hattie and Elaine," Lady Sarah said. "Catherine, have you any news from Anne on that subject as of yet?"

"No Sarah, no news yet," responded Lady Catherine, "and you know me too well enough to know that it was not from lack of inquiring on my part while I was with them." The self-deprecating statement drew a laugh from all of the ladies.

"We can only pray to the Lord that Marie will enter that state again soon," Lady Elaine stated, "and this time may there be no problems for my daughter-in-law."

"As I recently told Lizzy when she was worried that she was not yet *enceinte*," Lady Anne offered, "when it is time, it will happen. I have no doubts that Marie will get her wish."

"Lizzy told me that she talked to you, Anne," Lady Sarah said as she patted her friend's hand. "I became with child with Tom within a month of my marriage to Thomas, and Jane entered the state within three months, so my impatient daughter could not understand why it was not her time yet. Thank you, Anne, for opening her eyes to the fact that it takes some much longer than others. It was a good lesson for her to learn."

"I was just like my niece," Lady Catherine admitted. "It took me almost two years to become pregnant with Anne, and then a few years later I had a miscarriage and was never in that state again," she said sadly.

"It seems that some of us are only granted a few children like myself, Catherine, Anne, and Elaine," Hattie Philips said, "while others, like Sarah and Maddy are able to produce a brood."

Jane who had been silent as she listened to the matriarchs of the family talk interjected, "I wonder how many I will be blessed with," she stated as she rubbed her swollen belly.

"You never know, Janey," her mother answered. "Your father and I were blessed with seven, and others have even more, but whatever God grants you will be a blessing, whether it is one or ten."

"If I have two like you and Papa," Franny said as she looked warmly at her mother, "I will be very happy." Hattie Phillips glowed at the compliment that she felt from her daughter.

The conversation turned to the upcoming evening after dinner when the men would share the plans for Lizzy's security and how they would deal with the criminals. Lady Anne rung for tea as they speculated about how the plan would unfold.

~~~~~~~~/~~~~~~~~

As the Duchess of Derbyshire sat on Mercury admiring the view that was laid out in front of her like a pretty painting, except this one was by the ultimate artist, the Lord Himself. After admiring the beauty before her, her mind inevitably thought on what was to come.

'*Why do they want to hurt me?*' she asked herself. '*I have never done anything to them. It is not my fault that Wickham tried to move against me and died trying. That reprehensible man, Tony's father, was not forced to participate, and all of the consequences were due to their own actions.*' She paused and thought about what she had just told herself. '*I am trying to find logic and sense where those involved have short supply of both! Just like the previous conspirators reaped the results of their own actions, so it will be with this lot.*

'*I do feel bad for Tony as his mother is one of the group. He has done everything that he can short of tying her up and kidnapping her to get her to change her course. If she chooses not to, then that will not be on his head.*'

"Lizzy, where did you go? I was asking you a question and you did not hear me," Kitty asked, snapping her sister out of her reverie.

"Sorry, Kitty, I was wool-gathering," Elizabeth said sheepishly. "What was it you were asking?"

"I wanted to know if you come up here often as the view is spectacular," Kitty repeated. "If we have time before we depart, I would like to return with my sketching accoutrements and make some drawings to paint later." Kitty had a natural talent for drawing and painting that had been honed by many lessons with masters.

"We leave in three days, Kitty," Mary reminded her twin sister, "If you want to come back here on the morrow, and there are no plans that we will be intruding on, I will come back with you as I would not mind making a sketch of the Peaks in the distance." Both Georgiana and Lorretta added their names to the group to return as the four looked at Elizabeth in expectation.

"As far as I know there are no plans that would be impacted by your returning tomorrow," Elizabeth agreed to expressions of joy form the four younger ladies. "As long as you have permission from your parents, and that your companions accompany you with two guards apiece, I have no objection."

"Were we like that when we were younger?" Caroline asked rhetorically.

"I know I was," Marie responded, "both Jane and I had our share of youthful exuberance."

"Not so much for me," Louisa said with a smile, "Caroline can tell you that I was a much more serious girl." Caroline nodded her agreement.

"Are we ready to return to the house?" Lizzy asked. There were no objections so with two footmen and grooms leading the way, they began the decent from the summit of the hill back towards the stables.

~~~~~~~/~~~~~~~

Edward Gardiner had just caught a very large carp and was most pleased with his efforts for he enjoyed angling above all sports. The group of men was spread out along the banks of the stream. He was in a group of the more mature men. His brothers Frank and Thomas were to his right with Reggie and Cyril to the left. The seven younger men were fifty yards downstream.

"I would rather be relaxing with some fine port in my son's library than swatting flies away," Lord Thomas joked. "Without inflating William's ego, I have to admit that this is a very pleasant spot, and these oaks give us ample shade and keep us out of the sun."

"If I were master of an estate like this, I would never leave it," Frank Phillips said as he looked around at the pleasant scene.

"Even I have to admit that Pemberley has more beauty that my Snowhaven," Lord Reggie stated, "but," he added with a large grin, "if any of you repeat what I said to William, I will adamantly deny that those words crossed my lips!" The men around him guffawed leading the younger group to wonder what had caused the group to laugh as they were.

"Something amused them." Bingley stated the obvious.

"Indeed Bingley," Graham Phillips ribbed his brother-in-law, "none of us noticed that fact!"

"Do not harass Bingley," Lord James warned his cousin, "unless, that is, you want stories of Lizzy beating you in a fight to be told."

"Hey, I was only eleven at the time!" Phillips defended himself with a smirk.

"You were, but how old was my sister?" James prodded.

"Six!" came the almost inaudible response, which was repeated by James, causing the men to laugh at James's expense.

"I will have to ask my wife for an explanation," Darcy said with amusement as he imagined a six-year-old harridan beating her older cousin in a fight.

"Graham is not the only one that took a beating from Lizzy, is he James?" Lord Wes shared.

"Same for you and Tom, so I would not crow too loudly if I were you, Wes," Lord James countered. Wes lifted his hands in surrender, he had lost to little Lizzy more than once, and not for want of trying to best her. Richard and Andrew looked on in amusement as both had heard stories about the wild girl that was their younger sister from their respective wives.

By mutual agreement Richard and William asked James to take a short walk with them while the others tended their lines. "You know that William and I share guardianship of Georgie, do you not?" Lord Richard asked. Lord James nodded to let them know that he did.

"We," Lord William said as he looked to Richard and received his nod for him to speak for both of them, "want to reiterate that we want Georgie to have a season before you, or any other, declare for her."

"The message had been received loud and clear," James said firmly.

"James, neither of us have an objection to you as a suitor for

Georgie," Lord William said, just in case James felt that they were warning him off. "As long as you are her choice and you love one another, we will not stand in your way."

"Thank you, William, Richard," James said appreciatively. "It gladdens me to hear you say that. I promise you that if Georgie feels the same for me as I do for her, her happiness will be my life's mission."

"Make sure that it is," Lord Richard stated as he slapped his brother on the back. James was well aware that although the words were said lightly that there was a strenuous warning behind them. James was determined that if his suit was accepted, that neither Georgiana nor her guardians would ever have cause to repine.

"One more thing," his other brother-in-law added. "We will require a long courtship, and if it comes to that, a betrothal period that would last until she is eighteen and you three and twenty." James agreed to the restriction as there was no length of time that he was not willing to wait for the young lady that held his heart firmly in her grasp.

~~~~~~~/~~~~~~~

Tom and Amy Bennet received an express from his father three days after they arrived at Dumfries Castle. The express briefly told them that the intelligence that they had been waiting for had arrived, that the family was all at Pemberley, and that due to the information in the letter, the stay had been extended.

It took no time at all for the decision to be made. The rest of the tour would be put on hold and the couple would head for Pemberley on the morrow before sunrise to join the family. They issued orders for their trunks to be packed and the carriages to be readied for an early departure.

~~~~~~~/~~~~~~~

Tony Álvarez had been informed that a missive from the men who had infiltrated the *Stealthy Runner's* crew had been received. He was further informed where the showdown would take place and when. He also knew for sure that his mother had chosen to ignore his pleas. It saddened him, but he felt that he had warned her as much as he could. The report that the men had sent had clearly stated that his mother was still with the Younges and was as keen as ever to execute their plan.

Tony had sat with the Elliots for a few long conversations and they had helped him come to peace with the fact that he had no control over his mother's choices, and helped him see that there was naught more he could reasonably do. He had become very close to the Elliots, so much so that he was treated as a son by the couple who accepted him for who he was and wanted nothing from him but his friendship in return.

Young Álvarez was to leave for Oxford in a sennight, before the confrontation was to occur. He thought back to the meeting he had been party to in the parsonage's sitting room with Mr. Elliot, the Dukes of Hertfordshire and Derbyshire, and the Earl of Brookfield.

"*I want to stay at Pemberley and be of assistance,*" Tony had requested.

"*That would not be wise, Tony,*" Mr. Elliot said.

"*I agree with the reverend,*" Lord Thomas stated. "*You have worked so hard to be accepted to study at Oxford, do you really want to defer your studies for a year complete?*"

"*No, but,*" Tony's determination wavered, "*I feel a responsibility...*"

"*You have none!*" Lord Richard cut him off. "*You have chosen to live a good life, and that is what you need to do. In fact, I believe that it would be better if you were not here when we have to deal with the criminals.*"

"*I agree with my brother,*" Lord William added. "*It may become very unpleasant, and we have more than enough men here. You deserve to start your studies, that is what you need to do.*"

"*I will write to you once it is over, Tony,*" Mr. Elliot promised. "*Remember that you are part of my family now and that there will be chambers waiting for you when you have your term breaks and holidays.*"

"*I agree with my sons and the vicar,*" Lord Thomas said encouragingly. *"You need to start the new path you have chosen, and it will do you no good being here when it all happens. Choosing right over wrong and good over evil is not always easy, but you have made the correct choices. You will have all of our support, and if you need any help at school all you need to do is write to Mr. Elliot and he will let us know."*

As he was readying himself for his journey to Oxford, Tony knew that he had again made the correct choice to not stay. The men could have ordered him to, but they treated him as a man and left the decision to him. Tony Álvarez was at peace as he climbed aboard the Darcy carriage that would bear him to university, seen off by the three Elliots, with young Grace bestowing a hug and a big wet kiss on his cheek before he entered the conveyance. With a wave to the people who were so very supportive of him and allowed him to make his own future, the carriage jerked a little as the driver put the team in motion.

<div align="center">~~~~~~~/~~~~~~~</div>

On the eleventh day of August, the year of our Lord 1812, the *Coastal Trader* docked in Bundoran. The Younges, and Johanna Álvarez felt the excitement building, after she departed on the morrow, it would be a few short days later until the *Stealthy Runner* set sail, bringing them to the riches that they felt were justly deserved.

The End of Part 2

ABOUT THE AUTHOR
Shana Granderson, A Lady

I have three children and after a disastrous first marriage, I found my soul mate who I believed I had lost forever over 25 years ago until we miraculously reconnected. We are now married so I am with the love of my life for life. I live with my soul mate in Australasia and we have three pets, two cats, and a golden lab.

Pride and Prejudice was assigned to me in an English literature class when I was 15. It was not my favourite book, which was true of any book I was forced to read at that period in my life. Under protest I read it in order to pass the class.

I forgot about the book until I was in my 30's when in 2004 I discovered and watched, and then fell in love with, the 1995 Pride and Prejudice version made for TV in England. I purchased a copy of the DVD which has been watched more times that I care to count.

The tipping point was seeing the 2005 big screen adaption of P&P. Not long after I acquired and read the complete works of Jane Austen on Amazon. Reading e-books is my way of giving back to the environment. I read them all starting with Pride and Prejudice. P&P is my favourite by far of all of Miss Austen's great works, in fact my favourite, full stop. After I read it three of four times over, I wistfully said to myself: 'it is a great pity that Jane Austen never wrote a sequel to her seminal novel.'

I was searching the Kindle Store for books and for the hell of it I entered "Pride and Prejudice Sequel' into the search bar not expecting any results. The rest is history. I discovered the myriad of JAFF books. Once I devoured all of the sequels and continuations that I could find, I reluctantly tried a variation. I had the wrong-headed belief that I would not enjoy a variation as much as sequels. Boy was I ever wrong!

The more that I read, the more I started thinking of plot bunnies and hear stories in my head. Eventually I decided to start writing, something that I never imagined in my wildest dreams that I would ever do. Today I am the proud owner of well over 1,000 JAFF novels that I have acquired on Amazon. 'A Change of Fortunes' was the first book that I wrote. 'The Hypocrite' was next with the Duke's Daughter my third book and first series. It is in three parts; part 1 & 2 are available and have been edited professionally and 'The Duke's Daughter Part 3' in progress. It seems that the more I write, the more I want to write.

BOOKS IN THIS SERIES

The Duke's Daughter

This Story follows the Bennets and the Darcys from the days of Fanny Bennet to what we hope will be happily ever after for some and just rewards for others. In this series Lady Anne Darcy is alive and the impact of her living is examined and far reaching. As would be expected, our dear couple, Elizabeth and Darcy are the main characters in this series while giving others their day as well.

Part 1: Assumptions And Consequences

Lady Elizbeth Bennet is the Daughter of Lord Thomas and Lady Sarah Bennet, the Duke and Duchess of Hertfordshire. She is very wary of people's motives based on an event before she was born that could have been disastrous for both her beloved father and mother's felicity. The result is that she is quick to judge and anger and very slow to forgive. She does not see it yet, but she has far too many prejudices that colour her perceptions.

Driven by his life experiences, including the loss of his beloved father, almost losing his sister to a blackguard and relentless hunting of his person by unmarried ladies and their families of the Ton for his wealth and status, Fitzwilliam Darcy has learnt to rely on his own judgement above all others and had developed his haughty mask of pride, disdain and indifference. Once he believes that something or someone is a certain way, he does not allow anyone to change his mind. He ignored his mother about the hiring of his sister's first companion and the result was the Ramsgate debacle, but he had not learnt his lesson yet.

He misinterprets information that he heard from his Aunt, Lady Catherine, about her parson's relatives and the estate that is entailed upon him and with assumptions and surety that he is never wrong coupled with his failure to listen to his friends the Bingleys when they try to correct his perception, he makes a huge mistake at the infamous assembly in Meryton and faces a very angry Lady Elizabeth Bennet. They both make assumptions about the other and we see the consequences that follow.

Wickham arrives in Meryton to join the Derbyshire Militia to hide from his main creditor, the Spaniard, he tries to ply Lady Elizabeth with his lies but to his chagrin she is forewarned and not only exposes him for what he is, she dares to deride and laugh at him in a very public forum. He leaves Meryton just before the Fitzwilliam brothers return and swears revenge on the woman that has moved his nemesis Darcy out of his top spot of his hated people list.

Will Wickham get his revenge and will our couple work out their misunderstandings? Lady Anne Darcy is alive in this series and has a lot of influence on various characters and their expected behaviour. This is the first of a three book series.

BOOKS BY THIS AUTHOR

A Change Of Fortues

This "what if" looks at what the Bennet's life would have been like if unlike canon they had sons. How would the parents have been different and what kind of life would the family have? How would Bingley behave if he had backbone and stood up to his siter Caroline?

In this variation, there is no insult at the assembly and Darcy meets the Bennets knowing that they are very good friends of his uncle and aunt, Lord and Lady Matlock. Fanny Bennet is not to the flighty character of mean understanding that we are used to seeing. Most of the characters from canon that we love and hate are present as are new ones that are used to give breadth to the story.

The Hypocrite

What would happen if Miss Elizabeth Bennet took Darcy to task over the hypocrisy that she sees in some of his behaviour after his horrendous proposal and her reading the letter in Hunsford. What if the Bennets were not penniless and unconnected? For the purposes of this story great wealth is assumed, the source of the wealth is explained in the book. Will Darcy choose to acknowledge the rectitude of Miss Elizabeth's reproofs or will he reject them in pride and conceit?
Does he have the fortitude to change and how will knowing the Bennets affect those around him? Bingley in this variation is closer to his irresolute character that we see in canon. That

is the only similarity that your will see in him my dear reader.
There are villains but they are not the focus of the story.
You will find all of your favourite characters from canon with a
few added to broaden the tale. Sit back and enjoy.

I want to thank my Alpha reader, Will Jamison and my dedicated Beta readers Kimbelle Pease, Kristen Mitchell and last but not least, Leah Pruett. You have all made my work better with your time, dedication and assistance. You have my undying appreciation and thanks.

COMING SOON

March 2021: Part 3 of the Duke's Daughter:

The third part is the conclusion of the series. Are the villains successful? How does the family move on from the death of a loved one? We see the younger ladies come to the fore and are shown how their lives develop. Do not worry that the main characters are forgotten, they are not and figure prominently in the final part of the story. As in life, there are ups and downs, but in the end love wins.

Later in 2021: The Discarded Daughter - Volume 1

Fanny Bennet is convinced that her second daughter will be the son that is needed to break the entail on Longbourn. When she bears another daughter, she is furious and takes all of her frustration out on her new baby. She refuses to feed her and wants her sent out to one of the tenants. Thomas Bennet will not hear of that, he hires a wet nurse as he instantly falls in love with his dark haired hazel eyed daughter.

As she gets older, the resentment and hate that Fanny feels intensifies exponentially as her husband showers her second daughter with love. Even at an early age, the babe shows intelligence far beyond anything the blond three-year Jane has. She starts to walk at nine months and to talk before her first birthday. Convinced that Elizabeth is the devil's spawn, Fanny secretly pays an unscrupulous man to make her eighteen-month-old daughter disappear and to end her life. When it is discovered that his daughter is missing Thomas Bennet is shattered while his demented wife is secretly beside herself with joy.

This book will be a series that follows our heroine through the trials and tribulations of life as she grows up as the Discarded Daughter.

www.ingramcontent.com/pod-product-compliance
Lightning Source LLC
Chambersburg PA
CBHW061955170626
46813CB00006B/2655